AF270542

TOM
STERN

VATICAN GOLD

VATICAN GOLD

VATICAN GOLD. Copyright © 2003 by Tom Stern.

All rights reserved. Printed in the United States of America. No part of this book may be reproduced in any manner whatsoever without written permission except in the case of brief quotations embodied in critical articles or reviews. For information, address AEI Titan, 9601 Wilshire Blvd., Box 1202 Beverly Hills, CA 90210.

Design by Mitzi Fine

Library of Congress Cataloging-in-Publication Data
    Stern, Tom.
        Vatican Gold/Tom Stern.–1st ed.
        p. cm.
        ISBN 0-9703056-1-3
        1. Vatican Gold–Fiction. 2. Vatican–Fiction. 3. Gold–Fiction.
        4. France–Fiction. 5. Treasure Hunting–Fiction.

    Library of Congress Control Number: 2002111797

Published by AEI Titan and Greenleaf Book Group, LLC
9601 Wilshire Blvd., Box 1202
Beverly Hills, CA 90210

This is a work of fiction. All names, characters, places and incidents are either products of the author's imagination or are altered fictitiously.

FOR MY CHILDREN

MARJORIE ORTEGA
JORDAN ADAIR
LINDSEY GAVARNIE
THOMAS MONTGOMERY

ACKNOWLEDGMENTS

MY DEEPEST THANKS TO MY WIFE, YOLANDA,
AND TO MY MANY FRIENDS WHO HELPED ME
AT EVERY TURN, TO KEN ATCHITY FOR HIS
ENCOURAGEMENT AND REFINED INTELLIGENCE,
AND TO ANDREA MCKEOWN FOR HER
EDITORIAL LEGERDEMAIN.

DISASTER

Paris, France

In the instant before his body could react, Dr. Todd Ellison already knew it: the grisly catastrophe exploding in front of him was one he would never forget. The deadly stroke came out of nowhere, as if from another plane of existence like Thor's bludgeon of horror. Just a moment before, reveling in the vivacious beauty of Paris, Ellison had been on a solitary stroll, enjoying a postcard panorama of the Eiffel Tower as it soared over its manicured park. A sight beyond compare, so perfect was the mathematically harmonious derrick, with its four curved rails probing skyward toward a distant apex, striving, arching to reach union high in the Parisian sunset.

To him, a man given to reflection, the tower seemed a likely metaphor of his life, for he knew that his own existence, like the apex of Monsieur Eiffel's tower, had soared beyond where most would have believed it possible. Just a year ago he had been a beleaguered surgeon wading through a divorce and seeking escape. When, as part of his ill-formed plan to reconstruct his life, he volunteered for an American medical mission to the Philippines, he had inadvertently become an explorer and adventurer in a reckless treasure hunt that turned wildly successful. After triumphing in kill-or-be-killed battles with Filipino Muslim terrorists, he had heard his own voice echo in a chamber stacked to the ceiling with gold bullion, a golden mountain of Japanese treasure hidden during World War II. His partner in adventure was now his wife, Miranda, a talented and adventurous beauty from the upper crust of Asian society.

On the Eiffel Tower's observation decks far above him, he could see tourists waving gaily at friends waiting below on wrought-iron park benches. He was about to tear the end piece of his fresh baguette, still hot from the bakery's oven, which he planned to eat with Normandy cheese while sprawled on the lush grass where he could fully enjoy the view. But obliterating Ellison's enjoyment of the scene without warning, two devastating fireballs blossomed like huge, deadly roses beneath the tower's famed Pillar of the West and Pillar of the North.

Barely half a mile from Ground Zero, Ellison instinctively shielded his eyes from the shock wave he could already see coming, a seven hundred mile per hour distortion lens in the atmosphere that made everything shimmer for an instant. At the same time, the very air itself had become an orange-colored sea of fire. Before he could take cover, the shock wave hit him like a football linebacker, blasted him off his feet, and left him gasping at the base of a suddenly leafless tree.

Stunned and lying prone, out of the corner of one eye Ellison saw the erector set tower wobble in a slow harmonic oscillation. Nearly as tall as the destroyed World Trade Center, briefly she stood still and beautiful once again. For fully twenty seconds, before the remaining twin pillars collapsed under the unbearable strain, he had a fleeting hope they might be strong enough to take the weight. But like a robotic giraffe with two of its four legs amputated, or a mighty redwood felled by some god who had called out "timber!" the tower inclined past a critical point of no return. Accelerating as it fell, and with tourists tumbling from it like hundreds of seed cones, the Eiffel Tower became a cracking, shrieking one thousand foot long whip snapping toward the earth.

Torn from its moorings by the whip-cracking downfall, the crowded observation capsule near the top of the tower fractured off to become a hurtling projectile in solo flight. It launched into a short, turbulent arc, all the while spinning tourists into space before it speared into the River Seine with a titanic splash. The rest of the doomed tower accelerated as a unit until, with a deafening crash that rammed another burst of pain into Ellison's already bleeding ears, it smashed itself into the apartments along the Left Bank. All that remained was a billowing cloud of dust that obscured a jumble of twisted, smoking girders and the setting sun.

Ellison, still on the ground, had wanted to avert his gaze from the sight of twenty schoolchildren dressed in regulation blue uniforms flailing in slow motion plunges into the Parisian cement. When they hit ground, he felt an immense wave of nauseating horror wash over him, a horror so great it threatened to paralyze his thinking. But he knew already that he would have to help. Who could have done such a thing? Why?

After struggling to his feet and testing himself—plenty of pain, just a few scrapes, nothing seemed to be broken—Ellison began to run through the dust cloud toward the disaster. Like a rangy cowboy spurring his horse into a herd of crazed stampeding cattle, his athletic strides carried him against a swelling tide of screaming, fleeing, grime-covered or burned tourists hell-bent on escape.

As he neared the rubble, time shifted into low gear. His mind became a camera recording each horror, frame by frame: the dead and the dying everywhere, mangled arms mixed in with rebar and glass shards, detached legs, heads without bodies, and bodies without heads—all scattered akimbo in the dust. Despite the adrenaline putting every cell in his body on alert, Ellison's blood felt like ice water coursing through him. Adding to the revulsion caused by what he could see, he heard the mournful sounds of the air filling with emergency sirens above the wailing cries of the wounded and the grieving.

He had come upon seven disasters in his medical career: a hotel fire that killed twenty-nine, an overturned bus, a man stabbed in Central Park in New York, and four fatal highway crashes. In the Emergency Room at San Francisco's Parnassus Heights Hospital, he guessed he had saved nearly a hundred lives during his five years as a general surgeon; and he had seen plenty of lives lost, but nothing like this. There were a thousand dead and dying in plain view.

Ellison knelt at the first victim in his path, an old woman lying in a pool of blood, not breathing, her head twisted at an impossible angle. Dead. Across a pathway, an Arab woman wailed near three crumpled figures, clutching at them for signs of life when a falling girder crushed her body before his eyes.

He had thought about death and its implacable enormity often during moments snatched between surgical cases. It was a mystery, but this was no time for philosophy. Now it was a time for peak performance. Action. A test.

Twenty feet away a toddler howled at the sight of her intestines oozing blood on the sidewalk beside her. His heart skipped a beat at the sight of her, for no baby could survive such a wound. With a final gasp, she closed her eyes and died before he could reach her. Desolate after he felt her tiny wrist for a pulse, he beat his fist on the ground in frustration. How ape-like. Professional composure, he reminded himself.

It was a battlefield of innocents. The size of the explosions and the number of casualties exceeded anything he had seen, even during his volunteer days in New York at *Ground Zero* helping with the few survivors, or the weeks in the Gaza Strip and the West Bank, when his Doctors for Humanity tents had treated hundreds of refugees from Israeli bombs, or in Jerusalem itself, where they treated Jews maimed by Arab suicides. At the time, he couldn't imagine more hell. In reaction to the international horror, with more money than he thought he could ever spend, Ellison had thrown himself into voluntary efforts that he hoped would contribute to peace on earth. As part of his strategy, he visited all of the international peacekeepers to hear their ideas. But the more he learned of the sheer number of blood spilling contests going on worldwide at any moment, the more he felt at a loss over what he could do that would really make a difference.

Though chaos and madness ruled around him, Ellison willed himself to concentrate. Cutting through the klaxon warble of converging ambulances, a gasping cry galvanized Ellison into emergency action.

"*Aux secours!* Help me."

From ten feet away, Ellison could see a teenage boy's situation was desperate. His own ribs had gored a hole through his chest and torn open a gaping wound that sucked air with every breath. Ellison knew he had to seal the leak before the blue-lipped boy suffocated, and with reflex speed, he jammed his bare hands over the hole. Giving the boy an encouraging smile, he said in high school French, *"Je suis un medecin. Tout sera bien.* I am a doctor. Everything will be okay." But he was unsure what to do next and knew he needed help.

A fleet of emergency vehicles sped toward him across the manicured lawns. Ellison waved frantically at the first ambulance, a Citroen with its blue light flashing, and felt a moment of soaring relief when the driver slid to a stop beside him. A French doctor eased himself out of the tailgate door dressed in a crisp, stylishly trimmed white uniform. Like Ellison, the doctor was a very tall man, and while Ellison had curly blonde hair, medium-short, easiest for a busy man, the Frenchman wore his hair long like a woman's and hid his chiseled face behind a perfectly trimmed chestnut beard. Except for his hip swiveling limp, the Frenchman looked as athletic as he, though Ellison guessed him to be three or four years older. When Ellison forced his eyes away from the doctor's abnormal legs, he couldn't help but notice a powerful chest, a narrow waist, and arms like a body builder.

Surely sensing Ellison's tension and trained to deal with high anxiety, the Frenchman spoke first. His voice was so loud that it crashed through Ellison's shock. *"Mon Dieu! Monsieur. Qu'est-c'e que s'est passé?* What happened?" The man had a curiously mystical face, full of gravity yet immediately friendly, and despite its bullhorn volume his voice had a soothing gentleness. Ellison wondered why this particular voice had such an effect, which contrary to the horror of the situation put Ellison more at ease. He couldn't recall ever hearing anyone with a louder voice, pleasant though it was.

Ellison shook his head, partly because he was experiencing the after-effects of the explosion and partly because he was not certain how to answer in French. He willed himself to be calmer, just as he knew the French doctor would advise. He hoped his English would be understood, though he had little enough to say about the disaster. "Two bombs went off."

With brown eyes sparkling from behind all the hair, the Frenchman studied Ellison closer. He inhaled mightily and boomed, "Are you American?"

"American, yes." Relieved to be able to communicate, Ellison continued, "I don't know how this boy got hurt. But you can see he needs a chest tube, and right away."

"A doctor?"

"Trauma surgeon. Todd Ellison's my name. San Francisco."

"I've been there," the Frenchman remarked with a lilting English. "Pierre Francois" he said, clapping Ellison on the shoulder. "Also Trauma Surgeon. Let me look closer." When Francois hiked up his trousers to squat next to the boy, Ellison could see why the Frenchman limped. He had two artificial legs, their flesh colored plastic and metal hinges extending as high as Ellison could see.

"*Sacre bleu!* Your boy needs surgery right now."

"Do you have a chest tube?"

"In my satchel," Francois said. Swift in his work, Francois tossed his hair back with a turn of his neck that revealed a large ruby stud in his right earlobe. He moved with skill and experience. With his right hand Francois slid a rubber tube through the hole in the boy's chest, while with astonishing dexterity of his left hand he deftly inflated a balloon at the tip of the tube now satisfactorily inside the patient's chest and perfectly placed to seal the hole temporarily.

"Can I help?" Ellison offered, impressed by Francois' medical performance placing the plastic chest-tube. In Ellison's estimation it had been sheer mastery.

"You can start this bag of Hextend and give it as fast as his vein can stand. What do you think of my First Aid, *monsieur?*" Francois inquired with a collegial nod.

"Great work. It should hold him."

"Stay with him, *monsieur.* I will be back after we pick up five more."

Ellison steadied his fingers and got the intravenous on target on the first stick. With the life saving fluid flowing, Ellison had a moment to study the chaotic scene around him, where several dozen doctors and ambulance crews attended to the wounded. They were France's fabled *Medicins D'Urgence*, the most highly trained disaster team on earth, but Ellison could see the *Medicins d'Urgence* squad was wholly inadequate for this scale of carnage. As ambulances full of bleeding cargo screamed away to their pre-assigned hospitals, they left the park littered with unattended victims who would have to stay alive on will power and little else until the ambulances could return for more of the injured.

In two minutes, Dr. Francois returned. "Good, your boy lives." They slid his stretcher into the ambulance. "Well, are you coming?" Francois asked, nodding his head with encouragement.

"Do you want me?"

"It is one of the first rules in our manual of disaster response: mobilize all qualified personnel."

"I'll stay here or come with you. You tell me."

"Another rule is to use a man at his highest level. More first aid people are on the way. My idea is to commandeer you as my surgical assistant."

"You bet."

With a practiced hand, Francois made an all-inclusive sign of the cross over the victims and Ellison. "Bless all of you. And you, *monsieur.*"

Moments later Ellison stood beside his worsening patient for a weaving, jarring ride toward the *Hôtel de Dieu Hôpital,* across from the Nôtre Dame Cathedral. Seemingly unconcerned by the mad Parisian traffic, Francois twisted to face him. His large, brown eyes hypnotically sad, Francois wore a grim look that made him resemble an Old Testament prophet. In the confines of the vehicle, his voice was so loud that Ellison had to ask himself again why anyone would talk with such a loud voice. Though he seemed to understand everything Ellison said, maybe Francois was partially deaf, due to the same process that had cost him his legs, whatever that might be. "We have received word from our dispatcher that the situation is worse than we knew, *monsieur,*" he shouted. "It is unimaginable. More than we can manage."

"Tell me."

"When the top of the tower fell into the River Seine, it broke into a subway tunnel under the river. Twenty thousand or more have drowned in the Metro."

"Twenty thousand!" Ellison could imagine the uncountable men, women and children screaming as a wall of river water roared toward them. It reminded him of youthful experiences on the North Dakota truck farm his father had struggled to grow to feed his family during a 1980's recession caused by Arab oil embargoes and inept government responses. Growing rows of vegetables required a never-ending fight against the prairie dogs and gophers that burrowed long tunnels beneath the carrots, corn and potatoes so they could feast on the tender roots. After his father, Owen Ellison, decided he had to feed his family no matter what, he ran irrigation water from the Missouri River through canals, along the tractor-furrowed Chernozem soil of his fields. When the river flowed in, torrents of brown water ran into the holes of the countless gophers and prairie dogs, threatening to drown them. As soon as soaked animals emerged from holes, Ellison's job as a twelve year old was to shoot them with his pellet gun. After studying the fatal results of his aim with a child's scientific curiosity, he vowed never to kill them again. Later, when his father noticed him shooing the mammals out of the field with a stiff broom, he smiled and rubbed the top of Ellison's head with fatherly understanding. They were very close, and everyone expected Ellison to follow his father into agri-business.

A good student, to everyone's surprise Ellison had worked his way through college and ultimately chosen medicine, something no one in the entire family had ever studied, since he was the first of the entire family to graduate from a four-year school. After careful consideration in medical school, he refused to kill the dogs during anesthesia experiments, and advised the professors, "If I have to kill living things to get through medical school, tell me now; because I refuse to do it." He could understand the terror of the people in the subway, where the River Seine forced them to scramble like drowning gophers fighting for air. Finally bursting with panic and air hunger, they'd had no choice but to fill their lungs with water. It must have been a miserable death. He tried to encompass the reality that he had just witnessed the Eiffel Tower bombing, but it was too big to get his mind around, something he wished he had never seen.

Ellison thought of himself as a complex man, someone who often took his time making decisions; but simultaneously he recognized a fundamental simplicity in himself as well. In the end he either liked someone, or he did not. He could see Francois' jaw grinding over the news of the watery catastrophe. Probably because they were on the same professional plane, he recognized an immediate appreciation of Francois. Ellison acknowledged a peer and gave him credit, for to become such a man is not easy. Like most doctors, both of them had seen too much death in their careers. In the end, by virtue of having gone through an ordeal by fire, they had become part of a brotherhood. Or sisterhood. "How much longer to the hospital?"

"Three minutes," Francois responded, optimistic. "Stay with me, and we will operate on yours first."

But it took closer to half an hour. They hit grid-lock two blocks from the Emergency Entrance and had to abandon the ambulance and commandeer youthful bystanders to help them carry the stretchers. After racing through the narrow streets of Paris with their patients, worse awaited them inside, for instead of the carefully practiced efficiency Ellison had hoped to find in the Emergency Room, wild-eyed disorganization greeted them. With the staff overwhelmed by the tidal wave of injured and dead, no one in the hospital seemed to be in control. Except Francois, who served as chief of this division of *Medicins D'Urgence*. Struggling to manage without canes, Francois led Ellison slow-footedly down the corridors, shouted detailed instructions to the staff following him, and moved his six patients to the head of the line for surgery. Elective cases scheduled before the disaster would have to wait.

While they prepared to begin surgery, Ellison took stock of events around him. It was a nightmare that already seemed might never end.

CARDINAL VERDI

Vatican City

With its imposing square leading to the largest cathedral in the
world, St. Peter's Basilica seems to offer a magnanimous welcome
to visitors, but Vincente Cardinal Verdi knew it to be a false im-
pression. Except for the great basilica itself and its adjacent museums, the balance of the smallest sovereign nation on earth remains
off-limits to all but a select few. Behind its thick walls, Vatican
City, the kingdom of the Pope, hides shrouded in nearly two thousand years of mystery, its inner workings comprehended by few,
even of those allowed inside. Some of them have rashly believed
they understood the system. But they were fools and Verdi knew
the truth. He knew that Vatican secrets are sealed deeper than any
other.

Swiss Guards in their colorful Medici costumes recognized him
despite the pre-dawn darkness, saluting him and stepping aside to

allow him to pass through the towering bronze doors into the church that can accommodate sixty thousand of the faithful at once. After he made the long walk down the right aisle past Michelangelo's *Pieta*, Verdi fell to his knees before the High Altar built above the tomb of St. Peter himself.

"*In nominee Patris, et Filii, et Spiritus Sancti*," In the name of the Father, and of the Son, and of the Holy Spirit," he began.

In this time of great conflict in the world, Cardinal Secretary of State Verdi prayed for God's guidance and wisdom in fulfilling his duties to The Church, which tasks were many and weighty. Despite a nagging headache from a bit too much wine the night before, he felt the Holy Spirit suffuse his being with certainty of purpose, steeling him for the challenges ahead. Crossing himself after his solitary devotions, he rose and strode through the arched corridors to the Apostolic Palace beside the great basilica, to ride the elevator with its fourth floor stop at the Papal Apartments.

As he entered the chambers of the Pontiff, an ornate mirror reflected his handsome figure: Cardinal of Calabria, nearly the youngest bishop in a thousand years, one of the youngest ever to be created cardinal, and definitely the youngest Vatican Secretary of State since the post was established. Just forty now, Verdi's chiseled features recapitulated the genetic history of his Italian province: the sculpted chin and Roman nose from the Empire, engaging blue eyes that were vestiges of the Viking kingdoms that ruled his region of Italy for two hundred years, thick shoulders and an olive swarthiness from the African Arabs who held sway for centuries, strong white teeth from his peasant mother. Trim and powerful as a middleweight boxer, Verdi had never doubted he cut a dashing figure in his chasuble.

A young priest greeted him from behind an ornately carved desk in the ante-room, "*Buon giorno*, good morning, Your Eminence."

"How is His Holiness today?"

"No better, the doctors say, though they say little enough to me."

"Praise God he is no worse," Verdi responded, passing through the double doors into the spacious residence of the Pope.

Italian Giuseppe Cardinal Strizzi, the *camerlengo* or chamberlain in charge of much of the day-to-day operations of the city state, stepped to Verdi and spoke in a low voice. Verdi responded with whispered answers, out of habit rather than need, for they were alone in the room. Though magnificently dressed in the robes of immense power, Strizzi suffered from pinched facial features and a long nose. "Dr. Morra reports the Pontiff's liver is failing." His narrowly-spaced eyes grew calculating. "Elections are near."

Wordlessly, Verdi folded his hands behind his back and strolled to the window used by Popes to speak to the vast crowds that gather in St. Peter's Square. *Elections are near!* Strizzi's words spread sweet honey all through his body. Gazing out over Rome coming awake, Verdi felt consumed by the desire to be himself the Pope, Vicar of Christ, Successor to Peter, Supreme Pontiff, *Pontifex Maximus*, Bishop of Rome, Servant of the Servants of God. When Satan took Jesus to the mountaintop and showed him the world spread at his feet, it must have been like this place here above the square. But in Verdi's case, he felt certain it was God himself, not Satan, who had brought him to this opportunity.

It was his destiny to rejuvenate Christianity before it collapsed. As a percentage of total population, attendance at Mass was down worldwide, and eighty percent of the faithful no longer believed in an afterlife. Deep in their hearts, most Christians even doubted the divinity of Jesus. Particularly in developed nations, fewer and fewer young men took the cloth, and many of those who chose to become priests rejected central authority, tolerating rebellion in their parishes, where they allowed women to become nearly priests. Often a priest came from such a different culture that he could not truly understand the lives of his parishioners, as when a Nigerian priest found himself the only available manpower for the position in rural Louisiana. Some said that inevitable changes lay ahead when the priesthood itself became openly more than half homosexual or bisexual. And as if the internal weaknesses of the priesthood were not enough, Verdi felt added pressure on The Church from the international situation. Because of the insane terrorism of the Islamic fanatics, he worried about access to the sacred sites. Jerusalem and the Holy Lands had been under the rule of non-believers since 1157—since before the printing press, or steam engine, or automobile, or telephone, or electricity, or penicillin. Enough is enough, he thought.

From his experience as a diplomat on the world scene, Verdi

knew it is men who create history, and if his great dream indeed came true with him as Pope, he would be the one to declare a Christian Renaissance, an expansion of Christian civilization in a holy undertaking sure to spark a fire of piety around the globe. If anyone asked him "Why now?" Verdi answered that the Christians of the Holy Land and Middle East have become nearly extinct in the past century. Christians who escaped death fled to the ends of the earth. Camping under the tent of Islamic revivalism, Mohammed's forces had toppled Iran, Libya, Algeria, Egypt, Lebanon, Syria, and the periphery of the Soviet Union. Around the world, in the aftermath of the Allied crushing of the terrorist networks, intellectuals of Verdi's caliber sensed global religious war coming, a more serious conflict than any before that could lurk ahead of mankind's progress, ravenous and beastly.

More millions of Muslims now worshipped in *masjids* in America than did Jews in United States synagogues; while in Europe, Christian culture in nearly every nation felt the growing pressure of Islam. Across the world, Muslim expansionism threatened to attract converts from a straying Christian population. More than half of the people alive on the earth have never used a telephone. Ignorant and disadvantaged, large population groups can be controlled with relative ease with modern methods. As the frictions increased with more and more people on earth, apprehensions and mutual suspicions mounted. Less than five minutes after the Eiffel Tower bombing, the news broadcasts of every nation listed Islamic Terrorists on the list of suspects.

Verdi could see the future. Without his leadership from Rome, fifty years from now St. Peter's would be a mosque filled with sixty thousand Muslims, all bowing in rows with their arses in the air above Peter's tomb, praying to Mecca beneath walls stripped of crucifixes.

When another cardinal objected that his thinking was preposterous, Verdi told him, "History gives the lie to your belief it can't happen. You must look at world events over long periods of time to understand what is really happening. Look at Istanbul, where the Turks desecrated the great cathedral of Hagia Sophia, a place so holy and great that it was the center of the Byzantine Church. Thousands of Catholic churches have become mosques. Weak leaders make mistakes. Now is the time to change the course of history."

Convinced the time for action was imminent, for the past four years Verdi had been promoting his plan; and already a third of the cardinals generally if reluctantly agreed with him. Others simply feared Verdi, for as Secretary of State he also held a seat on the Congregation for the Doctrine of Faith, the modern name for the Universal Inquisition. In the Vatican pecking order, most considered him number two, just behind the unquestioned autocrat, Pope Hildebrandt III. The *Most Outstanding Cardinal* some called Verdi, a phenomenon of a priest with a career skyrocketing toward great things.

When the red-clad *Camerlengo* spoke to him again, Verdi turned away from the balcony and shut off his daydreaming. "His Holiness will receive you now, Your Eminence," Strizzi said, gesturing to the open door into the Papal bedroom.

In the bedroom, under an embroidered awning, octogenarian Hildebrandt III waved away the ministrations of his barber and extended his gnarled hand toward Verdi.

"Bless you, Vincente."

"It pains me to see you so frail, Your Holiness. I'll control your schedule to permit you to rest."

The Pontifex Maximus struggled to raise his head. "I feel I am dying."

Verdi held his breath, unsure how to deal with his own guilt about a tinge of gladness at the Pontiff's report.

FRANCOIS

Hôtel de Dieu Hôpital, Paris
Minutes after finally reaching the operating room, his Nordic blue
surgical scrub suit exactly matching the color of his eyes, Ellison
stood next to Francois at the operating room sink. While they
talked, Ellison brushed his enormous hands with a stiff brush, not
missing a single place from his soft fingers to the sun-bleached
hair on his sinewy arms.

In stark contrast to the weakness in his lower body, Francois'
hands and arms looked even stronger than Ellison's. He noticed
Ellison studying him.

"Yes, *monsieur*, a god on top and a hell below the groins."

"Do you mind telling me how it happened?" Based on many
deep discussions in the course of his life, Ellison had concluded
that a sincere, well-intentioned question never led to trouble. Sometimes people want to talk about something, and sometimes they

don't. Ellison wouldn't have been offended if Francois had deflected his question.

Francois paused for a moment, lost in a long thought. "Landmine in Cambodia, near the big temple at Angkor Wat. I was with Princess Diana on a tour before she was killed in Paris. The area was supposed to have been swept; but at least one went undetected. The one that took my legs."

"Very tough," Ellison said as he rinsed soap from his hands. "What else can I say? You must be one tough guy to be here now."

"Tough? I do not know, *monsieur*. Is quitting the priesthood a sign of toughness?"

"Really?"

"I had nearly finished seminary; but when I got out of the hospital almost a year later, I felt too angry at God to become a priest."

"So you went to medical school instead."

"Yes, but I had done one year of medical school before I entered the seminary. A little mixed up, I guess," he said with a charmingly authentic Gallic shrug. "In fact, I might have gone back to medicine anyway, though as a priest."

"And your voice?"

Francois laughed easily. "Yes, everyone notices. Sorry, *monsieur*, it is my opera training."

Ellison wanted to know more about Francois. There was something about the way he moved his upper body with such presence, chest out and shoulders back, and a steady, competent look in his eyes. Ellison guessed Francois had a competitor's confidence in his body, like great athletes have. He also sensed that Francois wanted to say something more to him, but was measuring him before forging ahead. Ellison enjoyed conversation, thinking, and new ideas. With the world outside gone mad, Ellison himself needed to talk, as if the act of communicating could keep the pain of the disaster at bay, at least until they plunged into the total concentration of surgery. The focus required with a scalpel in hand would repel all worries like a drug. "Say, doc, speaking of arms, how did you develop yours? You look like Mr. Universe."

"Training for wheelchair races first." He took a subtle deep breath and eyed Ellison as he spoke. "When I got up to a certain level, I did some bodybuilding for the Gay Games." Francois watched him for a reaction and seemed satisfied by what he saw. "Good, we are done," Francois concluded, nodding for Ellison to follow.

They shoved their way through the double doors leading to a state of the art operating room. Already prepped and shaved for surgery, Henri Cartier—Ellison had learned the name of his young patient—slid from his gurney to the operating table. Henri gave Ellison a terrified glance, but mustered a brave smile just before the anesthetic took him.

A French nurse, Giselle her name tag read, a brunette beauty openly intrigued by Ellison's tall athletic frame and Scandinavian good looks, helped him into thin gloves and a sterile gown. He could see she was a natural leader who wanted to use her own merry manner to keep everyone's spirits up amidst the anxiety of it all. After she patted him on the shoulder, he took stock of the surgical suite. Except for the joking Giselle making bright conversation with the team one by one, obviously French patter about him, there was none of the operating room banter he was used to at Parnassus Heights Medical Center in San Francisco. With the disaster outside, it was no wonder.

Shortly after surgery began, Francois eyed him with appreciation. "You have a way with the knife, *monsieur*."

"Five years in California trauma. I've seen just about everything."

Francois stopped working with his scissors. "To hell with regulations, *monsieur!*" he said with a boiler room shout. "They need me upstairs. Can I leave you to do your boy's case?"

"If your nurses agree, I can manage." After Francois gave a rapid-fire explanation in French, Ellison saw nods of agreement from the entire crew.

While Francois pulled off his gloves and corkscrewed out of the room, Ellison took control. "Table up," he ordered, adjusting the height to his lanky six foot four inch frame.

Now that a mechanical ventilator was breathing for Henri, Ellison felt confident the boy would not die of suffocation. Since the chief danger was hidden damage, he widened the incision so he could inspect the boy's heart for lacerations.

"Not good," he muttered. "Blood in the chest, and lots of it." It took him five minutes to locate the source. "Hmmm. The heart looks okay. Guess I need to look at the great vessels. Yes. There it is, a big bleeder."

Just as he was about to pass fine sutures through a tear in the largest artery in Henri's body, the cellular phone dangling from Ellison's belt broke the silence in the room with a ring that jangled everyone's nerves.

"Do you want to answer, doctor?"

"Not now! I'm on the aorta!" he snapped, before he remembered it would be Miranda, worried and calling from the outskirts of Paris. With everything that had happened, his wife's early morning departure to speak at the United Nations Women's Conference already seemed ages ago.

"On second thought, nurse, get the phone, okay?"

The slim Giselle reached under Ellison's gown and answered in French before shifting to English. "It's your wife." She pretended to pout and held the receiver to Ellison's ear so his gloved hands could remain sterile.

"What's up, Miranda? Are you okay?"

"Fine. Where are you?" He could hear the anxiety in her voice. When he had tried to call her, the airwaves were too overloaded to transmit his message:

"I'm in surgery at the hospital across from Nôtre Dame Cathedral. It's terrible here. Of course you know someone blew up the Eiffel Tower."

"We saw it on CNN, Todd. None of the politicians at the conference have an explanation, since most think the Islamic bombers have been controlled. In the nineties, an Algerian group plotted to crash into the tower. Still, it may be a French domestic group, though no one can fathom any probable suspects."

"I hope they find out something soon. How was your speech received?" She was to speak for thirty minutes on *The Economic Power of the Modern Woman in a Transnational World*.

"The attendees applauded for two minutes."

He was very proud of her. Six months ago, when they had left her ancestral hacienda in her Philippine homeland to take up primary residence in San Francisco, Miranda had enrolled in California Law School. She was acting on her almost life-long theory that to have access to the levers of power a woman must have a license to practice law. Their marriage had caused her to reconsider where she would attend law school, which she had expected to do in Manila or Hong Kong, but the American school was highly regarded. Without a law license, she felt women could not hold the field against naturally more aggressive males.

"Gotta go, beautiful. I'm doing the toughest part of the case right now."

Three hours later Ellison shared a round of high-fives with his newfound team; but his jubilation ended when Giselle took him upstairs to the temporary morgue, where sagging body bags were stacked in rows and layers.

He found Francois glumly watching the number of corpses increase minute by nightmarish minute. "We just brought one of my cases in here," Francois grumbled. Ellison wondered if he was talking so loud that he was trying to raise the dead. "And yours?"

"Stable."

"What do you want to do, *monsieur?* I was told your wife called you. Giselle thinks maybe your wife needs you. This is not your obligation here."

"Look, with that team I've got downstairs, I can help if you need it. My wife will understand."

"One of the nurses recognized you from the photograph in *Newsweek, monsieur.* We appreciate the offer of such a famous man." Francois bundled his hair under a net in preparation for his next case. "I recall photographs of your wife. Most men's dream. From the minor puffiness around her eyes, I guessed she might be pregnant."

Ellison winced inside. "No children yet." The look on Francois' face invited a return question, "You?"

Francois shrugged with an operatically theatrical smile. "Once a priest always a priest."

Not that it mattered to him, but the way Francois spoke made Ellison nearly certain Francois was homosexual or bisexual. Ellison knew many gay men in San Francisco, and though he sincerely enjoyed their company, he had never experienced any sexual interest in any of them. And from personal observations, he knew that sexual orientation had no influence on surgical skills, in fact he recalled the best neurosurgeon in San Francisco cross-dressed when off duty. "If you need a surgeon, I'm your man."

Francois laughed a great huge laugh curiously full of genuine mirth. *"Merci.* Thanks a lot. Stay beside me if you like."

After that, Ellison moved amongst the living, doing what he could as a volunteer member of Trauma Team Francois. For the next thirty hours, he spent most of his time on his feet in the surgical suite, amputating limbs and repairing lacerated organs.

As he moved from patient to patient, he saw many who died because the disaster readiness plan was deficient: not enough doctors or nurses, ambulances stuck in traffic, panic in the city. Perhaps quicker than anywhere on earth could match, Paris put forth a heroic response to the crisis, but human society is simply not organized to react instantly to a true disaster.

Between cases he thought about the year just passed, twelve astonishing months of near perfection. Though he had felt himself a bit of a wreck before he met Miranda, his spirit damaged by a bitter divorce, he knew he had always been favored by fortune. He had not expected to fall in love with Miranda during a medical visit to the Philippines, but an irresistible resonance of pheromones passing between them during a Presidential Ball had created love at first sight. Her love had transformed him. He came from the rural class in America, but some unnamed urge inside him had always driven him to explore. With her he was unafraid to plunge into the exotic life of her tropical islands. With Miranda his life had rocketed to the realm of dream adventures, to what every man would give everything just to taste for one hour. He knew that a miracle had hit him and bestowed him with everything, except a child.

He wasn't sure he had really adjusted to the undeniable fact of having one billion dollars in the bank, his personal share of the Yamashita Gold, but he had begun to think about his options, which seemed endless. It could be almost disorienting at times, as if he were back on the prairies without a single tree in sight for a reference point, just spaces and directions that all could be interesting. He knew he wanted to deal with his sudden wealth in a philanthropic way, to give something back to the world for all the good things that had happened to him. But he had not donated it yet because he hadn't felt the right opportunity had arrived.

Almost everything was perfect, except for the miscarriage Miranda had experienced in the third month of her pregnancy, now six months past. Because Miranda enjoyed excellent health and vitality, the loss of the child had been heartbreaking for both of them and had left him with a nagging suspicion that stress was the underlying cause, for before he could rescue her, Miranda was held prisoner by the masters of the Yamashita Gold, when she was already pregnant. He winced as he thought of fighting to rescue Miranda. He'd spent a lot of energy forcing himself to forget pulling the trigger with men in front of him. Not doubting he had killed several men, he had never felt completely relaxed again. Though they had spent hours talking about their feelings, in the end he felt a disturbing storm inside himself. During many dinners alone they both sat and stared into space, wondering what they could have done differently, and what their child would have been like.

He and Miranda talked often about what he should do with his fortune, particularly since her much larger share removed all financial worries for generations to come. The world suddenly became full of people with ideas about how he should spend his money. Rich and well-known as he was, Ellison had dozens of proposals come to him every week, an assault that ranged from sophisticated business schemes to abject begging for help.

His original idea of funding an Advanced Surgical Unit at Stanford had finally struck him as redundant; though as a memorial for their unborn child, they did pay for construction of the largest children's hospital in Asia. Still, after considering all the ways he could use his fortune for the common good, nothing seemed to feel just right. Confused by the massive changes in his life, sometimes feeling lost as though adrift at sea, he had taken Miranda to Europe to get far enough away for a clear decision. They needed uninterrupted time together, as both of them felt the time was right to try to have another child. They were in love, very close and wanted to explore their closeness in every way. And now this.

He was just passing by the hospital morgue again when an idea hit him like a beam from a lighthouse: he would create a vast emergency medical team that could race around the globe on a moment's notice, something big enough to make a difference in anything short of outright war. There would be nothing like it in the world. The concept came into his mind fully formed, something he was sure he could do. His idea felt like a vision, heavy with certainty, perhaps a product of sleep deprivation combined with hours of adrenaline, stress, and caffeine. Laughing to himself, he recalled the Sioux tribe across the Missouri River from his family farm who in their quests for a prophetic revelation fasted and stayed awake to the point of exhaustion, hoping for an empowering vision. He felt as if he had just experienced his.

He found Francois sipping coffee and slapping his face to stay alert. It took Ellison just a moment to outline his plan for a world-wide rescue team.

"Commando Doc is born! *C'est magnifique!*" Francois exclaimed. "When I was in the seminary, people had all kinds of generous ideas but never enough money to put them into action. You are one in a billion."

"Thanks, but—"

"I will help you any way I can, *monsieur*. In fact, I will contribute everything I have learned. If you want me, I will be your teacher and number one helper."

Ellison studied Francois' animated face. All people are students of the rest of the human race, watching them and learning from their behavior, and Ellison felt himself a good judge of character. Though Francois at first seemed almost too eager, Ellison sensed his enthusiasm to be genuine and to come from a warm and caring heart. As for being helpful to Ellison, Francois was years ahead of him in knowledge of organization of a trauma unit. Francois seemed a likely choice as a *major domo* for Ellison's new project.

"We can talk later; and maybe you should be my number one man. But for now, just tell me what to do here."

"Give as much of yourself as you can, *monsieur*. Save lives!"

After dozens of surgeries, on the evening of the second day–or was it already night?–he no longer cared much, Ellison began to experience bursts of sleep while standing at the operating table. Once he would have clamped the wrong artery to a patient's heart if Giselle, the surgical nurse for that case, had not taken his hand in her firm grip. Recognizing he was becoming a hazard, not a helper, Ellison admitted to himself it was time to go. After completing surgery, he offered profuse thanks to his nurses. He found Francois and the other haggard doctors, who smothered him with parting Gallic embraces and encouragement to return as soon as he could. Unlike Ellison, they had been working in rotations that allowed them at least a few hours of rest. Sickened by the slaughter around him, he made one last check of his patients before leaving. Exhausted but partially satisfied by knowing he had done his best, Ellison shuffled to the taxi station for a ride to Le Grand Hotel, the five-star edifice across from the Opera House. The palatial stateliness of his roomy suite relaxed him like a safe harbor in a storm.

Smiling at the note Miranda had left when she drove to give her second speech, he pushed himself away from the ornately inlaid desk, staggered to the bedroom, called room service to place an order, and drenched himself in a steamy shower. Once toweled off, he collapsed in front of his television, where he blew steam off several mugs of strong coffee and tried to fight sleep until Miranda returned. What a horror show this nice little vacation in Europe had turned out to be.

The television forced him to suffer through seven commercials before bringing the gray-bearded personality back onto the screen. For once he looked agitated.

"This just in on the Eiffel Tower Bombing. A group calling itself Sword of Jihad has claimed responsibility. The Paris office of UNESCO, the United Nations Educational, Scientific, and Cultural Organization, received a call demanding the release of Ramzi Ahmed Youssef and Sheik Umar Abd al-Rahman, an Egyptian cleric, from American custody. The men are serving life sentences for bombing New York's World Trade Center in 1993, and Youssef was also convicted of bombing a Philippine Airlines 747 that same year. The anniversary of their convictions coincided with the suicidal jet attacks on the twin towers. In total, he is serving a sentence of life plus two hundred forty years in isolation in America's highest security prison. Sword of Jihad threatens more bombings if the men are not flown to Libya immediately."

Those guys again, he thought. I heard about them in the Philippines, friends of Osama bin Laden, who had several brothers and one or two concubines in the Philippines. Bin Laden was a regular visitor to the archipelago and had trained hundreds of men, in Philippine camps for the rank and file, in Pakistan and Afghanistan for the officers. One of their secret cells in Yemen did the suicide bombing of the *USS Cole.* When the Philippine terrorist group, Abu Sayyaf, kidnapped the SCUBA divers and fifty others, their first demand was the release of Youssef and The

Sheik, whose supporters were the prime suspects when TWA 800 blew up just after takeoff from New York City. They had even sent a note beforehand, threatening terror if Youssef was convicted. The TWA 800 explosion, notwithstanding the fuel-tank cover-up story concocted by the American government to calm nervous travelers, bore all the trademarks of a Ramzi Ahmed Youssef group. Very few who had access to classified documents failed to recognize their characteristic *modus operandi.* They always liked to put the bomb in row 26, at the weakest site of the 747. Row 26 happens to be near the fuel tanks, so that a proper detonation causes the nose of the plane to fall off before the aft of the plane plunges from the sky in flames. Sure, the media reported conclusive evidence of a problem with the aircraft itself, but Ellison never believed it was true. Now, probably from frustration that Youssef and The Sheik had been rotting in prison for so many years, the supporters had wanted to prove they could still operate despite tightened security world-wide and had done the Eiffel Tower.

The taxi driver and the doormen at the hotel had told him that all the world sat watching replay after replay of the collapse of the Eiffel Tower, which had been captured on at least nine home video cameras. Ellison assumed that the military of every nation had gone on heightened alert. Embassies everywhere would redouble their guards, public places would be placed off limits, and all the world would become a less friendly place as an inevitable temblor of suspicion shook the planet. Big time bombers, he winced, easing himself into bed. But he knew the CIA and FBI would be on them, along with Interpol, Mossad, French Intelligence, and every other investigative agency on earth. It made him sick to realize the surgical strikes after the airliner bombings of New York and the Pentagon hadn't gotten the cancer out.

Hope they catch the bastards soon, he thought, because America will never let Youssef and The Sheik out of jail alive. Despite a world going wild, he needed sleep and would have to think about the bombers later. He had barely gotten his head on his pillow when sleep crashed down on him like a theater curtain.

A POPE

Only the 264th Pope to die in all of history, Verdi thought. He patted Hildebrandt III on the arm but said nothing. Instead, he arranged the Pope's pillow and detected the smell of morbid flesh.

"You are like my son," the Pontiff croaked. "I could have helped you."

"Preserve your strength, Holy Father," Verdi said, attending to the man but at the same time thinking of Church history. On at least two occasions during the past two thousand years Popes had transferred the papacy to their own sons, bastard Popes born out of wedlock. "Your succession is the furthest thing from the minds of the Curia, and certainly from my thoughts. I pray continuously for your speedy recovery."

"Bah! It is too late for me. I pray that God gives wisdom to the Electors when I am gone, for when I think of the future, I fear for The Church."

"As do I, Your Holiness."

"Then abandon your mad idea."

"Mad?"

"It is of another time."

"The idea consumes me, Holy Father. What more can I do than follow the call I hear?"

"We all know your forehead was touched by Christ, Vincente; but as with all great men, you must beware believing any inner voice that claims to be divine."

"True, I believe God speaks to me on this."

"It is usually your own ego speaking, not God's voice."

"To guard against that error I will beseech Christ's guidance, Holy Father." Verdi smiled at the dying man, who reminded him of his own father in his purity of soul, though in contrast to his father's agricultural earthiness, Hildebrandt III had an extreme sophistication as a byproduct of The Church's emphasis on knowledge and finesse. At times like this Verdi actually felt quite close to the old man. "Do you wish Confession?"

"I, a dying sinner, need to rest now, my son." He grasped Verdi's hand with his waxen fingers, lonely fear in his eyes but with an iron will of optimism fending it off. "What will be, will be. Instead of talking about peace and goodwill with men who are not disposed to listen, I now prefer to talk about them to God alone."

"Rest now." Verdi brushed a silvery hair away from Hildebrandt III's eyes. Despite everything, things he suppressed in his mind whenever he could, he still loved the old man, but in a very unusual, complicated way. "I will be working in my office."

In the salon, *Camerlengo* Strizzi approached him. "What do you think?"

"He might live a few months at most. What news?"

"If he dies tomorrow, there will be one hundred fifty one cardinals under the age of eighty eligible to vote in the conclave. Assuming full support of the Italian cardinals working in the Vatican, I estimate you have fifty of the one hundred one votes you need. Now that election is near, there are several more I can persuade to help you reach the two-thirds plus one votes required to be elected."

"If God wills it. Who else is strong?"

"Many who think you too young favor Cardinal Muldowney

of New York. He is popular and capable, though without your visionary talents."

"There will never be an American Pope! John Paul II, the great Polish traveler, was the only non-Italian Pope since 1522, and there has never been anyone but a European."

"True enough. But Cardinal Obunse in Nigeria will speak for Muldowney against you, as will Cardinal Alvarez in Argentina; and they can sway many cardinal-electors, particularly those from the Third World."

"Obunse and Alvarez are old, infirm. Perhaps they might be too ill to travel to Rome to vote."

For several seconds the *Camerlengo* said nothing. Drawing his breath in, he hissed, "For the good of the Mother Church, that might be arranged."

They were both Calabrians, from the province next to Sicily, where a harsh code of brotherhood reigns supreme. In a pinch, a Calabrian inevitably chooses one of his own. With Strizzi a decade older than he, Verdi had watched him from afar before Verdi's own star ascended. In diplomacy, Verdi modeled himself after Strizzi's Machiavellian style. Strizzi liked to think of himself as a king maker, which he vowed he could be for Verdi at the right time, subject only to the will of God.

Like Strizzi, Verdi's path to the Vatican began in a rural Italian family, as the youngest of four children. His father, also named Vincente Verdi, grew grapes and olives at their four-acre farm near the wall of the village. In the heat of Italy's August, grapes ripened to be pressed in the traditional ways, with the village maidens inaugurating the crush with a glorious dance in the vat that splashed scarlet juice on their long legs. Verdi loved his family, and felt himself the happiest of young men. At night, in their cozy home inside the village, his mother served crusty bread made from her own wheat and baked in her own oven, a heavy loaf sweet with a yeasty scent claimed to come only from the magical yeast of his province. Without fail they made a prayer of thanks before each meal, and she was a daily communicant at the local church. His father sang in the men's choir, gave as much of his hard-earned money as he could to the monsignor, and often assisted the priests during Mass.

Whenever Verdi visited home, his family regaled him with the many legends that existed about him in the village lore. When he was born, all the women in the village took turns nursing him, so that when he became the brightest child at school, the mothers joked, "He sucked out all the intelligence, and now my own son is not as smart as Vincente Verdi."

During his baptism, a woman dressed in flowing gray robes, a stranger to everyone in the village, joined the circle of Verdi's family around the baptismal font. She fell to her knees and worshipped Verdi, kissing his tiny feet. After she swished out the door, she was never seen again. When Verdi was created cardinal, no one could be convinced the mysterious visitor had not been an angel come to pay homage with an annunciation of his future, simply not understood at the time.

By the time Verdi was a teenager, everyone regarded him as the finest village son in memory. He had the hard-muscled body of a gymnast and a beautiful, clear-eyed face. True, he had kissed some of the girls, but not one ever said he had gone too far with them, though they later admitted they would have been responsive to any show of lust.

The priests controlling the upper school invited him to explore the mysteries of The Church with them and were delighted to find their encouragement seconded by Verdi's aunt, Sister Carolina, identical twin of his mother. Verdi knew his mother would have followed Carolina to the religious life had it not been for her irresistible attraction to Verdi's father. Coming from such an ideal background, Verdi felt the call, gave up everything of this world, and entered training for the priesthood. Seven years later, at his ordination as a Roman Catholic priest, his parents beamed with pride. Their two daughters had given them grandchildren, Vincente's elder brother owned a successful olive exporting company, and now their youngest son was a priest. During the ceremony, Verdi felt his heart and soul soaring with feelings of satisfaction that he was living a life of conscience. Years later he thought of those ecstatic feelings as secret amulets that could shield his soul against the labyrinthine intrigues of Vatican City. Yet a day had come when he realized power held more attraction than did unattainable purity, that through some mysterious alchemy he had become one of them, but that since it was according to the will of God, it was for the best. Later, by applying himself with all his might, Verdi had risen to the top.

Verdi put a cautionary finger to his lips as he whispered to Strizzi, "Say nothing."

*Science without religion is lame, religion without
science is blind.*

—Albert Einstein

THE FORCE

San Francisco, California
When the landing gear of his gleaming, red and white trimmed
Boeing 747-400 hospital plane touched the ground at the newly
privatized Alameda Naval Air Station, Ellison felt a great sense of
accomplishment and relief. Accomplishment that in just ninety
days following the bombing of the Eiffel Tower, he, Miranda and
Francois had created a complete rescue team; and relief that their
first mission had gone so well.

He kissed Miranda lightly on the cheek, but she barely stirred
in her recliner seat. She and everyone on his team were weary after
the eleven-hour flight from Tokyo, where a 7.4 magnitude earth-
quake had leveled flimsy residential districts of the city at the precise epicenter of the quake. Like San Francisco in 1906, much of
what remained standing soon burned to the ground in the ensu-
ing fires.

Named after the horseback Viking goddesses who carried slain warriors to Valhalla, *Valkyrie One* cleared the runway just ahead of *Valkyrie Two*, another 747-400 flying hospital with ten surgical suites, recovery rooms, and an Intensive Care Unit. The 561 doctors, nurses, and support staff of Rescue Team International followed in two more 747s, just ahead of the tankers and slower cargo planes carrying the vans with their portable hospital tents. Altogether, with Francois' advice and guidance, Ellison had committed every last cent of his billion dollars in three frenzied months putting his Rescue Team International together, ram-rodding construction, and hiring the many surgeons he needed, from Orthopedists to Neurosurgeons. He had reasoned that something as ambitious as Rescue Team International required first class thinking in every way. If he could control his costs, he calculated he had enough funds for four years of operations, but after that he would have to raise money, and lots of it, according to his accountants. For the moment, though, by paying top dollar to overworked physicians and nurses, he had created a stellar medical team that—unexpectedly finding itself caught up in something new—was happy and excited.

Not long after they'd finished their first training session, world events galvanized Rescue Team International, referred to as R.T.I., into action. Every newspaper on earth headlined the Tokyo quake *The Big One*.

Surrounded by devastation, R.T.I. had performed round the clock surgery in Tokyo, with Ellison himself completing six or eight major operations every day for two weeks. While Ellison toiled in the operating suite, Miranda, using her communications skills to advantage, went into the leveled city to work with the local politicians on emergency responses.

Miranda was a product of the finest educations available in the Philippines and America, with a degree in Economics from the University of Chicago. The second child of Don Margarito Santiago and Donna Eliza Santiago, patriarch and matriarch of vast Hacienda Teresita on Mindanao, Miranda was born in a tiny village far from the hacienda. Her parents had gone into hiding because they had violated the rules of Eliza's strict family. As full-blooded Chinese, her mother's family had not wanted Eliza to marry a Spaniard. Full of fire, Margarito and Eliza eloped to distant Katipunan, where their first-born, Eduardo, was mid-wifed into life by the light of torches and the smell of burning garlic, both powerful magic against the forces of evil. In those days on the still wild island of Mindanao, the lovers were able to remain hidden for more than two years before trackers hired jointly by both sets of parents found them, and by that time Miranda had come into the world. After couriers ran the news to Hacienda Teresita, the relieved parents arrived sixteen days later. Overjoyed at seeing their prodigal children, the parents showered the babies with love, gave their belated blessings to the union, and convinced Margarito and Eliza to come home. Ready to resume the life of wealth and privilege in the tradition of the Spanish culture, the young couple took up residence with Don and Donna Santiago at Hacienda Teresita, a vast plantation that had prospered for more than a century. There they, too, rose in the world and raised their children.

Destined and trained for greatness, Miranda had never found her match until she met Todd Ellison. She wanted a man with *gravitas*, a man who was not afraid to live according to his own lights. And she had committed herself to do whatever she could to make Rescue Team International a success.

Tokyo had been a learning experience for the entire organization, with the overriding lesson that Rescue Team International needed more security. Chaos brings out animal instincts, and in desperation the law can become kill or be killed. In Tokyo, looters in surprising numbers had set upon them, first singly, then in groups when local food supplies ran out. What made Ellison edgy was that somewhere less civilized and orderly than Japan, his force might have been put in the paradoxical position of having to fight civilians in order to save their countrymen.

Once on the tarmac, he stood with his legs apart and his hands on his hips, enjoying a blustering wind from the Golden Gate that tousled his blonde hair. Miranda stood beside him, now alert and looking like a victorious Polynesian princess surveying her island from the prow of a war canoe. Everyone said they made a beautiful couple, she with her Asian exotic beauty, he with his All-American good looks. He knew that to be as svelte as she was only eight months after her miscarriage reflected Miranda's discipline. With her stomach already as flat and firm as ever in her twenty-four years, she was even more beautiful than her Miss Philippines year. Maybe both of them had exercised so intensely to block the pain over the loss of the baby. Right alongside her, he had worked hard to keep his athletic frame in shape; and though at thirty-two, he was not as lean as at Stanford, he was stronger, and Miranda told him he had a body like a Michaelangelo statue. Eight years older than Miranda, he anticipated their age difference would become an issue if he let himself get flabby. Dressed in his customary linen shirt, pleated gabardine slacks and a woolen sweater to fight the wind, Ellison scanned the sky until he spotted the approaching specks of the transports that carried his security forces.

When the first of the transports landed, it taxied at unusually high speed until it executed a perfect turn and stopped precisely next to a gate. It's remarkable pilot, General Mark Beecham, the wiry little cowboy who had given up his star to command security for Ellison, bolted from his seat and stepped smartly down the steps. With his black ten-gallon hat, ostrich cowboy boots and two-gunned revolvers, the tiny man looked more like the hero of a silent Western movie than the former chief of Delta Force that he was.

"Well, doc, ma'am," he drawled. "I'd say we were mighty lucky."

"With the world so high-tech now, no one's prepared for a breakdown of basic services," Ellison said, struck as always by how bow-legged Beecham was. "A couple of clicks on a computer and most people figure they can do anything from buying movie tickets to ordering groceries."

"I reckon every one of them cowpokes was on half rations by the second day after the quake."

"It takes trainloads of food every day to feed thirty million people in Tokyo," Miranda told them. "With the freeways and rail lines down, people got hungry in a hurry."

"It was tough to see that," Ellison agreed, "but we can only do so much. Haven't you always said we have to focus on our mission, which is to help the injured?"

"Just remember, pardner, if we'd been in Rwanda, instead of them polite little yellow fuckers we'd have been seeing big black guys coming over the fences with head axes." Beecham thought of himself as tall compared to many of the Japanese and liked to discuss anyone shorter than he whenever possible.

"I've been thinking about that scenario for days; and there's no doubt we have to improve our readiness."

"Fuckin' A," Beecham mocked.

"What do you suggest?"

"More hardware, especially half a dozen choppers for perimeter guard, and another hundred men. My guys got worn out by the round-the-clock duties."

"I'm just about broke, General. You're used to making requests from the guys who print the money."

"Then what do you say, Miranda? You've got plenty of dough."

"Hold on," Ellison interrupted. "This is my project, and I don't want to ask for any financial help, especially from my wife." He meant what he said.

Beecham never gave up easily. "How about from Eduardo, then?" He brightened, "Say, he's waiting for you 'n Miranda at the Sheraton Palace Hotel."

Eduardo, Miranda's brother, former playboy adventurer and thanks to the Yamashita Gold now the third richest man on earth, seemed to spend most of his time racing around the world on his new fleet of airplanes like a pasha on a magic carpet. Lavish as Eduardo's life was, he was a highly principled thinker who thought of the common man more frequently than anyone Ellison had ever known. After Eduardo donated a fortune to the Catholic Church to refurbish all of the cathedrals in Asia, Pope Hildebrandt III made him a Knight of the Golden Spur, one of the five knightly orders a Pontiff can bestow. Now, in addition to limitless wealth, a magnetic charm, and good looks, Miranda's brother deserved to be called Sir Eduardo.

"He called me on the plane," Beecham continued, raising his eyebrows. "Said he was flying in from Rome to speak with you about something urgent."

"I got his message," Ellison acknowledged. For Eduardo to fly halfway around the world to talk in person meant something big.

Though everyone was dead tired and needed rest, once through Immigration and Customs, they dragged themselves to a waiting limousine for the drive to San Francisco.

"Ah! Eduardo wants to speak of Rome. My roads used to lead

to Rome," Francois mused, to himself.

Eduardo, slim and perfectly dressed in a white linen suit, opened the door of his Presidential Suite. Worry nearly erased the smile on his face the moment Ellison walked in.

"Great to see you, Eduardo!" He and Eduardo were like blood brothers. Up close in a mutual bear hug, Ellison could not help but notice the long scar on Eduardo's cheek, the best plastic surgeons could do with the damage from last year's knife wound suffered during the struggle over the Yamashita Gold. It was the only mark on Eduardo's otherwise handsome face, which wore a tight smile that indicated Eduardo felt he had no time to waste.

"Trouble, Todd. I need your help."

Though he had just showered on the plane, Ellison sensed a sudden layer of perspiration on his upper lip. Trouble, it seemed, was everywhere. "Tell me."

"It's a long story; but I'll give you the executive summary.

"Shoot."

"I'm managing *Opus Spiritus* for the Catholic Church in Asia. Heard of us? We're a group of business and political people who both help the Church and watchdog the clergy."

"That, too, Sir Eduardo? Sure I've heard of them. Very powerful, and a secret society, isn't it?"

Francois cut in, explaining, "Centuries ago, yes, but not secret in modern times. Now all of the members of the Orders are identified. At least that is the rule," he said with a wink.

"Still, we can handle delicate matters when the need arises," Eduardo resumed. He rose to gaze out at the night sky, silent for a moment, his face twitching in an unsuccessful search for some comfortable expression. "Anyway, three days ago I spent the night at a resort outside of Manila."

"Someone new?" Miranda interrupted with a knowing smile.

"Karina Garcia is her name. I'm serious about this woman, Little Sister. You'll see. Anyway, about midnight a stranger knocked on my door. My security people told me I had to talk with him. You will never guess who it was!"

"Tell, Eduardo," Miranda teased. "Was it a woman dressed as a man coming to steal you away from your sweetie?"

"Hush, sister. No. It was Cardinal Lopez from Manila, disguised as a kitchen helper. He said someone may be trying to kill the Pope. I tell you my heart almost stopped."

"But why?" Miranda asked, shocked. "Pope Hildebrandt III is a friend of the people."

"Every Pope has enemies," Francois declared, his voice booming.

"Surprised me, too, but reality is as Francois says. So I called the Pontiff's personal secretary, who told me in strictest confidence that His Holiness has been so ill for two weeks that his look-alike has had to bless the crowds at St. Peter's."

"Did you talk with the Pope's doctors?" Ellison asked.

"I went to Rome to question one of them who belongs to *Opus Spiritus*. He's my friend. In fact, he's the Pope's chief doctor, who carries the official title of *Archiatra*. He says the Pope is dying, and to bring specialists because they are losing him."

Anticipating what was coming next, Ellison felt his stomach churn.

"So," Eduardo continued, I want all of us to fly back to Rome right now. I simply cannot decide how seriously to take Cardinal Lopez's rumor until you have examined the old man. In a matter this delicate, I need you, brother."

Not many months before, Ellison had made a solemn, solitary vow that he would never again expose his wife or himself to dangers like the ones he had survived in the Philippines. Instinct told him he should turn Eduardo down, but Eduardo was still talking, giving the details, and it was hard to imagine how accepting the great honor of being asked to consult on the Pope himself could lead to difficulty.

What could he do? He glanced at Miranda with the question in his eyes.

"It's up to you, Todd. But why not?" She gave him an encouraging smile. "We could ask His Holiness to bless your project."

"What do you think, Eduardo? Can I bring Francois? I know he's familiar with the Vatican medical services."

"My husband's right hand man," Miranda added. "In fact, I think Todd spends more time with him than he does with me."

With all of them aboard two hours later, Eduardo's powerful new business jet banked left over San Francisco Bay, climbed to an altitude higher than any commercial flight and made a beeline on the polar route to Rome.

Ellison woke hours later to see Iceland in the light of the rising sun, its smoking volcanoes venting clouds that rose skyward like sea serpents blowing flame. It would be Rome soon, The Eternal City, and beyond his excitement about traveling to a favorite city, he had to admit that he felt fascinated with the prospect of practicing medicine on a Supreme Pontiff.

❊   ❊   ❊

Verdi was praying alone inside the Pope's chapel when Strizzi walked in briskly, with news in his eyes. "I have been campaigning for you. You have an excellent opportunity," Strizzi whispered, kneeling beside him.

"Good," Verdi said.

"I promise you the two cardinals will not vote."

"Tell me more."

"They will not even speak against you. Obunse has gone into isolation after revelations that he plundered the diocese's coffers to support two mistresses. And Alvarez fell and broke his hip." Strizzi's face revealed nothing.

Men in high places regularly feel compelled to destroy enemies, Verdi knew, one face of power. Verdi felt satisfied that his chances in an election were being maximized. It was time to return to his duties as Secretary of State. "Now let me look at the Pontiff's schedule." When he looked at the list, Verdi started and barely concealed a gasp. "Eduardo Santiago?"

"Sir Eduardo now," *Camerlengo* Strizzi corrected. "You recall him. From *Opus Spiritus*."

"And Todd Ellison from America? Another doctor? How unnecessary, and with His Holiness so weak. I will not allow this intrusion, especially several hours from now when he is sure to be fatigued."

"The Holy Father himself gave permission. He says it is his final responsibility to the world to be examined by others."

"*Opus Spiritus!* Order of the Golden Spur!" Verdi grumbled, waving his arms with a gesture of dismissal. "A collection of meddling, corrupt weaklings who know nothing of our sacred work."

"As you wish, Eminence. I'll refuse them entry."

After pacing the room, Verdi controlled himself. "No, Eduardo Santiago is richer than a king and has many friends. You must avoid a scene. Let him in. As for another doctor? I would like to keep him out, but I suppose we have to allow this Ellison his day."

TAILSPIN

Over the North Sea

"Listen to this!" Eduardo shouted through the cockpit door to anyone in the *Gulfstream V's* cabin who was awake. "Two airliners just went down over Europe, both American."

"What!" Ellison gasped, not believing he had heard Eduardo correctly. He sprinted to the copilot's seat, with Francois right behind in his wheelchair.

"I just heard it on my side-scan radio. A Delta flight and a Northwest bound for Detroit. Simultaneous crashes, and both out of Amsterdam."

"Are you sure?"

"Listen for yourself." Eduardo flicked a switch to broadcast the transmission throughout the aircraft. "They're talking about it."

Ellison felt a churning in his stomach when the announcer confirmed both planes blew up in mid-air. "Youssef's supporters again," he guessed. "They've been quiet since the Eiffel Tower."

"Youssef for sure," Eduardo agreed. "When Washington refused to release him or The Sheik, their organization was certain to do something sooner or later."

"See if you can get General Beecham on the phone. He'll know what's going on."

Beecham answered on the first ring and Ellison cut in, "Is it true about the planes, General?"

"Confirmed. The second one blew up two seconds after the first, in broad daylight about an hour after takeoff from Amsterdam."

"Son of a bitch," Ellison muttered.

"Timers, don't you think?" Miranda added, squeezing into the cockpit and rubbing her eyes. "Why Amsterdam?"

"For the same reason they allow marijuana, hashish, and flesh to be sold in the open," Beecham answered. "The citizens of Amsterdam are the laxest in Europe, even in airport security at Schipol International Airport."

"Correct, *monsieur*," Francois added. "The rest of us in Europe think they are madmen. For example, the Dutch have their doctors out doing mercy killings, lightly supervised. It's too much of a paradox for the average European mind."

"Remember how Youssef and his gang planned to bomb a dozen airliners out of Manila on the same day?" Ellison mused. "There was plenty of evidence. Project Bojinka, the Philippine investigators called it." On a trial run to test the explosive scanners at Ninoy Aquino International Airport in Manila, Youssef got one bomb aboard a Philippine Airlines 747. It detonated when the aircraft was six miles in the sky, killed the passenger sitting above the briefcase and blew the legs off another, but was not a big enough blast to bring that airliner down. "His terrorist cell must have found a way to get multiple bombs through Amsterdam."

"Yeah," Eduardo said. "Right now is like waiting for the other shoe to drop."

"How much longer to Rome?" Miranda asked. "I've got a bad feeling about being up here now."

Eduardo studied his electronics. "Three hours and nine minutes to Aeroporto Leonardo Da Vinci."

Miranda possessed an uncanny intuition about trouble, and

her worries made Ellison feel so tense that he could taste his own fear, a rancid flavor that persisted until two hours later, when they merged into the flight corridor for Rome with Eduardo smooth and steady at the controls. Beecham suddenly broke into the tense mood with shouts over an open line.

"Two more confirmed down! This time when they descended through twelve thousand feet."

"Flag?" Eduardo asked.

"Continental and United. Both originated in Amsterdam."

"Traffic Control notified me that we're following a Delta airbus into Rome."

Miranda cut in, her voice raspy. "I hope it didn't originate in Amsterdam."

"What's its flight number? I can check its flight plan in a second," Beecham said.

"Delta 748."

They heard Beecham tap some keys. After he hesitated, his voice sounded as if he were reading the obituary of a friend in the newspaper, "Amsterdam to Rome."

"Damn!" Ellison cursed, punching his own fist.

Around the world, flight supervisors recognized the pattern and notified every one of the thousands of aircraft in the air at the moment. Rome Traffic Control broke in, "Delta 748, hold at one five thousand." Fifteen thousand feet, higher than the detonation altitude.

"Request immediate clearance, sir. We have a sick man in Business Elite Class."

The air traffic controller gave it to the pilot straight. "Four flights out of Amsterdam have been destroyed. You may have a barometric bomb on-board."

"Request advice." Beneath the matter-of-fact response, Ellison could hear the terror in the pilot's voice.

"Circle and hold. Search your aircraft. Consult your *Emergency Manual*. Also contact your headquarters." The traffic controller turned his attention to Eduardo and snapped out orders. "Gulfstream niner five yankee, circle and hold one nine thousand."

"Circle and hold one nine thousand," Eduardo repeated.

When Francois forced his wheelchair into the cockpit entry, Ellison felt the stump of Francois' leg brush against him. Whenever he could, Francois removed what he called his instruments of hell, accepting the involuntary stares at his stumps, which without artificial limbs strapped on looked like the over-sewn closures of hams. Over the months of working together, no matter how difficult the situation, Francois had manifested an indefatigable joyfulness and brilliance. Ellison had known genuinely happy people in his life, but Francois was different. He wasn't like Porter's *Pollyanna*, who was foolishly and blindly optimistic, nor like Voltaire's *Candide*, who believed everything was for the best in this best of all possible worlds. Francois had barely escaped death, and now his friend was a two-legged cat who had used up eight of his proverbial nine lives, and through some grace had come to total love of every breathing moment. No, Ellison had never met anyone who enjoyed simply being alive as much as Francois did.

Tense silence ruled the cockpit. Ellison calculated their aircraft held little risk, but had no way to make a reality-based estimate of the danger to the Delta flight just below them.

Francois spoke, wanting to break the tension. "I know the Muslim mind very well, perhaps as well as anyone can who converts from another religion."

Ellison looked up, wondering.

"I've never told anyone I was a Muslim for almost two years."

"No," Miranda said, surprised. "I'm shocked that we've never known."

"It was a chapter in my life, at a time very painful for me to discuss. While learning to live again after I lost my legs, I met a man, an Algerian physical therapist raised since elementary school in Paris. A lithe *café-au-lait* colored man with a French soul, Akhmed became my best friend and roommate. He spoke perfect French, Arabic, German, and at least six other languages. I loved and respected him. He believed in Allah, and since I no longer believed in Catholic dogma, going directly to Allah came naturally enough for me. He is after all the same god. But after an intense beginning Akhmed and I grew apart because his desire to overwhelm and possess me came into conflict with my need to live my own life, my way. Two years later we parted the greatest of friends. Sometimes I even see him now. But living away from him, the conformity of Islam grew tiring, and my old culture drew me back."

"To exactly what?" Ellison asked.

"I still love Allah, though I am a Christian of sorts again. You might call it my own esoteric school of thought. To quote the philosopher Ludwig Wittgenstein, a philosopher from before the millennium, 'I believe religion is the calm at the bottom of the sea at its deepest point, which remains calm however high the waves on the surface may be.' I believe, *monsieur*, that love and god are a unity inside each human being."

"Under that definition, Youssef and The Sheik might not qualify as members of the human race."

"Difficult to forgive," Francois agreed. After he adjusted straps on his thighs in preparation for putting on his legs, he told Ellison, "You know, *monsieur*, this trip to Rome has some feeling of Fate about it, as if I am coming back to something."

"What do you mean?"

"Like everyone, I am on my search. Even if you do not know it, and like it or not, you are on a search as well. This feels like part of mine."

After an hour of circling on a thirty-mile racetrack pattern four thousand feet above the Delta flight, Ellison and everyone on board felt exhausted by the tension. Finally the voice of the Delta pilot came through. "We've searched the plane and found nothing. Low on fuel, we have to land."

"Godspeed, Delta 748."

Through his binoculars, Ellison could see the big plane below them ten miles ahead. With its nose tilted downward, the pilot carved a smooth line through space toward Aeroporto Leonardo Da Vinci approach. Ellison almost closed his eyes for a moment, afraid to watch but at the same time aching to see the aircraft make a safe landing.

Half a minute later, precisely when the Airbus descended through twelve thousand feet, an explosive flash appeared at the rear of the plane. To Ellison's horror, he saw the tail and ailerons blown away from the plane in an appalling display that doomed Flight 748.

At Miranda's scream, Francois braced himself against the door of the cockpit. Tears of anger and outrage were in his usually calm eyes.

"Nothing can fly without a tail," Eduardo gasped. "It's going to go down!"

Like a gladiator plowing forward despite fatal injury, for five agonizing seconds the jet defied Eduardo's law of aerodynamics by maintaining its arc of flight. In the sixth second the aircraft flipped onto its back, flew upside down for what must have been the most terrifying few seconds of life for the passengers on board, gave off belches of gray smoke from fires beginning in its wings, and rolled into a spiraling dive, rotating like an augur until its wings tore off and it exploded a mile above the earth. No one could have survived.

Ellison struggled to find some philosophical meaning for what he had just witnessed. Unable to think clearly, he forced himself to remember the *Rescue Team International Psychological Manual*, which had been developed by the best mental health professionals he could find. Francois, as if reading Ellison's mind, quoted from the document. *When confronted by a great horror, the human capacity to think is obliterated by a variety of overwhelming emotions, but only for several seconds. Although for several hours the aftershocks of the perturbation cause the intellect to wobble like a weakened boxer, initial problem-solving begins as soon as the emotional shock undergoes rapid adaptive responses.*

"What should we do?" Ellison asked.

Francois quoted *Psalms* and Miranda sat still, pensive, and horrified. All of them recognized that conversation might make them feel less isolated in the universe, but that in fact talk would accomplish nothing else. They looked into each other's eyes and fell silent. Ellison forced himself to formulate a rational response. He contacted Beecham with a question. "Should we start the entire R.T.I. force moving right away, General?"

"For starters, we'll saddle up *Valkyrie One*."

"I suspect we can be helpful, even if it's just dealing with grief-stricken families."

"I'll make sure all our shrinks have their voodoo ready."

Shaken by the downing of Delta 748, Eduardo needed to muster all of his skills to land the Gulfstream V. Worse, the kill count reported by General Beecham increased even as Eduardo taxied to the private terminal. By the time their limousine arrived at Rome's Hassler Hotel above the Spanish Steps, a baker's dozen had gone down in total: one each from British Airways, Quantas, Lufthansa, Air France, KLM, and Alitalia, and four more American carriers after the initial three.

The whole world sat mesmerized by the media spectacle, with Ellison and the others joining humanity as soon as they could snap on their television. It was like the Eiffel Tower bombing redux, with sovereign nations rattling swords at potential suspects, worldwide restriction of civil liberties, and widespread anxiety. Coming as these bombings did in the aftermath of the Eiffel Tower catastrophe, world reaction threatened to lose all civility. The Sword of Jihad claimed responsibility and proved it by directing investigators to a service truck at Schipol International Airport that contained two items: a probably untraceable example of the explosive used, and a letter that repeated their demand for the release of Youssef and The Sheik. When the American FBI confirmed the Sword of Jihad story, nations and leaders fought to get in front of a camera with their opinions of what should be done. Some trumpeted the idea that America should fly Youssef to Libya before more innocent people died for him, while others argued that caving in to terror invites more of the same. Beecham reported calling his friends at the Pentagon and receiving Joint Chiefs of Staff interest in his Draconian solution: to execute both Youssef and The Sheik as killers anyway, and to follow their executions by combing the world until every last one of the terrorists had been run to ground and killed. Government lawyers gave the immediate opinion that such vengeance as killing the prisoners could not be countenanced, unless entirely new charges could be made. Besides, the prison warden was known to have convicts inside who could be convinced to assassinate other prisoners in special circumstances. Beecham figured that politics would dictate a measured response suitable from a nation living by the rule of law. Judging by the reaction from Washington D.C., the consensus in the White House seemed clear enough. Youssef's prison was surrounded by a battalion of tanks and armored personnel carriers, half of them facing in, and half facing out.

Though Ellison felt the need to rest from jetlag and sift through the events of the hellish day, after a shower and a shave before putting on his finest business suit, he barely had time to catch his breath before a chauffeured limousine and two escort cars flying the flag of Pope Hildebrandt III rumbled at the curb outside the Hassler Hotel's palatial lobby.

LEVIATHAN

Vatican City
One hundred eight acres named after one of the Seven Hills of
Rome, the Vatican Hill, the home of the Holy Roman Catholic
and Apostolic Church, and despite being the smallest sovereign
nation on earth, the walled tract of land serves as spiritual center
of one fourth of humanity. Majestic power, Ellison thought, as
they motored over the Tiber River and along the *Via Del Concili-
azione* toward St. Peter's Square. Directly in front of them, an
obelisk stolen from Cleopatra's Egypt pierced the sky, its beveled
apex pointing to the cross topping the massive basilica ahead. In
Rome, nothing can be higher than that cross.

"I shook hands with Pope John Paul II before he died," Francois told Ellison. "Popes are men of flesh and blood. My advice?
Remember that fact, *monsieur*, because as you will see, a Pope is
also a king."

Ellison marveled at the glorious dome designed in 1486 by the Renaissance architect, Bramante. The dome reared over the mighty cathedral that wore it like a hat. "Magnificent. Very impressive."

Enthused at being in Rome, Francois acted as tour guide. "Yes, *monsieur*. Built over the site identified as the true crypt of Saint Peter himself. The First Apostle, the most favored of the disciples, who died crucified upside down because he felt unworthy of dying like his master, Jesus."

"Are they sure of the site?" Ellison asked.

"Completely. It is one of the amazing true stories of our time. For centuries, no one dug into the ground beneath the altar, whether out of respect, superstition, or dread of finding Peter's relics gone. But building reinforcement work in the crypt of St. Peter's in 1939 uncovered an archaic pagan cemetery. As excavation proceeded it became clear that the ancient workmen had gone to enormous trouble to orient the entire basilica toward a small niche datable to 165 AD. This shrine, though damaged, contained bone fragments declared by Pope Paul VI to be the relics of St. Peter."

"Amazing!"

"At first it was a simple altar built by a few Christian survivors who survived Nero's persecution. They pooled their coins and built small, but what they built lasted until now. When Christianity became the official religion of the Roman Empire, the emperor ordered the first basilica to be built precisely centered over Peter's grave. Constantine built a magnificent structure that lasted almost a thousand years before it had to be demolished and rebuilt by Bramante and Michaelangelo."

"It looks almost new," Ellison marveled. "Very beautiful."

"The Curia believes in beautiful gardens and many luxuries, at least in Rome. They have a large budget to constantly attend to the buildings."

A motorcycle escort led them to a heavily guarded tunnel through thick fortress walls, then down a maze of narrow cobblestone roads until they reached an ornate covered carriage entrance from the era of the Three Musketeers. There, a reception party whisked them to the Papal Apartments. Before Ellison could absorb the sensation of being at the beating heart of the largest branch of Christendom, in its very castle, he became awed by the artwork, majestic creations that adorned the walls and ceilings. He was surprised to feel his own heart throbbing as they passed through a magnificently carved double door, and across the polished marble floors of the spacious Papal Apartments.

It seemed ironic that he found himself attending a Pope. Raised a Lutheran in the Great Plains of the Dakotas, for Ellison, organized religion was not necessary for a religious life that respects everything there is. In that simple concept lay Ellison's religion. Devout believers, his parents had forced him to attend Sunday School, to go through Confirmation with its endless memorizing of the books of the Bible, and to participate in youth groups that met twice a week. Despite his small income, Ellison's father was a pillar of the Lutheran community, sang in the choir, and was a deacon. To help his struggling parishioner, the Bismarck minister gave Ellison's father odd jobs at the church. Ellison had to help his father clean the church every weekend, another of the several janitorial jobs Owen Ellison held to support his family. As a teenager, Ellison hated throwing sawdust on the floor and sweeping the church from one end to the other with a long push broom. Perhaps as a result of this forced servitude, his adolescent formulation of religion became one that viewed religiosity as a mutual-belief reinforcement society, a fraternity bound together by shared fears of the unknown. He despised the sight of everyone bowing and kneeling at the prescribed moments in the service, more often looking around to make sure their neighbors noticed the proper observance than asking their innermost selves whether they were honoring God. The hypocrisy of ritual behavior grated on his rebelliousness. In the end, he concluded that by obscuring the goal, an institution can become more of an obstacle than a help in everyone's journey. But as he had grown from youth into manhood, he had become more moderate in his criticism of religious institutions; and in St. Peter's, he felt awed by the power and sophistication around him. An institution that has ruled much of the world for two thousand years should not be underestimated. It and all religions must appeal to some basic need of man, or soothe some primal fear. Enveloped in the immensity of it all, Ellison felt like a tiny speck in history.

Though there were nearly twenty black-robed men in the room, Ellison's attention was instantly drawn to three men who stood huddled in a corner of the room, tailored in red and white, with scarlet belts and scarlet capes and scarlet skull caps. "The cardinals, right?"

Miranda answered before Eduardo could, for he was already nodding to a splendidly dressed man carrying a stethoscope and a grim look on his face. "Princes of the Church" she said. "They are all powerful men."

Eduardo shook the hand of the approaching doctor. "Dr. Morra, allow me to introduce my sister, Miranda Santiago Ellison, and her husband, Dr. Todd Ellison of America."

"*Bellissima,*" Morra sang as he bowed to kiss Miranda's hand. About the age to be one of Ellison's professors, the *Archiatra* flashed an equally friendly smile at Ellison, "*Buon giorno, dottore.* We are glad you have come, though helping His Holiness may be beyond the talents of any human."

"That bad?"

"As you will see, his condition is grave."

"What is the diagnosis?"

"Liver failure, heart failure, kidney failure...even his adrenal glands seem to have shut down. Five months ago he was healthy as an ox."

Odd, Ellison thought, not quite sure why he decided to keep his thoughts to himself, though any doctor would have to be a suspect if the rumored assassination were true. "Does he need a hospital?"

"We have everything we need here, and the best consultants have done their utmost. Come, my friends, follow me. His Holiness is expecting all of you."

In the company of a cluster of clergymen, their group passed across a room where a dozen chairs surrounded a raised dais topped with a throne for the Pope. Exiting the salon, they followed a hallway into a suite of bedrooms. An exquisitely decorated chapel opened into the private passage leading to the royal-scale master bedroom. In contrast to the typical way of dying in America, alone in a hospital or nursing home, or at best with close family at the bedside, the Pope's chamber included more than twenty people. With three nurses bustling about him, the Supreme Pontiff lay on a bed, intravenous bottles dripping fluids into a vein in his neck and an oxygen mask on his face.

"His Holiness took a turn for the worse a few hours ago," Dr. Morra whispered. "When his temperature spiked, we got a chest X-ray and found pneumonia, both lungs."

Ellison studied the Pope as Morra led him to the bedside. An old man, and with the multiple organ failures described by Dr. Morra, an old man in the process of dying. For Ellison it was a sad sight. The Pope turned his eyes on them one by one, first toward Eduardo, then Miranda, then Ellison, finally Francois. *"Dominus vobiscum*, the Lord be with you," he whispered.

"Your Holiness," Morra said. "Sir Eduardo Santiago has brought a specialist from America, his brother in law, Dr. Todd Ellison."

"Deo gratias. Thanks be to God. His excellent medical reputation has reached our ears before we became ill, as has his history of adventure." As king of a nation, the Pope used the royal we. "Welcome, Dr. Ellison, and please proceed. We are surprised to find ourself dying, but we have little doubt."

"Thank you, Your Holiness."

"Take off my mask so I can speak without hindrance. If it is time for me to die, I live in joyful anticipation of everlasting life with Christ. During my illness I have learned much of the mystery of Christ's crucifixion and salvation through suffering. *Sursum corda.* Lift up your hearts, and do not mourn for me."

Ellison felt a deep respect for the old man. To rise to such stature, like any president of a nation or chairman of a large corporation, usually happens only to hard-working men. And beyond that, Hildebrandt III's famous holiness was acknowledged by almost everyone. All who knew him felt he was a man of supreme importance, a human as they were yet at the same time quite unlike them. No one ever spoke cynically about him. He was a combination of human genius and Divine Grace. In short, he was a complete man.

"May I examine him?"

At a nod from the *Archiatra,* Ellison listened to the Pope's heart and lungs, noted the jaundice in the Pontiff's eyes and the many hemorrhages in his skin. The only organ that seemed to be working was the Pontiff's brain, and that was surely weakened by the bacteria swarming through his bloodstream. Ellison tried to keep telling himself that the Pope was a man like any other man, but the Pontiff exuded a sense of institutional majesty that could not be denied. When this man died, history would be changed. In a relatively short term of four years, he had done more for the suffering people of he world than any Pope in recent history.

Dr. Morra handed Ellison the Pope's medical chart. One look at the numbers told him that it would take a miracle to save this patient. He needed a liver transplant, yet he could never survive the surgery, at least not for more than a few days. Still, it was the only chance, one probably considered by the Roman specialists already. He moved out of earshot of the Pope. "Do you have a donor for a liver transplant?"

"Of course, but we fear His Holiness would die in surgery."

"What do you think, Francois?"

"He would never wake up, *monsieur*. His condition is hopeless."

Noticing a few wisps of white hair on the Pope's pillow, Ellison swept them into the palm of his hand. Francois saw him and gave an approving nod.

"May I, *Archiatra*?" Ellison asked.

"Of course," Dr. Morra answered with a distracted wave.

Ellison slid the hair into a small envelope, just enough to run a complete series of special toxicology in his new lab aboard *Valkyrie One*, which was ruled by his old friend, Dr. Zahar Zaharian. In the scant downtime Rescue Team International experienced, Zaharian had developed a new generation of scanners for analyzing for chemicals. It relied on Epoch Biosciences technology in a Perkin-Elmer Analyzer. No one else on earth had Zaharian's refined scanner.

While the Pope blessed each of them with the sign of the cross, Ellison noticed one of the scarlet-caped cardinals striding toward him with a frown on his face.

❋　　❋　　❋

Verdi felt a sudden anger toward this intruding physician. Not that he could do any better than all the others. But what was he doing at the end of his examination? Did he take hair? The sacred hair of the Pope? If it were not for Eduardo Santiago and the rest of *Opus Spiritus*, he would simply order Security to confiscate the stolen hair samples, but Verdi knew it was politically better to present a statesmanly mien.

He saw Eduardo Santiago, and the beautiful woman, probably Eduardo's famous sister from the looks of her, bowing to him. He extended his hand and gave his most gracious blessing. But before he could speak, a wavering voice called to him.

"Vincente, I need Confession."

"Yes, Your Holiness."

"And I command you to have Eduardo watch over the gold. Who could be as helpful?" Forcing himself to a sitting position, the Pope grabbed both Eduardo and Ellison by an arm. "I know of you both. You are gold men. Protect it."

Verdi noticed the doctor stiffening, full of questions. "What gold, sir?" Ellison asked.

"The Vatican Gold."

It was strange the Pope would bring up the gold, Verdi thought, particularly in public. Hildebrandt III had already questioned him in private about rumors of Verdi's plan to use the gold for his Christian Renaissance. He seemed not to believe Verdi's denials. That was when their filial relationship had turned sour, at least in Verdi's mind. Hildebrandt III continued to love him, he knew, but Verdi feared he had lost the Pope's confidence in his judgment in the political arena. If Hildebrandt III lived much longer, Verdi feared the Pontiff might remove him from the Secretary of State position.

In the end, the Pope was obviously taking the safe route, and as his last act was putting a ball and chain around Verdi's ankle with this Eduardo and Dr. Ellison. He wondered what other obstacles Hildebrandt III might have hidden in front of him. Everything was developing according to God's plan. It made him so excited his mind leaped to imagining himself up all night planning, pacing, and letting new and wonderful ideas into his head.

As for showing these interlopers the gold? Verdi felt no fear of them. The gold would be his if he became Pontiff. Seeing the Vatican Treasure now struck him as a good idea, as it had been more than two years since he had last ventured deep into the bowels of Vatican City. Yes, it would be exciting to look at it and imagine his revitalized institution on the move.

He smoothed the pillow case of the Pope, saying, "Yes, Father,

I will show them." He turned to speak to everyone in the room. "Please excuse us now. I must be alone with His Holiness."

SULLIED
TREASURE

Minutes later, Verdi emerged from Hildebrandt III's chamber with a troubled look on his face, no doubt due to his concern for the Pope's condition, Ellison thought. At Verdi's signal to follow, Ellison fell into step beside the dynamic cardinal, who led them to his Secretary of State's office one floor below the Pope's quarters.

"Excuse me while I get everything ready for us to gain entry," Verdi said, motioning for them to wait.

As soon as they were alone, Miranda asked in hushed tones, "What did you think, Todd?"

"He was vigorous five months ago. If someone's trying to assassinate him, it could be poison. But at this point, there's nothing in his medical records to support that explanation."

"Except history," Francois whispered. "Rivals murdered at least nine Popes, and one of them people suspect was in 1978."

"John Paul I," Miranda nodded. "His reign lasted less than a month."

While they stood alone in the corridor, Francois lectured, "This area is completely unknown to the public. It's called the *Galleria delle Carte Geographica*, the Gallery of Geographical Maps."

Ancient murals, world maps taller than six men, marked the entry to the State Secretariat. Ellison marveled at the pale blue circles with continents in the Western Hemisphere incorrectly drawn because they indicated no route around South America. That told Ellison they had been painted before Magellan's discovery of a passage around Cape Horn in 1520 A.D., since the maps showed South America joined directly with Antarctica. Something about the perfection of the colors, like Gothic rose windows in the great cathedrals, made Ellison alert, aware. He felt the history of the place permeate him, making strong in him the sense of being at a precise moment in time, in the belly of an all-powerful whale.

Disrupting Ellison's ruminations, Verdi, once again in a seemingly buoyant mood, returned with a hooded, black-robed bishop who positioned himself shoulder-to-shoulder with Ellison. After they registered at a security checkpoint and descended in an armored elevator, they emerged into a broad, ancient tunnel hewn into solid rock. Filing cabinets and library shelves crammed with thick books sometimes pushed so far into the tunnel that their group had to pass single file. Though now illuminated by bright lights, the better for the surveillance cameras to do their lonely work, in places the ceiling of the tunnel was smudged with soot from centuries of passing torches. Ellison noticed the air getting cooler as they penetrated, and the smell of mold and old paper filled the air with antique ideas.

Cardinal Verdi guided them, his vigorous stride setting the pace for their hike through long caves filled with filing cabinets and bookcases.

"Seventy-five kilometers of documents," he said with pride. "Everything about the history of Christianity is in here."

"Including the Crusades?" Ellison asked pointedly. While en route to Rome, he and Miranda had reviewed dossiers on several Vatican officials, but it had been Miranda who first noticed references to Verdi's anti-Muslim philosophy.

"Ancient history," Verdi said with an easy laugh. "Now we have to live with the Muslims."

"The airplane bombings today won't promote peaceful coexistence."

"True, doctor, but my secretariat believes these are the acts of deranged extremists, not state-sponsored terrorism. No one can blame the vast majority of the Muslims, or any government."

"Some will," Miranda cut in. "Scratch the surface of most people, and the impulse for a religious war will not be hard to find."

"Forgive us for being so forward, Eminence, but we have all lived through Muslim-Christian war first-hand," Eduardo added.

"And your *Opus Spiritus* knows all about me," Verdi said, a mocking smile on his face. "But we are almost at the vault now, the sanctuary of the Vatican Gold. What does *Opus Spiritus* know about that?"

"That the Pope, the Secretary of State, and the dean of the College of Cardinals are the only people who know the entire collection inside," Eduardo answered. "Workmen have seen one part or another, but no one outside of the inner circle knows the full extent."

Verdi nodded. "And as the Pope's order was that I show you the gold, please do not be offended if I concentrate our visit in that section."

"Can you tell us more about the history of the gold?" Ellison asked.

"Basically it began with a few Roman gold coins hidden in catacombs beneath Rome, used by the early Christians to support their activities. Along with the Church, the treasure grew gradually, but when Rome adopted Christianity four hundred years later, the treasure began to grow rapidly. Some of it was taken by Alaric in 410 A.D. during his three day sack of Rome, but he was a Christian himself and spared a thorough search of the church properties. At that time the wealth was hidden in multiple locations in and around the city. Luckily, he never found King Solomon's Gold, which was already here."

"King Solomon's Gold?" Ellison asked, astonished.

"From the Ethiopian mines. Legend says that when King Solomon built the Temple in Jerusalem, there was nothing on earth to compare with its golden treasure."

"And you have it here?" Miranda asked, as amazed as Ellison.

"When Rome conquered the Jews, the spoils came to Rome,

of course."

"I thought Attila the Hun conquered Rome. Why didn't he take the gold?" Ellison asked.

Pope Leo I persuaded Attila to spare Rome, persuasion in the form of a payment from the Pope to prevent wholesale destruction."

"So the Vatican Treasure has been concealed beneath St. Peter's for centuries?" Ellison queried, his credulity strained.

"Since the first St. Peter's was built." Verdi answered. "Not all at once; but over the centuries the treasure made its way here from all over the globe. The Crusaders brought a fortune back with them; and the Spaniards contributed mightily when they ruled production of most of the world's gold for centuries."

"And the artwork?" Miranda asked.

"Valued at one dollar on the Vatican's financial statement," Eduardo reported. "And the same for all the billions of dollars worth of real estate owned by the Pope. One dollar. Amazingly understated, but I have seen the balance sheets with my own eyes."

"True," Verdi responded. "Just one dollar for all of the art and one more dollar for the combined value of the worldwide real estate holdings of all cathedrals and churches, all tracts of land, and all other buildings, such as bishops palaces. But how can any price be put on such things? Portions of the art we display in the Vatican Museums, but some is reserved for the bishops. Much is never displayed to anyone."

Verdi waved his arm at a security guard standing in front of a heavy vault door. "We are here. In addition to artwork, we have rare seeds and relics from all over the world; so we will all change into protective suits. Our scientists advise we do it this way. You can change your clothes in the locker room. Signora Ellison, this way for you."

When they emerged dressed in white suits and masks, surprisingly comfortable, Ellison thought, they walked through a final vault door that clunked shut behind them. They entered a cavernous room marked by eight tunnels running like great octopus arms from the cathedral-like center, probably copied after the ancient catacombs that wandered beneath much of Rome, especially outside the Empire walls. They waited, as Verdi had instructed, with Ellison and Miranda exchanging glances, already awed by what they could see.

"Astonishing!" Ellison whispered.

"Paintings in that tunnel, as far as the eye can see," Eduardo pointed.

Miranda, equally awed, said, "I recognize Rembrandts, Michelangelo, Da Vinci."

"It looks like a mile of Great Masters," Ellison observed, just as the vault door eased open for Verdi to join them, the black-robed bishop staying behind.

"Ah, my guests. Are you ready?" Verdi asked, looking entirely human in his white suit. And friendly? For a cardinal, Ellison thought, Verdi seems overly friendly, though the elated smile on his face shines real enough.

"My heart is pounding," Eduardo responded.

To his left, Ellison read a sign over one tunnel marked Reliquary. "Can you tell us what's in there?"

"Why not? In fact, we will go in," Verdi answered. "You are dressed for it. The first exhibit is the left leg of John the Baptist."

They paused in front of a glass vitrine in which a shriveled, blackened limb sat on silver prongs, its skin rolled back in several places to reveal strands of dessicated muscle and bone. "His arm is in the Topkapi Palace in Istanbul," Francois told them, shaken by the sight of an ancient leg.

"Next you will see three relics brought back from the First Crusade that are claimed to be the foreskin of the penis of Jesus."

"For a man of the cloth, you've certainly got a sense of humor," Ellison laughed. "That's got to be a tall tale."

"I could tell you the details, but believe me, doctor, it is true. In addition to killing as many Jews as they could find, the Crusaders sacked a Christian cloister in Southern France reputed to venerate the True Foreskin. Actually they collected two foreskins of Jesus even before they left France, and found more on the way. Of our three, we are not sure which, if any, is authentic."

As they strolled down the tunnel, Francois clanked ahead to the next display. "Are you going to tell us this is The True Cross?"

"We have had it since 336 A.D., at first in Constantinople, then here as a gift of Emperor Constantine, through his mother. Empress Helena, now beatified as St. Helena, is the one who convinced him to become a Christian and make Christianity the religion of the Roman Empire. Before that, the Church was struggling, persecuted. After she converted to Christianity, Empress Helena visited Jerusalem, bought the most priceless relics she could find, and gave her Emperor son the True Cross as a gift. In honor of the new religion that had helped him hold power in the Empire, it was he who built the original St. Peter's Basilica."

Verdi was talking easily as they approached another door, even heavier than the first, which opened with precision ease under Verdi's touch. When they stepped through the vault door, Verdi announced with a sweep of his arm, "The gold!" and Ellison let out an involuntary whistle.

They entered a chamber similar to an Olympic football stadium, its oval banks terraced with wide, tiled avenues lined on both sides with jeweled crucifixes, diamond chalices, and whole altars made of solid gold. Ellison's breath was taken not only by the wealth and opulence of the mind-boggling display, but because even from a distance the workmanship was of such beauty that he could see the work exemplified the finest goldsmith artisanship possible by an inspired man. He had always felt that when looking upon such creations, one feels the great essence of the human race. No other creature can create like man. For several seconds Ellison stood silent with the others as they took in the sight of a metal with so much power, in its own way more powerful even than the uranium or plutonium used for nuclear weapons.

"Not as much as the Yamashita Gold, right Todd?" Eduardo asked with hushed tones.

"Not even close, I'd say."

"But with the other treasures here, more valuable in total," Miranda added.

"Priceless," Verdi agreed.

The terraced cavern sloped away to a plain in the center that looked like a small town railroad yard. In the center, he could see two strings of boxcars, five per strand, stretching in long gray lines. A massive pair of locomotives sat quiet at the front of the gray train, their livery in the colors and symbols of the *Reichsfuhrer* Hitler's Train. In one corner of the chamber, the rail mainline ran against a tunnel, now cemented closed.

"The Nazi Gold," Verdi told them, his face revealing his awareness of the paradox of the Pope doing business with Hitler. "I assure you the Vatican acted with the welfare of Christendom in mind. When Pope Pius XII saw the opportunity to take ten box-cars of gold out of play, he took it."

"How did that happen?" Ellison asked, feeling slightly disoriented. Too many things were happening too fast, the way they had on his eighth birthday. His mother had planned a big birthday party for her favorite son and they were anxiously awaiting guests when torrential rains swept into the Dakotas from Canada. In two hours the Missouri River swelled and went over its banks in a flash flood. Years earlier the Army Corps of Engineers had built dams and levees and told everyone all dangers had been tamed. Believing them, his father had risked everything he had saved for years to build the house himself. It wasn't much, but it was his; and he and his wife decorated it with rough-hewn furniture and swirling rose vines painted on the imperfect door frames. Years later Ellison remembered it as looking like a little cabin from a Norwegian forest. From high ground on a bluff, his family had watched their farmhouse float off its foundations and drift downstream. He wasn't sure if that had been the saddest day of his life, though it was the only time he had ever seen his father weep, but that day had created in him an appreciation for inexorable forces. Try as he might, Ellison had never been able to give up the doubt about whether his birthday celebration had somehow caused the universe to be unhappy. He had been so excited by the smell of molasses cookies and the rare treat of a pheasant roasting that his father had shot in the wheat stubble. The pace of events at the Vatican reminded him of that day. He needed time to think about the Pope, the bombings, and the gold. Normally he would have spent days grinding the facts of the situation into comprehensible grist before he decided the most promising plan. But the one luxury he wanted most, he simply did not have: Time.

Verdi had been eyeing him, wondering whether to reveal how Hitler's Gold could have gotten into the Vatican vault. "In brief," Verdi answered, "Pius XII rose to the papacy in 1939, on the eve of World War II. Before that he had been one of my predecessors as Vatican Secretary of State, and before that served as papal nuncio to Germany from 1917 to 1929. He knew Hitler well, and in fact negotiated the Reich Concordat with Hitler in 1933 that guaranteed that the Catholics of Germany would not oppose the rise of the Nazis."

After the war began with Mussolini's Italy as an Axis Power allied with Hitler, Pius XII remained in regular communications with Berlin. Though he struggled for safety of the Vatican, Catholics and Jews, Pius XII retained a secret negotiating channel with Hitler."

As Verdi spoke, he became more voluble and seemed to give up censoring his own thoughts. "When the tide of war began to turn against the Germans in early 1943, Hitler needed a safe harbor for the gold stolen from Russia, Poland, Belgium, France, Croatia, Denmark, and all of the other conquered lands. Hitler never trusted the Swiss. Believing that putting the bullion in Swiss banks would mean he could never recover it, he made an offer to give the gold to Pius XII, some have argued in exchange for his silence on the question of the Final Solution. Most of us who know the entire story believe, however, that Pius XII simply outsmarted Hitler. In March, 1943, the secret train came by night. Pius XII assumed the Nazis would never dare recover the gold if Hitler changed his mind. But four months later, when the Allies invaded Italy and threatened to conquer Rome, Hitler said, 'I'd go straight into the Vatican. Do you think the Vatican impresses me? I couldn't care less. We'll clear out that gang of swine. Then we'll apologize for it afterward.'"

In that same month Mussolini fell, and the new government said it would back the Allies instead of the Axis. Hitler did invade Italy and captured Rome, surrounding the Vatican but not storming the citadel. At least a fourth of all the SS Troops were Roman Catholics, and Hitler reasoned that as long as the gold was surrounded, there was no need to retake physical control of the bullion anyway. Vatican City remained better than any other hiding place. Pius XII, for reasons never well understood, set strict limits on knowledge of the train. It has been here ever since."

Miranda spoke up. "In our day it is politically correct to accuse him of being Hitler's Pope. But in fact, the head of the rabbis in Israel said at the end of the war that Pius XII saved close to a million Jews with his quiet efforts."

"Public opinion does not follow that line for now, but the gold is no secret to the Swiss Bankers," Eduardo added. "I've heard about it in Zurich. How to handle the gold is the problem."

"Each rail car in the vault has fifty tons of gold," Verdi reported.

Ellison did a quick calculation in his mind. "About 120 billion dollars."

"The richest train on earth," Verdi added. "Sir Eduardo, have you seen enough?"

"My remaining questions have to do with security issues."

"Impregnable."

"Can you be more specific?" Ellison asked.

Verdi made an expansive gesture like a magician sealing a box, "Every kind of sensor monitored round the clock by a squad of guards in an underground bunker in an adjacent tunnel. To get in here, someone would have to capture Italy first, then Vatican City, something Hitler's *Wermacht* didn't relish attempting."

Eduardo took his charge from the Pope seriously. "May we speak with your security people?"

"The *Corpo di Vigilanza*. Certainly." Verdi nodded to them, "They are separate from the Swiss Guard and are responsible for protection of the Pope and the Papal Household. Anything else?"

"We thank you for this great honor," Eduardo responded.

"His Holiness accorded it to you. I am but his humble servant." Verdi eyed Ellison, "He has little time left, yes?"

Ellison nodded, "I see little reason for hope."

Miranda said, "Even I could see the Pontiff needs a miracle."

"We can all change at once," Verdi instructed them when they reached the dressing rooms. At his locker, Ellison reached into his jacket pocket. The tiny envelope containing the Pope's hair was gone.

"Your Eminence, did you see an envelope on the floor?"

"Envelope? *Non, dottore.*"

Ellison checked the pocket again, inspecting with his eyes instead of his hands, even sensitive as they were. The envelope was gone, there was no doubt about it; and he had been mindful of the precious sample all the while they walked through the labyrinth. True, several times he had been bumped by the black-robed bishop; but his pocket was deep and he doubted the cleric was an accomplished pick-pocket. How could he have dropped it? But if someone had taken it, the bishop or Verdi had the best chance. But why?

Ellison focused his eyes deep in the pocket of his jacket. A thin white strand nestled in the lining of the pocket, the sight of it causing Ellison's heart to accelerate. It was surely a sample from the Pope, one that had fallen from the envelope during what must have been a hasty search of his clothes. With a red suspicion light flashing in his mind's eye, Ellison felt an urgent need to get the hair sample to his laboratory.

TOXIN

Rome

Five and a half hours had passed since departing the Vatican. Cool inside his just-arrived personal aircraft, Ellison noticed a hot sun turning the sky outside white with mirages shimmering off the black tarmac. While mechanics swarmed around *Valkyrie One* in its private hangar, Ellison took a deep breath to help settle his mind, in turmoil since Hildebrandt III's locks disappeared. During their wait for *Valkyrie One*, agitated discussions with Miranda, Eduardo and Francois about what to do next had done little to put him at ease, particularly when Miranda reminded him of his sometimes slovenly habit of leaving things in his pockets and not finding them for days. Finally, though, everyone agreed with Ellison that as soon as Dr. Zaharian arrived to activate the special testing equipment aboard *Valkyrie One*, they needed to test the hair sample for poison. The wait while the R.T.I. team completed its flight from San Francisco to Europe had been agonizing.

Ellison's alarm gongs were going off, and he wanted his strongest people at his side, though for security reasons, Ellison had not given any hint what the urgent mission entailed, only that Beecham and the chief scientists should be ready for a meeting as soon as they landed. "What?" Beecham complained on the radio. "Come on, doc, I'm a damn good cowboy but I can't round up cattle in the dark, and if you want me and this here Nose Man to help, we need to know exactly what's going on in that so-called mind of yours."

Once in the secure conference room aboard *Valkyrie One* he reported his Vatican observations to Beecham and Dr. Zahar Zaharian, Chief of Laboratory Services. Miranda, Eduardo, and Francois added their impressions. General Beecham, who had slept during the flight across the Atlantic, was bright-eyed as a rooster exulting in his crow at dawn. When Ellison finished his report, Beecham pursed his lips and whistled. "That's deep, pardner, someone poisoning the Pope."

"Farfetched, I know," Ellison mused, "but it has happened before." Ellison handed Dr. Zaharian the single strand of the Pope's hair. "We need to know if any poison can be detected."

"Small sample," Zaharian grumbled, peering over his long Armenian nose. Many considered him the most brilliant pathologist on the planet, but he had the pale face, receding hairline, and bookish stare of someone who had spent too many hours pouring over data in the bowels of hospitals and morgues. With his faintly cadaverous appearance, he had never been a big success on the social circuit. But he had published over five hundred scientific articles, one of them sooner or later destined to win him a Nobel Prize. Ellison had total confidence in him. Zaharian squinted his eyes, studying the hair. "Maybe too small."

"This is it."

"Can you get more?"

"Not without good reason," Eduardo interjected. "We just cannot ask for locks of..."

"The Pope's hair," Francois said, finishing the sentence for him with a Gallic wave.

Zaharian turned his nose toward Ellison with a cool interest before he folded his thin white fingers in a peak. He gazed into space for several seconds, pondering. "Ah, I see. In that case, we will use techniques that do not consume any of the sample, like nuclear magnetic resonance and spectrophotometry." His voice had the measured sonority of a mortician.

"How long?" Miranda asked.

"Before your finish your second cup of coffee, Mrs. Ellison."

Francois cut in, "And if we come up empty with the non-destructive techniques, Todd, then what?"

"Use half."

"Right," Zaharian said. "Dr. Francois and I will be back with the answer."

"Be careful with that sample," Ellison added as they left. It was a miracle that he had one at all.

Ellison led Miranda by the hand through the door to their faux-marble stateroom, which occupied most of the Boeing 747's upper deck bubble. Several of his ancestors had worked with wood, as master cabinet-makers or carpenters. He appreciated the sheen and texture of mahogany, teak, and cherry paneling and had designed their stateroom to have the aged patina of the Captain's Quarters in the stern of a British sailing schooner. Antique furniture was bolted to the polished floor to prevent slipping during turbulent flights, and a king-sized bed with a canopy beckoned across the room.

Taxed by the flood of events and lack of time, Ellison and Miranda desperately needed rest and each other. All of his life, Ellison had appreciated beauty, whether in nature, music and art, or the physical beauty of the human, and particularly he enjoyed beautiful women. Beyond any dispute, Miranda ranked with the most beautiful and alluring women on earth. What separated her from other beauties was her rare combination of intelligence and goodness, things that would not wither with time, and whenever he looked at her he experienced a smooth current of pleasure. Always ready with a smile, she had a broad, youthful face that showed the earliest crinkles of crow's feet when she squinted against a tropical sun. The skin of her thighs glowed a velvet tan, with a silken texture when he touched her. As a matter of personal hygiene and lifelong training, her fingernails were always perfectly manicured, with matching toenail polish. She insisted on a daily bath and fresh sheets every night.

As a child, she was attended by an *amah* who slept beside her cradle. If she started to cry, she was carried to her mother, showered with love, and rocked back to sleep. Ellison believed the child-rearing practices of the Filipino upper class produced adults who were usually open and confident.

Miranda liked intensity and wasn't afraid to live for it. She loved to leap astride a spirited horse to gallop against the wind along a beach, her long black hair blowing behind like a comet's tail. Her soul was as dark and mysterious as a jungle, influenced by exotic legends, by moths that seek the moon only one night a year before they die, of whisperings about ritual circumcisions of teenage boys, of spirits that could fly from the mountains, half woman, half flame. Before Ellison came into her life, she was a plantation owner and adventuress who had joined her brother exploring caves filled with bars of nickel babbitt. When Miranda concluded the bars were simply lead brushed with nickel paint, she shifted plans. Using what had already become her legendary business judgment, she decided the best strategy was to identify an existing smelter willing to buy the lead itself. She located one in New Orleans, and just as Hacienda Teresita regularly did under her stewardship, the venture made an excellent profit.

When she kissed Ellison invitingly, his jet lag disappeared in an instant. He kissed her back, enjoying the sensation of her warm, moist lips against his. Such a woman, he thought, the rarest of the rare, the crème de la crème. His life had been a whirlwind of change and excitement since he had met her, and he liked it. Life was exciting, and though tired as he was, he felt a surge of loving lust for her.

Not long ago, in connection with pregnancy planning after the miscarriage, Ellison had estimated the number of times he and Miranda had made love since their marriage; and except for the several days after she lost the baby, their loving averaged once a day. Today would not reduce the average; he could sense that she really wanted him.

"I'm fertile, darling."

Ellison felt something go off in his brain, a neuro-endocrine signal that brought him more in touch with the senses of his body, made him more aware of the pleasure of her lips against his.

Knowing they would not be disturbed, he relaxed and gave himself over the private experience of body against body, relinquishing awareness of everything around him. She was in the private sphere with him, her senses tuning out the world and honing in on giving physical pleasure to him. He sensed urgency in her when she pushed her hips against his.

For someone who had remained a virgin until he met her, Miranda took a surprising interest in sexuality. Soon after their marriage, she brought home a book named *Netsuke Dolls*, about carved ivory figures of Japanese couples experimenting in the one hundred sixty Japanese sexual positions. Ellison responded by finding a Hindu book of Tantric sex which encouraged delaying orgasm until the need reached exquisite, aching, and accentuated climax. Between the two books and their own strong libidos, there was little they had not tried together.

But when Miranda was really excited, as she was now, what Ellison liked to do was go down to kiss every inch of her, which he began to do, kissing her neck and breasts. She had little body fat, a narrow waist, and firm, perfectly shaped hips. She held his face close to her nipples and moaned with pleasure, until he moved across her belly, tasting her sex, probing with his tongue, bent on pleasuring her. Miranda responded with her own mouth, taking him in, until he felt driven by the need to be inside of her, making wild love, throwing caution to the winds.

It was passionate and fast, both of them racing toward a joyful hammering home, an exultation from a primal level riveting their two bodies together, fulfilling the act nature has programmed all life to perform, passing bits of deoxyribonucleic acid in forty-eight chromosomes in a wild explosion of pleasure that jolts across the brain and swells in waves of sensation from the erotic nerve fibers.

They slept, for an hour Ellison judged by the shadow of *Valkyrie One's* tail on the tarmac. Miranda dozed with a satisfied smile on her face, cozy under the blankets. He loved to watch her while she slept, and he always felt amazed that she was his. He believed they understood each other through the wildness of their sex. He knew from experience that he could lose his veneer of civilized demeanor and become a savage. He would never have believed it about himself, but battle brings out a hidden side in everyone.

Once again concentrating on the world around him, Ellison splashed cold water on his face, donned his favorite robe-satin with broad vertical stripes of burgundy, navy and gold...the pattern of the Royal Army Medical Corps, the *Licensed Lancers* formed in 1898—and strode alertly to the conference room.

"Francois and Zaharian are on the way," Beecham told him.

"Any news on the hair?"

"They haven't told me anything."

"It goes without saying you are welcome to sit in on their report."

"Thanks, pardner. While you were sleeping, to kill time I checked with Washington, D.C. No more planes have gone down."

"That should be over for now," Ellison said, relieved. "Their kind of work takes time between acts."

In response to a soft hum, Ellison punched a button and saw Zaharian and Francois waiting outside the door. Another button slid the door open for them.

"Nothing, boss," Zaharian reported, while Francois nodded in agreement. "No evidence of any known toxin, drug, or poison."

Ellison pushed himself out of his leather chair and walked around the room with his hands clasped behind his back, pondering for several minutes, until finally his face brightened. "Then how about unknown toxins, secret stuff?" He looked at Beecham. "Come on, General, you guys in the U.S. military must have something secret, maybe at Dugway or Maryland."

"Sure. As weapons systems, a thing or two you haven't read about in the New York Times; but our kind of stuff is designed for big populations, not to take out political targets."

"Poisons?"

"Sure, but very fast. Too fast for the clinical picture you described of a patient going down hill over a few months."

Ellison resumed pacing the room, hoping for an insight. When none came, he turned to all of them, "Any ideas?"

Zaharian squirmed in his seat, spread his alabaster hands on the table, and straightened his arms as if bracing himself to speak. "During your initial presentation, you mentioned the Nazi Gold. I know they were doing research on slow poisons."

"Nerve poisons?" Ellison asked.

"Maybe, but also biphasic toxins, specifically two harmless substances that combine to produce fatal effects. Like epoxy glues that come in two separate tubes and only become active when you mix them."

"I recollect seeing a report about that sort of thing in some papers the Ruskies took from Berlin to Moscow at the end of World War II," Beecham said. "Some experiments they did on the Jews, but our scientists decided the same as the Krauts did—not suitable for warfare. Couldn't kill enough people."

If anyone had come from poorer roots than Ellison, it was Beecham. He'd grown up in the West Texas desolation around Midland, where his whore of a mother had gotten pregnant with an unidentified cowboy's sperm. Just before his ninth birthday, she died from an overdose of sleeping pills and Beecham was taken in by an illegal Mexican family. Forced to work cleaning the portable toilets near the oil rigs that bucked up and down day and night, pumping oil for America's restless drivers, Beecham grew to hate every minute of every day. Unless he did the dirtiest work, Beecham was sent to bed without his supper of tortillas and beans. At age ten, Beecham ran away from the daily whippings Señor Martinez gave him, climbing out of the adobe hovel on the night of a particularly brutal, cocaine-driven, lashing with a lariat. After nearly starving to death living on the streets and trying to catch rabbits in the endless brush around the city, he had been apprehended and pronounced a ward of the state of Texas. He suffered through two years at an orphanage before a miracle struck him. A former cowboy movie star had built a ranch and adopted almost a hundred orphans. Beecham never figured out what Mr. Roy had seen in him during one of his high-profile visits to the orphanage, but that evening he and three other children were riding in the plush seats of a van as it barreled across the open land toward Dallas. Once in a loving environment, Beecham had excelled in school, graduating near the top of his class in a fine high school. The United States Senator from Texas was a personal friend of the movie star and recommended Beecham for admission to West Point. Ellison believed that Beecham had spent much of his life trying to escape the memories of his past. He had never married, and Ellison realized that he, Miranda, and Eduardo had become Beecham's first and only real family. Beecham would do anything for him. Classified or not, Ellison needed to know about poisons.

"Well, inasmuch as we are out of options, General, how can we get access to those reports?" Ellison asked, feeling he had to keep moving forward to delay the frustration of defeat.

"Easy. With my security clearance, I can access most anything on the Defense Intelligence Agency website." After an elaborate sign-on procedure, Beecham was in.

Using its translating ability, the computer in Virginia presented the original German studies in nearly perfect English. Ellison scanned a list of five substances, whose chemical structure and physical properties were followed by detailed scientific studies performed for each substance on one hundred Jews in Bergen-Belsen. "Autopsy reports on five hundred human beings. Ghastly," Ellison sighed.

The chemical pentasulfiram attracted his attention, a potential analgesic created at Heidelberg University before the war but not used for treatment after it was found to be fatal in the presence of alcohol. Its molecular structure looked much like disulfiram, a drug he knew well from using it to treat hopeless alcoholics, though the Nazi drug had five sulfiram rings instead of just two. Disulfiram, or Antabuse, disrupts the normal metabolism of alcohol. Usually, the liver breaks alcohol down into carbon dioxide and water; but if a drinker has disulfiram in his body, the alcohol gets shunted along another pathway and becomes acetaldehyde, a poison related to formaldehyde. Drinking thus becomes an auto-embalming process, with vomiting, fever, rapid pulse, and sometimes death. If taking disulfiram every day, an alcoholic simply cannot drink.

"According to the Nazi studies," Ellison observed, pentasulfiram is even stronger than Antabuse. And look, it makes alcohol into a potent liver toxin."

"So five hundred Jews had their livers destroyed for the glory of the Reich," Francois interrupted, his voice thick with disgust.

"The Pope has liver failure," Zaharian reminded them, brightening up for the first time.

"Did you test for pentasulfiram?" Ellison asked.

"Maybe, maybe not," Zaharian answered. "We did test for Antabuse, but this pentasulfiram is an unknown toxin, and I'm not sure if they cross react."

"Let's find out," Ellison said, then paused. "Can you?"

"Easy, at least in theory," Francois explained. "All we have to do is scan the molecule into the computer and the machine does the rest."

"But it will be our last shot," Zaharian added. "Testing will consume the remainder of our hair sample."

An hour later, Zaharian returned with a frown on his cadaverous face. "The best I can tell you is maybe," he said. "Pentasulfiram is not the kind of thing that goes into hair; and besides, Todd, you just got the ends of the hair, no living tissue. Most of our sample probably grew out of Hildebrandt III's scalp more than six months ago."

"Then what do you mean, 'Maybe'?" Ellison asked. "Did you find it or not?"

"Down at the end nearest where the root would have been, we got a weak positive readout." Zaharian peered over the top of his rimless spectacles. "But it could have been a machine error."

Ellison put his head in his hands while Eduardo stood to pace the room deep in thought. Ellison asked Miranda to join them. Fresh and happy, she stood behind Ellison with both arms around his neck, cuddling her face to his but paying close attention while Ellison summarized their findings to her.

"I believe we have to warn the Holy See," Eduardo announced, "Cardinal Verdi in particular."

"Not him," Ellison protested. "Though it is obviously unlikely, he could have removed the Pope's hair sample from my pocket."

"I know what you are saying, but protocol is to go to him."

"I agree with Eduardo," Francois said. "Besides, no matter who Eduardo tells, Verdi will hear of it soon."

"But we cannot make fools of ourselves," Miranda cautioned. "As one of the Pope's knights, going public with an accusation like this could destroy your-our-credibility forever."

"What we really need is more samples," Ellison protested. "Maybe we don't have to tell any priest yet. Morra is *Archiatra*, the Pope's chief physician. We could show him the evidence privately. Maybe ask him for more samples. Better yet, get some blood so we can test directly."

"What do you expect him to do?" Eduardo challenged. "Put yourself in his shoes. He got where he is by being two things: a great physician and a team player. He has to report anything we say through proper channels."

"Could we go directly to the Chief of Police in Rome?" Beecham asked.

"He will simply ask Dr. Morra anyway," Eduardo concluded. "No, to get more samples and to alert the Vatican to danger, I think we have to go directly to Dr. Morra and Cardinal Verdi. Agreed?"

Bowing to Eduardo's prestige and experience in the Vatican, Ellison stood by while Eduardo talked first with Dr. Morra, then Verdi by telephone. At dawn, Cardinal Verdi sent a car for them that brought them to his suite in the Apostolic Palace. A tape recorder rotated on his desk.

"Worrisome," Verdi muttered as Ellison finished his presentation. "Don't you agree, Dr. Morra?"

"His Holiness worsens daily," the *Archiatra* answered.

"We must put a triple guard on him," Verdi announced, closing the meeting. "Thank you for coming, Sir Eduardo, Miss Santiago. And, of course the Holy See thanks Dr. Ellison for his consultation."

"And the blood samples and hair?" Ellison reminded him. "Can I collect them?"

Verdi paused, his mind working at top speed. "He is too weak to give more blood, but as I am on my way to give him Mass, the hair is a possibility. Yes, when I return, I will have hair samples for you. You may all rest assured that we will do everything we can to protect the Pontiff."

LAST
COMMUNION

With eight priests gathered around Hildebrandt III's deathbed,
Verdi offered the Mass for their dying leader. *"Benedictus qui venit
in nomine Domini.* Blessed is he who comes in the name of the
Lord,"Verdi droned, chanting the Mass plainsong he knew so well
from his diocesan days as a parish priest. Were those three years
the happiest of his life? Verdi often thought fondly of the mar-
riages and baptisms, and of teaching the catechism to teenagers
from the village. It was a good life; but he knew early that a life in
Calabria was not his destiny, especially after what he called his
"spiritual crises" began to drive holy spurs into his twenty-seven
year old hide. He had felt differently about himself after the first
crisis.

Some thirteen years ago, Verdi remembered precisely, his way
of seeing life changed suddenly. The world opened up to him in
an exciting way. He felt marvelously alive, moved to tears by the

beauty of dewdrops on a fresh red rose, infinitely grateful for the blessing of living from one moment to the next, graced by a love for the smallest, most insignificant details of existence. In that state of being he felt more expansive, more in tune with cosmic harmonies, bursting with even more energy and enthusiasm than his prodigious vitality of the past. Unfortunately, with the enthusiasm came such surging energy that after two nearly sleepless weeks, everything about his parish life began to grate on him, from the paltry amounts in the church offering to the slowness of the altar boys during Mass. He began to snap at penitents during confession, and felt annoyed when the people fidgeted during his homilies from the pulpit. It irritated him beyond tolerance when he saw them grow restive after he decided to lengthen his preaching from fifteen minutes to two hours or more. At his wit's end from their abrasive behavior, he lectured them that they should be perfectly still to hear the message he brought before them. Perplexed by his own state of mind, he knew such things had not troubled him before.

Confused about his feelings in the midst of this remarkable episode in his life, Verdi went on retreat to a mountain monastery where he could practice religious exercises designed to clear his mind and soul. There he reflected on the new ideas flooding his consciousness, some so profound that he believed himself on the verge of a new theology. For days and nights he paced the monastery gardens, talking for hours to the Jesuit brothers about his new solutions to the old problem of how to retain religious faith in a scientific world. And when the brothers tired of listening to him, he hiked to the village below, where farmers displayed their produce and where a village lass named Maria sold fresh, crusty bread hot from an oven. Younger than he, and with the luscious, inviting curves of a woman ready for children, Maria had been mesmerized by his long theological discourse to her. Twice he held her hand to make a point, felt the gentle, tentative pressure of her fingertips in confused return, and was about to throw caution to the wind no matter what the cost to him, when the frowning eyes of Maria's father had driven him back into the street.

Trudging up the hill, with Maria already gone from his mind, he felt ideas crashing over him like endless waves against the seashore, great joyful ideas that would help all mankind see the light. And that very night, unable to sleep for the fourth consecutive night, he felt an ethereal certainty bursting through to him in the form of a visit from an angel, who told him that his life was ordained for a great mysterious purpose. His revelation, ineffable yet powerful beyond description, changed him forever.

At that moment, Verdi knew in his soul that God had a mission for him, still undefined, but a mission nonetheless that called him to transcend the confines of a parish priest's life in favor of the big stage. For him, the biggest stage possible had a two thousand year run going in Vatican City. He immediately offered his services to Cardinal Strizzi, former prelate of the capital of Calabria, and made himself invaluable to the older man. When Strizzi engineered his appointment as a junior priest in Vatican City, his tireless work caused him to be noticed by Cardinal Pacini, who eventually became Pope Hildebrandt III. Pacini sent him into the diplomatic corps because of his bright and gregarious personality. After that his rise was dazzling.

Verdi's instant of reverie ended, he focused on the present, the here and now. "*Dominus vobiscum.* The Lord be with you," Verdi prayed, blessing everyone in the Pope's sickroom.

"*Et cum spiritu tuo.* And also with you," the priests responded in unison.

"Do you wish Confession now, Holy Father?" Verdi asked with a solicitous bow.

Dehydrated by his pneumonia, the Supreme Pontiff croaked an answer from his parched throat. "*Quia peccavimus tibi, Domine.* Lord, we have sinned against you."

"Leave us," Verdi ordered. "I will hear the Confession of His Holiness."

Departing almost without sound, Cardinal Strizzi led the priests and nurses out, leaving Verdi completely alone with Pope Hildebrandt III, just as he had been daily for weeks, though only for minutes each time. The Pope may have had doubts about Verdi's political agenda, but none about his priestly services as an intermediary between God and man.

Verdi moved his chair closer to Hildebrandt III and made the sign of the cross over him. For several seconds the only sound in the room was the raspy breathing of the dying man.

The Pope eyed Verdi, gathering his strength. With great effort, Hildebrandt III rose up on one elbow. *"Kyrie, Elieson.* Lord have mercy. Forgive me, Father, for I have sinned. *Mea culpa, mea maxima culpa."*

Verdi brushed aside a matted lock of the Pontiff's hair, *"Mysterium fidei.* Let us proclaim the mystery of faith, amen." Verdi began the ritual repeated by almost two thousand years of priests listening to the sins of mankind. "I will hear your confession, Holiness."

A look of pain contorted Hildebrandt III's face as he whispered. "I allowed people to die in the African civil war when it was in my power to save them, but I feared our Church properties might be lost." A fit of coughing followed his effort, and Verdi was unsure whether the tears welling up in the old man's eyes came from coughing, from sorrow, or both. "When historians proved Jesus had a brother, James, I lost faith in the doctrine of the Virgin Birth and the Immaculate Conception of Mary. Thus I have heresy in my heart and mind. I wish to be forgiven, yet I have believed myself greater than other men."

In the end, a Pope, like any simple farmer, has to make his peace with the Lord. An act of perfect contrition, Verdi thought, vexed by the old man's piety. "Now I will give you the Eucharist, Holy Father," he said, standing to position himself behind the Pontiff, where he poured a draught of red wine while he chanted the Eucharistic prayer to transubstantiate the unleavened bread and wine into the true body and blood of Christ.

"Corpus Christi, the Body of Christ," he said, slipping the wafer into Hildebrandt III's open mouth.

After a quick glance at the sickroom door, he flicked back the sleeve of his robe, felt for its secret pocket, and found a tiny envelope filled with bluish powder. After he dropped a pinch of the drug into the wine, he swirled the cup and held the adulterated chalice to Hildebrandt III's parched lips, *"Hic est enim calyx Sanguinis mei.* This is the cup of my blood," Verdi chanted. "Shed for the remission of your sins."

Verdi inhaled involuntarily while Hildebrandt III drank the poisoned mixture, by Verdi's count the sixty-third dose. The Pontiff had already lived long beyond Verdi's expectations.

Exhausted by his eucharistic effort the old man sank back into his pillow, spiritually relieved by the *Viaticum*, food for his endless journey. Verdi fought off a stab of conscience. This Pope will be a saint, he thought, knowing that some influential churchmen were already calling for the beginning of the process leading to sainthood. Verdi rested his hand on Hildebrandt III's shoulder. "Your place in Heaven is assured when you are judged." And well, he thought, your time has come. It is God's will.

He looked at Christ's Vicar on earth, dozing now in the deep sleep that leads toward death. "I have loved you," he whispered, "and I have done what you would have wanted if you had really understood my vision. Time is wasting. The Church must move on."

With a last glance back at Hildebrandt III, Verdi opened the double doors to the antechamber and spoke to a large group now gathered there in a death-watch. "He is sleeping. Set up a vigil beside him." While a dozen cardinals and bishops surged past him, Verdi remembered a final task. He motioned Cardinal Strizzi aside. "Please, stand guard beside him."

"What?"

"In the name of God."

His face quizzical but asking no questions. Strizzi gave him a collegial bow, "Of course, Your Eminence."

With Strizzi temporarily fixed in place, Verdi spent less than a minute in the *Camerlengo's* office before finding enough white hair to foist on the intrusive Dr. Ellison. For months he had followed his plan in complete secret, unable to share it with anyone for fear of discovery. That his plot mirrored his own brilliance he had never doubted. He thought about new technologies and the danger that someone might detect a difference between Strizzi's DNA and the Pope's. To obviate that risk, he clipped off the root ends of the hair, leaving only the lifeless fibers of which hair is formed, where there is no DNA to be analyzed.

When Verdi returned to his suite, as expected he found Sir Eduardo, Miranda, and the meddlesome Ellison waiting, chatting with Dr. Morra and examining the leather-bound books on his shelves. Verdi presented Dr. Morra with a gilt edged envelope with a red wax seal hallmarked with his official stamp.

"Four hairs from the Pope. You said that would be enough?" Out of the corner of his eye, Verdi noticed Ellison studying him.

"Four, yes, that is what Dr. Ellison asked for," the *Archiatra* confirmed.

"Will that be all, then?" Verdi asked with a faint smile. He knew it was dangerous to gloat, but sometimes appreciation of his own amazing ingenuity made him forget. For most of his life people had been telling him again and again that he was a genius. He recognized in truth that his parents lacked his special spark, and like every genius, he wondered from whence the gift had come, for he could not identify its source in the warp and woof of his family tapestry. That he could rise to this level from the simple village of his birth gave proof of the intervention by God. Just the same, he couldn't help but appreciate the wonder of his own designs.

Ellison joined his conversation with Morra. "Now what?" Ellison asked. So direct, so uncouth, Verdi thought. Verdi's heart had almost stopped when during Dr. Morra's summary of the medical findings he heard Ellison utter the word, "pentasulfiram." It was a chilling experience for Verdi to hear the word that could bring his downfall, made worse by the way in which Ellison had confronted him, as if laying a trump card on the table and then watching him for a reaction. He didn't like Ellison, and he didn't like any of Ellison's friends. But something told him to be wary of the doctor, who reminded him of one of his mother's cautionary sayings. "A thorn in the foot can bring down even the strongest lion." Though he felt confident that no one—not even Cardinal Strizzi if he ever guessed the truth—would ever be able to prove he poisoned the Pope, still it gave him a burst of fear that persisted until, finally, his long-standing conviction that his life was divinely directed squelched his anxiety. Why was he so sure God wanted the old Pope dead? Why else would God have made Verdi the Vatican nuncio to Germany, where as an ambassador in his studies of the Holocaust he learned of the secret research? Why else would he have remembered that obscure scientific finding for so many years? And why else would God, just six months ago, just when he needed it, have led him to locate the small vial remaining in a laboratory at the ancient university in Heidelberg where it had lain forgotten for more than sixty years? Yes, one must discern the will of God in everyday events, and Verdi's history had begun to tell him the tale of his mission.

But Morra was telling Ellison, "Contact me when you have

repeated your testing. How long will it take?"

"Maybe two hours, depending—"

Interrupting their conversation, a bishop swished across the room, cornered Verdi and whispered in his ear. *"Il Papa e morte. The Pope is dead."*

Afraid his knees might buckle completely, Verdi held himself with two arms on the bishop's shoulders until, without uttering a word to anyone, he stumbled into his bedroom and fell on his knees beneath a gilded crucifix. Tears in his eyes, whether of joy or grief he knew not, Verdi prayed, "Forgive me if I have done wrong. Guide me if I have done your will. I am ready to be your sword."

At the sound of a gentle knock at his door, Verdi composed himself. It was Strizzi, functioning in his role as *camerlengo*, and Verdi knew it would be the beginning of a series of solemn rituals to honor the dead Pope, maintain operations of the Church corporate, and after properly mourning the old, to elect the new Pontiff.

Stay calm, he told himself. Strizzi may suspect, but he himself has much to hide; and besides, no one can ever prove anything. He is not here to accuse but to perform his duties.

When the pope dies, the prefect of the Papal Household informs the *Camerlengo*, who must verify the death of the pope in the presence of three cardinals and the papal master of ceremonies. According to the interregnum rules, no autopsy is permitted; and while in the past the absence of an independent post-mortem examination has led to wild rumors, the prohibition is absolute. Verdi felt secure that—Ah! But he had almost forgotten!

In a consuming panic, Verdi flailed across the room to his copy of *St. Augustine's Confessions,* extracted his vial of poison from its hollowed out pages, and flushed the vial down the toilet so that not a trace of evidence remained. As he watched the bluish-tinged water spiral down the drain, he remembered that residues of poison probably lurked in the secret compartment of his assassin's robe. Just before he opened the door for Strizzi, he threw the robe into the blazing fire in his fireplace. For a moment he felt certain Strizzi could see through his walls, but he caught hold of his wild imaginings when the robe blazed into ashes, rendering him calm enough to ease the door open for the *Camerlengo.*

Strizzi studied him with an inspector's eye, even and cool. "He is dead, Your Eminence. Please accompany me."

His heart pounding, Verdi eased out through the partially open door and fell in line behind Strizzi as the *Camerlengo* wound through the Apostolic Palace to assemble his verification team of Cardinals Muldowney of New York, Righetti of Rome, and Lopez of the Philippines. Speaking in whispers as they filed through the ornate hallways, Verdi told the others, "Doubts have been raised." All eyebrows arched in question, though of course they had already heard rumors. "And we have Dr. Morra working with scientists," Verdi added, to satisfied nods.

When they entered the death chamber, Verdi felt a surge of exhilaration and hope. Hildebrandt III lay with his eyes open, fixed on eternity, his face waxy yellow with his mouth wide open, but his chest not moving. As soon as he saw the motionless body, Verdi felt himself at the fulcrum of a universal mystery: does a man possess a soul that can survive his physical death, yes or no? And if it survives, then to become what? For a moment he felt the ghost of Hildebrandt III enveloping him with cold scrutiny.

With Verdi at his side, *Camerlengo* Strizzi approached the dead man and called him by his baptismal name, "Eugenio Pacini?" When there was no response, Strizzi tapped him on the forehead with a tiny silver hammer, for centuries used only to certify papal death. "Eugenio Pacini?" he said twice more as he tapped. After three sharp taps, the *Camerlengo* glanced at the faces of the cardinals standing in solemn array beside him before pronouncing the prescribed words, "The Pope is truly dead."

With the tenderness of a son, Verdi closed the unseeing eyes. He kissed Hildebrandt III's forehead and hands, reveled in the coolness of death, and understood how much they had loved each other. When the others crossed themselves in bereavement, Verdi shared their grief, though he simultaneously felt his soul soaring toward an unborn goal. For a moment, Verdi felt confused. He experienced a derealization, when for what he later estimated to be ten seconds, he felt completely lost. He couldn't remember where he'd been, or what he'd done, or what he'd planned to do. He experienced amnesia, an almost complete loss of his memory and sense of self. When his mind snapped itself back to customary functioning, all Verdi knew was that he had *never* experienced anything like it in his forty years.

At Strizzi's command, the muffled tolling of the single bell in the Arco del Campani broke the stillness of the moment. A brass giant that rings only to announce the death of a Pope, the bell sent out the news of Hildebrandt III's end. Verdi felt his body vibrating in harmony with the solemn cadence of the bell, its clang a deep and richly sonorous E flat. Like a wave spreading from a pebble dropped into still waters, other churches heard the news and other massive bells joined the Arco del Campani to toll out the sad news that the leader of Christendom had joined his maker. For a moment, the mad rat-race of life halted in its tracks. Traffic stopped, the faithful crossed themselves, knelt, and prayed, and all of Rome fell silent to listen to the mournful, slow message of the growing chorus of a thousand bells.

"Take him to the embalmer while the bell still tolls," *Camerlengo* Strizzi instructed. "When his body finally reaches the Sistine Chapel, let the bell stop."

"No autopsy," Verdi ordered, struggling to keep his voice and face impassive.

"Draining and destruction of the blood, but no desecration of the body," the master of ceremonies agreed. "That is the rule. Now it is my duty to notify the Dean of the College of Cardinals, who will inform all the cardinals of the world and summon them to Rome."

He had gotten away with it! He had assassinated the Pope and no priest even suspected that Hildebrandt III had been murdered!

While Swiss Guards moved the Pope's corpse in somber procession toward the embalmer, *Camerlengo* Strizzi led the others to Hildebrandt III's study, where they smashed the Fisherman's ring and the lead seal under which his most important documents had been sent. When they followed his body, Strizzi sealed the Papal Apartments with red ribbons held by waxen stays. His eyes sparkled at Verdi with friendly encouragement. The next person to enter would be the new Pope.

THE LIVING
AND
THE DEAD

Aboard Valkyrie One, Rome

Ellison studied the results on the slip of paper before him, the same as on the first set delivered half an hour earlier: not a trace of pentasulfiram in the Pope's hair samples.

"If it weren't for those stolen hair samples," he began to mutter.

"If you don't succeed on brilliance, you will on endurance," Francois said with a hearty laugh.

"With Todd's intuitions, we have to consider every possibility," Miranda cut in. "Any ideas? From anyone?"

"Chain of custody," Beecham offered. "You always have to look at that. On the last hair samples, I mean. Could anyone have slipped us a ringer? I mean there was no living tissue that had any DNA we could look at."

"Not once Morra put the samples in my hands," Ellison said. "But otherwise, we don't really know what happened before Verdi gave him the packet."

"And," Francois added, "we don't have freedom to ask a lot of questions here, as everyone has noticed."

"They are already talking about me," Eduardo complained. "Cardinal Lopez told me we have created quite a stir in the College of Cardinals, which takes displeasure at unsubstantiated accusations of murder." He frowned at Ellison.

"Sorry, Eduardo, but you do recall asking me to get involved in the first place, don't you?"

"Yes, but I am telling you to stop. We've gone far enough, and now you are ruining my reputation. What else does a man have? Answer me that."

"Truth, Eduardo, at least that is what I have to have." He saw the flare of Eduardo's temper but knew his arrow had struck its mark. He could always count on Eduardo to overcome his human temptation to rationalize the easy way. Time after time Sir Eduardo had proven he truly was a knight ready to sally forth. "Look, Eduardo, it's like the general says. Chain of custody. I'm willing to bet our hair samples are not from the same man."

"And if they are?"

"Then I will admit I've been wrong."

"Unhappily, we have no sample of living tissue from the Pope," Francois reminded them. "We just had old, dead hair."

"How about talking with Dr. Morra?" Ellison asked.

"We have to notify him of the negative test results anyway," Eduardo mumbled, rubbing his temples. "You want me to ask him for what? Blood or tissue from Hildebrandt III? God, I cannot believe I am going to do this."

After a relieved Ellison pounded his brother-in-law on the back, he listened to him get on the speaker-phone with the *Archiatra*. When Eduardo made his request, Morra sounded annoyed, "The Death Certificate will read **Natural Causes**. At the moment, the Pope's body is being prepared to lie in state in the Sistine Chapel, and we have none of his blood samples preserved, so as for DNA? Impossible. Thank you for your investigations and offers of support, but in view of your negative results, I believe we can all now agree there was no foul play."

Feeling like a trapped animal, Ellison looked at the faces around him.

"I guess it's over, Todd," Miranda comforted him.

Ellison had not been deceiving himself. He had little hope that Dr. Morra would provide additional samples. Morra's patient was dead, and now Morra would be violating strict Vatican rules by giving Ellison any part of the body. Ellison supposed that Morra would lose his job no matter what the outcome if he helped Ellison. And surely more important to the devout Morra, he would be thrown out of the Church, be denied the sacraments, and according to the teaching of Catholicism, be likely to find his very soul in hell on Judgment Day. When the Vatican makes a rule, it expects followers to obey.

Since realizing that depending on Dr. Morra would probably fail, Ellison had been brainstorming about his options, which he finally reduced to two: acknowledge defeat or break into the morgue before the morticians completed their embalming work. Once embalmed, Hildebrandt III's body would be on display in full view of an honor guard, unassailable. He needed to get tissue from the body, but he had less than five or six hours before the embalming was done. If Ellison followed his normal process of sleeping on a problem before deciding what to do, he would sleep through the final opportunity. He doubted if he could feel proud of himself ever again if he gave up, yet he recognized the arrogance of his notion that he had the right to become a grave-robber. Neither of the courses of action seemed right. It would be criminal to assault Hildebrandt III's body, and if caught, he would be imprisoned, no matter how rich and powerful the Santiago family might be. In an existentialist sense, it was absurd that he should find himself being forced to take action in an opaque universe studded with questions and mysteries. He wished he had never agreed to come to Rome and wanted to shout in frustration but knew it would do no good. Shaking his head, he sat down and assumed a posture exactly like sculptor Auguste Rodin's *Thinker*. He saw his reflection in the mirror, seated with his chin on his fist, considering the gates of hell below him.

It was ironic that this particular piece of sculpture came into his thoughts. He had been studying *The Thinker* at the Auguste Rodin Museum in Paris just before the Eiffel Tower bomb exploded. He had left the museum not five minutes earlier, strolling toward the tower in order to get a breath of joy infused into the weightiness inspired by the sculpture above its bronze doors.

When the bombs detonated, Ellison had seen the face of evil rear its head. Now, months later, he felt that if he gave in to Verdi's evil, he would be making his own deal with the devil: a nice, calm, uninvolved life in exchange for putting blinders over his perceptions. Self-deception was something he had done before, once when he convinced himself he could lie to his mother about where he had gotten the money for a train ride from North Dakota to California to look at colleges. His parents had no money to send him to college, and despite his perfect grades and near perfect SAT scores, they expected him to go to the local community college to study business and open an agriculture supply store after graduation. Ellison wanted to be a doctor, but there was no medical school in North Dakota. After watching reruns of *Baywatch* on Bismarck television, Ellison decided at age seventeen to get himself to California for college. At the instigation of his best friend, he had driven all the way to Fargo and stolen two fancy bicycles in a park by the Red River of the North. As he drove away with them concealed in his 1960 Ford F-150 pickup truck, he saw a boy of ten racing toward him across the thin ice of a pond by the river, with his father close behind. Ellison just knew that the boy would fall through the ice into the black water, but he drove away at top speed while looking back in his rear view mirror, imagining the worst. He drove two hundred sweaty, paranoid, tortured miles to sell the bikes in Minneapolis. He had never told anyone what he had done, and for years he had repressed his memories, but lately his self-deception had broken down. He realized that he had never forgotten. Sometimes he rationalized that it had been just a youthful indiscretion that he was mightily lucky to have escaped unscathed, but in his heart he knew that he had broken his personal rules for living because of desire for money. Worse, he knew that in a moment of truth, he'd proven to be a coward. He should never have driven away with the young boy in danger. He told himself he was no better than any other man, that he had no right to go after the Pope's corpse. He complained to himself that if he just hadn't experienced the series of events—the Eiffel Tower, the Delta Airliner, attending the Pope—he could rightly walk away. But in his mind the events had linked themselves into a chain that bound him, made him a prisoner of his time, and forced to him to do his duty, like it or not. He felt cursed and wondered if he was suffering some cosmic retribution for the killing he had done in the Philippines.

He looked at his wristwatch, wishing the second hand would stop moving. He knew he had come to one of those moments in life that give rise to the old saying his grandfather used whenever someone had to make a lonely decision, "Every man is an island." The second hand ignored his will. It was insane, but he had to choose: taking the incredible risk of invading a death house or letting a killer go free.

Ellison pushed himself erect and hoped the physical act would magically infuse him with a certainty he did not have. "It's not over for me," he announced. "Everyone can stay out of this if they prefer, but here is my plan."

Before he could finish telling them the details, they were shaking their heads in astonishment. Eduardo shouted that it would be impossible. Miranda advised him to think clearly. Beecham had an amused twinkle in his eyes, "I can give you some operational help."

Francois rolled his wheelchair to Ellison's side, grim-faced and with his voice louder than anyone had ever heard him. "I am with you. I don't give a damn what happens to me or what anyone thinks of me!"

Ellison reviewed his schedule one last time before he and Francois began their mission. It was Wednesday morning, time for the Pope's weekly General Audience, now held in the *Aule delle Udienze*, a six-thousand seat auditorium where some Popes give their deepest theological arguments to the common man. And what a day greeted them, one of the most spectacular days of a city blessed by good weather, a day when a gentle breeze wafted off the Mediterranean Sea and scrubbed the air to a polish that highlighted the pastel colors of Rome's matchless architecture. Despite tickets costing more than a week's pay for most workers of the world, thousands of visitors appeared at St. Peter's with precious tickets in hand on their scheduled day, not deterred because the Pope was already dead. The slow tolling of the bell in *Arco del Campani* reassured Ellison that the Pope's body still remained with the embalmers.

Francois passed him a plastic badge, hurriedly counterfeited by Beecham, that dangled from a red cord he placed around his neck. "Under usual rules, anyone needing to visit an office in Vatican City must first get a special pass, which the guards do not honor until they have called the office to verify that the visitor is expected. If you have not been invited into Vatican City's inner workings, you simply cannot get in. Once inside, a visitor is free to move about semi-public areas, but gaining entry to any of the private areas remains impossible."

To avoid recognition and facilitate acceptance, the men were dressed in the brown robes of Franciscan friars. After a quick trip to a costume supply store, Ellison's face was disguised with a bushy chestnut beard. Shocking everyone when he appeared, Francois had cut his hair short and shaved his beard completely off. Without it, everyone thought he had a handsome face that illuminated a room when he smiled. As soon as they felt prepared, Ellison ordered their driver to take them to Vatican City. As part of their plan, Ellison pushed Francois in his wheelchair. Their goal was the private morgue at the Vatican Health Services, a clinic with more than a hundred employees, where they expected to find the corpse of Hildebrandt III.

Beneath his robes, Ellison hid a plastic syringe, with a large bore needle carefully disguised as a straight pin he was using to fasten a photo of the dead Pope to his chest. Dangling from his belt, a tiny Swiss Army knife too small to be considered a threat was his second-option tool. If only they could gain entry to the embalming room, he planned to assemble his syringe and needle for a sudden plunge into the Pope's liver, followed by a quick pull-back on the syringe to create suction, and then withdrawal. It would all take less than three seconds, and based on half an hour of practice on dead chickens, he was certain he could strike such a huge target as a human liver, by feel in the dark if necessary. He believed the miniscule core of tissue that would be forced into the hollow needle would be enough to satisfy the hunger of Zaharian's machines and to resolve Ellison's suspicions once and for all. Failing the liver plunge, he would simply carve a strip from the Pope's hand. Time was of the essence, for once Hildebrandt III's blood had been replaced with embalming fluid for too many hours, testing for pentasulfiram would surely become unreliable.

Combined with the usual massive crowds and the predictable turmoil of the interregnum, or time between Popes, Vatican attention to detail declined. As Ellison had hoped, both the *corpo di vigilanza* and Swiss Guards were overtaxed by the massive public event inevitably moving forward.

They approached the Swiss Guards, who were examining documents of those lining up to enter the audience hall. A small notice said that the Cardinal of Milan would lead a mass for the gathered thousands, in place of, and in honor of the late pontiff. Gaining entrance without difficulty, Ellison let them be swept along in the tide of pilgrims, and gradually steered Francois toward a small stairway that led to a basement corridor.

"Over there," Francois said, pointing to the right. His voice boomed loud enough to make Ellison twitch. When excited, Francois forgot Beecham's strict orders for silence. Fortunately, no one seemed to notice, and Ellison could take stock of the situation. Fronted by only three guards, a red cordon prevented entry to a narrow doorway. "Just as we expected," Francois said softly.

Once they had positioned themselves directly in front of the guards, Ellison whispered, "Now!" With an ear-piercing scream that echoed above the rumble of the crowd, Francois threw himself from the wheelchair and feigned an epileptic seizure. In moments, two hundred visitors had formed a wide circle around Francois, horrified by the terrible screaming and thrashing clank of his metal legs on the marble floor. All three guards left their posts to evaluate the disturbance, which left Ellison able to scramble down the stairwell unnoticed.

At the bottom of the stairs Ellison stole a backward glance and heaved a sigh of relief when he saw no pursuit. With the layout of the basement memorized, Ellison knew he had to race to the right, into a connecting tunnel to an older building. The corridor reached too far for Ellison's comfort. Driven by fear, he broke into an all-out sprint for almost a hundred yards, before he recognized a side corridor with wall of aged brick smudged with soot. Almost as soon as he had scrambled through the turn, he passed a frosted-glass door stenciled, CLINICA, barely legible against a darkened room. Ten feet further along the same wall, a second door emitted a pale light that highlighted the sign, OBITORIO, or morgue. Once Ellison satisfied himself that he could detect no shadows moving inside the room, he put his hand on the doorknob. As he did so, he became aware of a preternatural silence. The bell of the *Arco del Campani* no longer rang. He sucked in his breath, desperately hoping to hear its muffled tolling, but it came no more.

Though the door was locked, it gave easily to Ellison's shoulder. Once inside, he began to glance around at the macabre hardware gleaming in the chamber, but he was momentarily distracted by a cool, acrid assault on his nostrils. He stopped short and sniffed the air, redolent with the smell of death and formaldehyde. In the middle of the room a stainless-steel table with a steel pillow lay empty, still dripping with the water of a recent rinsing. Large tools hung on the walls: autopsy scissors, three power saws, thick twine with long, curved needles, rubber tubing attached to large bags of embalming fluid. A selection of papal garments hung from a rack, Hildebrandt III's reading glasses rested on a side table.

Certain this room had recently contained the corpse of Hildebrandt III, Ellison noticed white tiles on the floor, many spattered with fresh blood just beginning to congeal. A stainless steel shelf held a three-gallon glass jar nearly filled with clotted blood.

Alarmed by the silence of the bell, he cursed himself for being too slow, for not getting into the morgue earlier; but they had decided their plan was the only strategy that held any chance. He had to assume the jars of blood were Hildebrandt III's, but he couldn't be sure. He regretted missing his objective by minutes, which Ellison calculated is all it would take for a procession to escort the body to rest in the Sistine Chapel. He wished he had been able to slip the needle between Hildebrandt III's right ribs into the liver. For his own sanity, Ellison needed closure on his doubts. He wanted to be sure Verdi was guilty. Unless he had seen his own hands jam the needle into the Pope's liver, Ellison doubted if he could ever be completely sure.

"I hope like hell that is the Pope's blood," Ellison mumbled to himself, quickly assembling his syringe and needle. He stabbed it through the thin latex membrane on top of the jar, and like a necrophilic mosquito, sucked up a full syringe of blood.

Seeing nothing more he could sample, he focused his mind on how to exit without discovery. He slipped out of the morgue into the ancient corridor. Returning to the *Aule delle Udienza* would require him to re-enter through the cordoned stairway with its three guards. Rather than retrace his entry, Beecham had advised Ellison to continue straight ahead, to a bank of elevators that would raise him back to street level on the plaza. His face now dripping with perspiration from exertion and fear, he raced along his planned escape route. In seconds he found the elevators, but while he waited for the slow grinding of the ancient hydraulics to bring the lift down to him, he heard his own heart pounding in his ears.

When the elevator opened, Ellison saw a Vatican physician in a white coat open his eyes with surprise. Ellison tried to shoulder by him to start the elevator upward. "Stop!" the doctor ordered.

Ellison ignored him and felt satisfaction as the doors begin to close. The doctor jammed his body between the doors and began shouting, "Help! Help!" To quiet him, Ellison swung a hard uppercut into his stomach. While the doctor toppled away from the door, momentarily breathless, Ellison bolted out of the elevator and past him toward a stairway he hoped led to St. Peter's Square.

He took the stairs three and four at a bound, spiraling upward until he saw light coming through a brick-arched doorway. Just outside the doorway, a Swiss Guard stood facing away from him holding a sharp pike. Without hesitation, Ellison crashed into the guard's back and knocked him flat. His brown robes flying, Ellison raced toward the immense crowd standing shoulder to shoulder in the square. Plowing into the middle, he tore off his robe and beard, threw them into a trash container, and allowed himself to be swept forward as part of the great mass of mourners. He forced himself not to look back for any pursuers, but he could hear shouts of security people far behind him. Ever so slowly his heart ceased its wild pounding in his ears. After several minutes, he worked his way to the far edge of the square, pushed toward a side street, and made his way to their rendezvous point at a taxi stand. Francois was already there, with a big smile on his face when he saw Ellison appear.

"They wanted to take me to a hospital, but I convinced them I could make it," he said.

"You are really special, Francois." Now that it was over, he felt amazed that anyone would have gone to such extremes to support him.

By the time their taxi reached *Valkyrie One*, Francois was shaking his head at their mixed luck. "By minutes, *monsieur*. That is all we missed by."

It was still light when Dr. Zaharian brought Ellison and Francois the chemical analysis report from the blood. "Potentially fatal concentrations of pentasulfiram in the sample. Mixed with just a few drops of alcohol, it would be enough to kill an elephant."

Ellison stood up to put on his suit jacket. "I am taking our evidence to the Chief of Homicide in Rome, since the Vatican Police aren't really independent enough to think for themselves."

"I cannot back you on this, Todd," Eduardo objected. "I am not so confident in your new technology."

"And you are only assuming it is the blood of Hildebrandt III," Miranda added. "Dr. Zaharian said so himself."

"Okay. I'll go alone."

"I will accompany you, *monsieur*." Francois offered. "As I say, I don't give a damn what anyone thinks of me."

Ellison looked at Miranda and saw a moment of questioning before she nodded agreement.

In the late afternoon slant of the sun, central Rome glowed with subtle pastels. Under the admiring glances of young Italian men smoking in outdoor cafes, smartly dressed women popped in and out of luxury shops on the *Via Veneto*. As their limousine ferried them to a large government complex, Ellison grew optimistic again now that he and Francois had gotten an appointment with a man powerful enough to confront the Holy See. In an ornate building just off the shopping district, Ellison looked across the wide mahogany desk of Commandante Helios Montini, the corpulent Chief of Homicide for Rome's police force. Francois sat in his wheelchair, his massive arms and firm jaw giving physical proof that he supported Ellison. Ten seconds into Ellison's presentation, Montini began chain-smoking and exhaling a sequence of perfect O-rings, perhaps to distract attention from the quickness of his eyes. Shaking his head at the complex computer graphs Ellison thrust in front of him, Montini seemed to be having difficulty controlling his emotions.

"But, doctor, consider my position. On the one hand, you tell me your unfathomable technical data say that Pope Hildebrandt

III was killed by a heretofore unknown poison; while on the other hand this Death Certificate—signed I might add by the *Archiatra* and three famous Roman doctors—says death by natural causes."

"I realize that, but—"

"In addition, I plan to investigate how you obtained your samples."

Before Ellison could continue, Montini's voice cracked like a whip. "This matter is already closed. By the way, you should be relieved to learn that all of Hildebrandt III's blood has been destroyed, in accordance with the rules." With an air of absolute finality, he folded the file and stood, his protuberant belly covering the documents. "Therefore I suggest you forget this quest. I advise you to stop this madness. In fact, I'm going to pick up my telephone to warn Sir Eduardo, whom up to now is a respected man, that if you persist, you will become *persona non grata* in Vatican City and in Rome. That would be most embarrassing for your family, *non?*" He shook his index finger in Ellison's face. "And if I find a shred of criminal action on your part, you will spend the rest of your life looking out of an iron cage. God help you if you were part of the disturbance in the Vatican clinic."

Ellison looked at his shoes, feeling defeated once more and hating it. Francois, his eyes fierce, whirled his wheelchair and took Ellison's arm without saying a single word. Ellison knew that for the moment he had reached a dead end. There was nothing to do but be polite. "Thank you for your time."

"Pearls before swine," Francois whispered as they left the police headquarters. "But I must be forgiving. The man was in a hopeless position."

"What is it you always say about people?" Ellison asked, calmed by Francois' tolerance.

"Every night I pray for those who live only for themselves and whose spirit is suffering under layers of pretense and vanity."

"My great grandfather lived to be a hundred and three," Ellison said. "He was a Norwegian immigrant who helped tame the Great Plains. Every night his prayer was, 'God protect me from the doctors and the lawyers.'"

They both laughed until Francois took Ellison's arm. "Let me take you to a special place near the Vatican. A surprise to cheer you up, *monsieur*."

They wandered through Rome side by side at first, two big men who stood out in a crowd, the older one struggling to keep up in his wheelchair but smiling and talking effusively until even he grew fatigued by the hills and heat of the late afternoon sun. Seeing him grow weak, Ellison ignored Francois' objections and began to push his friend along the hilly streets until they were alone in a Beaux-Arts style coffee shop across from a medical museum.

"Look, Francois. I really want to thank you for all of your support."

Francois looked over the brim of his cappuccino's foam into Ellison's eyes. "Let's talk about relationships. At first I simply liked you, *monsieur*, but now I've grown very close to you."

"Same here," Ellison said. "You are incredible."

"You should try me some time," Francois said, half joking.

"We both know that is never going to happen."

Francois looked away, his jaw working as if he were grinding up a problem and swallowing it word by word. "No, really that is not the kind of love I mean, though I would be the greatest you have ever experienced. But I agree, it can never happen. First of all I would never interfere with a marriage."

"That's one thing I like about you, Francois, that you live by a code of ethics."

"From time to time she looks at me with a question in her eyes. She lets me know she is watching me. We never speak about it, but Miranda and I both know there is a small competition between us over you. You and I have spent a great deal of time together and we have accomplished much."

"Miranda gets a bit jealous at times, but she is very secure."

Francois blew a kiss in the direction of Miranda, though she was miles away. "She is so fantastic, *monsieur*, I could imagine loving a woman again."

"She and I have talked about you plenty, Francois. We have a very close communication in our marriage. Actually she tells me to enjoy my time with you, because men, just like women, need some relaxed hours with their friends."

"It is that way the world around, *monsieur*. As a Catholic, Miranda understands the old doctrine that three kinds of love exist on earth. *Eros*, or sexual love, is familiar to everyone. *Caritas*, or charity consists of love directed first toward one's God but in large measure also toward oneself and one's neighbor as objects of God's love."

Ellison's mind stopped short. Loving oneself. It was a concept that grated on Ellison's nerves, ever since he had begun to sometimes loath himself for hurting those men in the Philippines. Since then, he didn't feel any god loving him. He felt he had lost the right to such love from a god, though he doubted any divinity cared much about human events, though it would be wonderful if it were true.

Francois reached across the table and put his hand on Ellison's wrist. "Finally there is *agape*, or spiritual love, which by definition is devoid of sexuality. Our relationship can be one of *agape*."

"I'm all for that," Ellison said with a smile. "There is nothing so wonderful as having a true friend." It was a strange coincidence that Francois would be raising the topic of their friendship for discussion, just now, when Ellison had been mulling over the nature of his relationship with him. Though Francois had been a stalwart supporter all through the development of Rescue Team International, helping Ellison get the blood sample was a whole new level, one involving criminal risk. There was no reason for Francois to undertake such dangers; and if Ellison put himself in Francois' shoes, he knew that Francois had helped him simply out of friendship.

Once before, back in North Dakota, he'd had a friend like this, a high school buddy named Bob Gibson. Together they had hiked through the springtime grasses, found grouse nests hidden on the ground and filled with eggs. They watched the unbroken blue enamel sky change with the hours and the seasons, eagles and geese recognizable by the way they flapped their wings. When Bob and Ellison grew old enough to be called responsible young men, their parents allowed them to camp in a tipi, Sioux Indian-style. Inside, they studied sexy magazines and talked incessantly of girls and what teenage boys would like to do with them. At graduation, they double-dated for the formal, and took their dates down by the river after the prom. Bob took Peggy Gustafson and a blanket closer to the Missouri River, while Ellison and Bonnie Sparks struggled to find a position to press their pelvises together so they could bump and grind in the bucket seat of Bob's ancient Camaro. After fifteen minutes of that, she put her hand on Ellison's zipper and tugged at him. Bob had sworn that he'd gotten Bonnie to go all the way during junior year. Without understanding exactly why, Ellison felt a bit unsettled about being second to his friend, but he assumed Bonnie would therefore be able to tell him what he should do. When they coupled for the first time, Ellison climaxed on the third stroke. Bonnie's continuing undulations were a sure sign she wanted more, and to his surprise he found himself able to give it to her soon enough.

They continued their intense relationship all summer, before he left for college. They walked hand-in-hand down the main streets of Bismarck, not caring what anyone thought of them. Swearing undying love for him, Bonnie went to the University of Minnesota when Ellison went to Stanford. Both of them had been selected *Most Outstanding Senior* for the yearbook; and most of their friends assumed they would marry some day.

Once apart they wrote daily, on paper in the days before e-mail. When he went home for his first Christmas, filled with anticipation at seeing Bonnie again, he found her waiting for him at her parents' home. In a few minutes, Ellison knew something had changed. She seemed distracted, not as close as he remembered. After the movie, he checked them in at the Roadside Motel, where they made love like old friends.

She sat in her bra and panties in front of the cheap mirror, watching the reflection of his face while she put on fresh makeup. "Look, Todd, I might get engaged to this guy from Detroit. I still love you, but I'm all messed up."

To his surprise, Ellison had experienced more relief than sadness. She was a fine woman, but he didn't want to get married young, particularly since Bonnie had always said she wanted to have a baby right away. He really understood they weren't meant for each other. He'd been right. She already had two kids with her accountant husband and, according to the *Bismarck Independent*, now lived happily in St. Louis working for the city.

It was his friend Bob Gibson he couldn't figure out. On that same first weekend home from college, Bob had announced that he was quitting college because he had become a monk in an obscure Buddhist cult based in Taos, New Mexico. He talked to

Ellison a lot, and told him that he had taken a vow of silence for two years scheduled to begin soon. Before he disappeared, he whispered to Ellison that he had become gay. Ellison had never seen his friend again. Through the grapevine he learned that Bob had become Father Palani and was healthy, but to this day, he never heard another thing, and whenever he thought about Bob, he felt a loss. No one else in town has seemed to understand the strange behavior either. Bob had been such an All-American boy. Ellison felt the same about Francois as he had about Bob.

"Yes, Francois, you are indeed my friend."

"Very rare, *monsieur*, something to be valued. In the priesthood we studied this kind of brotherly love. I will demonstrate it now. Go ahead. Tell me your problems."

"Mine?"

"Hesitant? Tell me your hopes and dreams, then, if you prefer to keep your problems to yourself," Francois said, easing back in his wheelchair and waiting with the calmest expression on his face. "Tell me whatever you want."

Ellison put his espresso cup down. He had not planned to think about himself, but he could put his finger on one problem for sure. "My experience in the Vatican has turned out to be different than I had expected. A cardinal is big game; and I'm running a bit scared now, Francois."

"Yes. Verdi is a prince of a hidden nation more than a billion strong, a nation sovereign but invisible, like the electricity flowing through the body. No wonder you are afraid."

Before Ellison could respond, a black sedan eased into a no parking zone just outside the café. A rear window rolled down and though Ellison couldn't see the face of the man inside, three perfectly blown O-rings of smoke belched the identity of the smoker. Two plainclothes policemen escorted a nervous young woman into the café, where they stood at the espresso bar and stared at Francois. "No brown robe, but I'm sure he is the one," Ellison heard the woman whisper. All three returned to the sedan, where Commandante Montini emerged to listen intently to the report. Montini strolled to the doorway of the café and blew smoke toward Ellison and Francois, ground out his cigarette butt on the travertine floor, and waddled back to his sedan.

Shaken, Ellison returned to their conversation. "For myself I am not afraid, but I worry for others who take risks because of me."

"Life overflows with mysteries, *monsieur*. My father died taking a risk on my behalf, trying to make extra money for my education when I was already old enough to have taken care of myself. I grew up in the coastal town of Arcachon, with its great beach on the Atlantic Ocean pressing against the border with Spain. He was a fisherman by trade but a musician at heart, who could play the violin with such emotion that people gossiped he must have Gypsy blood. And indeed, coming from our area, that could have explained his romantic soul, though my mother always claimed his intensity arose from his love for her.

"Papa fished alone at all times in those often stormy seas, except on the calmest of days, when he allowed me to skip school to accompany him. On those glorious mornings we sang together, using our voices to urge the sun to rise above the horizon. From him I learned the Gregorian chants and medieval harmonies that finally drew me away from my parents to study music in Paris. Believing I could be a great composer to rival Debussy, at the Sorbonne I studied music theory, counterpoint, harmony, and performance. When my singing talent became known, many sought my voice. I fell in with a group that made its money singing in tourist nightclubs in Montmarte, where we sang everything from French folksongs, to ballads, to American blues. I became a *bon vivant*, a singer who could charm the pants off women, though in retrospect I recognize that sex always left me with an unsatisfied appetite and a desire for yet another conquest. When my performance at school began to deteriorate and I was put on formal probation, my father asked me why. I lied and told him it was because I was working so hard to support myself that I had no time to study."

Francois paused for a moment, lost in thought. "I will never forget the last words he ever said to me. 'It is the duty of the father to help his son. Return to Paris, concentrate on your studies, and let me send you more money.' Just a month later, on a stormy day when every other fishing boat stayed in the harbor, he set out alone. His body was never found. To this day my aged mother wears black. At his memorial service I threw a red rose from the cliff into the Atlantic and almost could not resist the urge to kill myself with a dive into the rocks and surf. Instead I locked myself into my bedroom and wrestled with every issue and contradiction inside of me. I knew he had died for me. How could I repay that debt to my mother and the universe? To him? Surely not with my life as it was. For a year I styled myself as a Seeker of Truth, in the tradition of G.I. Gurdjieff, a mystic who tried to make sense of the world. Eventually I found myself at Confession, a young man with a weary old soul who felt responsible for his father's death. The priest heard my confession and wept with me. As penance he urged me to read the *Philokalia of Blessed Calistus*, which says, *If you wish to pray as you ought, imitate the dulcimer player; bending his head a little and inclining his head to the strings, he strikes the strings skillfully, and enjoys the melody he draws from their harmonious notes.*

Is this example clear to you? The dulcimer is the heart; the strings—the feelings; the hammer—remembrance of God and of Divine things; the mind draws holy feelings from the God-fearing heart, the ineffable sweetness fills the soul, and the mind, which is pure, is lit up by Divine Illuminations.

"Does it surprise you, *monsieur*, that I can recite the *Wisdom from the Fathers*, even now, lo these many years?

"Using the power of prayer, I turned my back on my restless, dissolute life. I swore I would never sing another note until I felt I had redeemed my sin. Once again I became an honor student, turned from the beauties of music to the beauties of science, and finally matriculated at the medical school in Bordeaux to be close to my mother. But medical school could not put out the fire of damnation I found scorching my heart every day. I believed my destiny lay in the spiritual life. In honor of my father I entered training for the priesthood, which no one could really believe I had done. My mother told me I was of the wrong cloth. I argued with her, but when I woke in Cambodia with my legs gone, I knew she was right."

"You have lived a life with too much pain," Ellison said.

"It helps to share it with a true friend. You see, *monsieur*, if I can admit these things to you, there is nothing you cannot tell me."

"I am learning from you, Francois. You are one of the bravest men I know."

"Try me, then. What is your deepest fear?"

Ellison was a man not afraid to question himself and as a consequence had developed a substantial awareness of his own flaws. By giving his unreserved love to Miranda, he had opened himself up to the risk of failing in love again, as he had in his first marriage. No matter how good everything seemed, he harbored worry that he and Miranda could repeat the natural history of his first marriage. He had never spoken of his fears in this regard with anyone. He studied Francois' earnest face and decided to take what for him was a plunge.

"I'm afraid that somehow this situation in Rome will sour my marriage. I worry that Miranda might stop loving me for some inadequacy."

"Go on, *monsieur*."

"I have never lived close enough to my emotions, a familial Scandinavian reserve, I suppose. I tend to suppress my feelings, often out of consideration for another person, but I know that I can accumulate resentments, until finally there can be too many nails in the coffin of a relationship. After my first wife, Vicky, and I broke up, I never expected to find such happiness again. I am a man who knows what he lost, one who feels as if he has been given a second chance, another bite at the apple. With Miranda, I want to maintain consciousness of paying attention to our relationship. In my prairie wisdom, I compare our marriage to a garden that needs tending, some work by me as a labor of love. A situation like this one in the Vatican can turn into a tornado that has the power to wreck the most carefully tended plot. I feel myself being drawn into a maelstrom here, yet for some reason I am determined to see it through to the end, no matter what, even if Miranda disagrees. What frightens me most is that I'm not really certain why I behave this way."

"In the end we are all alone." Francois said. Now I understand you better, *monsieur*. Like every adventurer, you have two faces: the secret one and the one you show the public. Tell me more."

Ellison stared into his half-empty cup. Thirty-three years old and already he had seen much suffering in the world. Memories and emotions surged through him. "I am afraid I am slipping into old emotional habits despite my effort to change."

"What habits?"

"Carelessness. Inattentiveness. Concentration on my own goals without considering their impact on others." For the first time in almost a year, Ellison felt he had nothing more to say.

Their eyes met, and Ellison could see deep pain in Francois, as if he were sharing his angst. "My dear *monsieur*. Do you wish my analysis and advice?"

"Analysis, yes. Advice so long as you don't assume I can or will follow it."

"Fair enough, *monsieur*. First, in your adventure seeking spirit you have qualities of heedlessness and inconsideration that can make you unpredictable and dangerous, to friends and enemies alike."

Ellison recalled the war he had lived through in Mindanao, of firing his automatic weapon in the midst of life or death battle. The part of him that had saved the gophers on his father's farm shuddered at the thought he had pulled the trigger. But another part of him reminded Ellison the only alternative had been to die himself, and after him, Miranda.

Ellison knew Francois had nearly chosen Psychiatry over surgery for his residency, and other physicians always commented on his psychological skills. "Second," Francois continued. "What allows the adventurer to have two faces amounts to a moderate problem during ordinary life, for the schizoid tendency that allows the two faces to co-exist almost always troubles mankind. You are a man divided."

"Who isn't? What did you learn at seminary about men like me?"

"That for all men there is the extreme danger of *hubris*, wherein you believe too much in yourself."

"Don't you, Francois? Don't we have to believe in ourselves, to the limit?"

"Listen to me, *monsieur*. There is a razor's edge you must walk. On one side is carelessness, on the other side excessive conformity and sloth."

Ellison sat silent, thinking. He was in the midst of a dangerous situation, no doubt about it. And he needed to move carefully.

Francois reached over to pat his arm, readying himself to leave the coffee shop. "I advise you to remain calm, to question yourself, and to struggle toward reconciliation of the different sides of yourself. If you wish my counsel, I will be available to you at any time. You have done well."

Ellison noticed a mysterious reduction of an anxiety that had been grinding away at his guts for months. "Thanks, *compadre*."

REQUIEM

Verdi smelled the wax-laden smoke of hundreds of candles flickering in the evening gloom of the Sistine Chapel. For three days
mourners had filed past the funeral bier of Hildebrandt III for a
last look at the *Pontifex Maximus,* the man who bridged the gap
between earthly and divine. Twice Verdi prayed over the dead Pope
while six columns of people passed by on each side. He wondered
at them. Though they might say they had come to honor the most
powerful man on earth, in truth what motivated the more than a
million mourners? Was it some kind of macabre fascination with
death, to see how even the high and mighty end? Or a form of
schadenfreude, the secret joy felt when a friend suffers adversity?
Or was it more like collecting experiences and autographs so one
could say, "I was there" or "Been there, done that"? Verdi wondered at the size of the crowds.

How different for Hildebrandt III than for St. Peter himself, a simple Galilean fisherman whose original name was Simon Bar Jonah. He was, with his brother Andrew, the first to respond to Jesus' call to abandon his old life and become "fishers of men."

Verdi had always felt that Peter towers over other New Testament figures. In all the Gospels Peter is mentioned first in every list of the names of the Twelve. And he is the first disciple permitted to witness Jesus' transfiguration on the mountain.

In the Gospel of Matthew, Jesus declares Peter's faith to be a direct revelation from God, and rewards it by renaming Simon as Peter, The Rock, and declares, "Upon this rock I will build my church, and I give to you the keys of the kingdom of heaven. And whatever you bind on earth shall be also bound in heaven."

After the death of his master, Peter led the Pentecostal proclamation of resurrection and set out to spread the good news. The new religion met fierce opposition.

Emperor Nero was celebrating the thirteenth year of his cruel reign when he entertained the Roman mob with the bloody spectacle of Christian persecutions. Peter, an old man by the time Nero captured him, was forced to witness every imaginable type of torture, all put on display to terrify anyone considering following the new god Peter preached.

Men, women, and children soaked in pitch and crucified were set ablaze to become human torches illuminating the circus on Vatican Hill. In the spectacles, Christians of all ages were torn to pieces by hordes of ravenous predators. Which would be easier, Verdi asked himself: to be killed by a bear? By a lion? In the middle of the racecourse, Simon Bar Jonah asked the executioners to nail him to his cross with his head downward.

And now, Verdi thought, millions pass by this dead Pope, Peter's direct descendent. Peter died yet still he lived on. Verdi had time to muse at length, since he had scarcely slept from the moment of Hildebrandt III's death. His entire being burning with doubts and questions, Verdi—like Jesus in the garden of Gethsemane praying before Judas Iscariot betrayed him—sensed that pre-ordained events were about to sweep him up. Yet he carried on his duties as Secretary of State, receiving kings and presidents, ambassadors and other forms of thieves from almost all the nations on earth, most there to ensure being seen on worldwide television honoring the beloved deceased. With sixty million

Catholic voters in America, even the President of the United States made the journey, his Secret Service making security demands that created unpleasant frictions in Vatican City.

Verdi rose to greet the tall American president when Strizzi ushered him into his office. Both of them had come far since their first meeting at the United Nations in New York City, when as a young senator, William Clark had given an impassioned speech for religious tolerance at a U.N. conference on conflict resolution. Though he had met Clark only twice since, Verdi recognized worry and concern written on Clark's Ivy League face.

"So good of you to come," Verdi began, extending his ringed hand to see if Clark, a Catholic himself, would kiss his ring or shake hands. To his surprise, Clark did both, probably because they were entirely alone.

"He was a great man, Your Eminence, one sincerely loved by the American people, Catholics and those of other faiths as well."

"Yes, yes. Please sit down," Verdi said with a motion to a plush sofa. "A glass of wine perhaps? I have a bottle of Chateau Petrus that should be drunk before it grows too old." He poured two goblets of the precious red liquid and sat beside Clark, who raised his crystal glass in a toast.

"To a fallen hero."

"And to continued closeness with the great Christian nation of America," Verdi answered sharply. Probably because of its Protestant beginnings and determined separation of church and state, for the first two hundred years of its existence, America eschewed formal diplomatic relations with the Vatican. Though before Verdi's time, the old situation lasted until President Jimmy Carter broke the ice in 1979 by putting an American ambassador in place. Verdi peered over his goblet to gauge the reaction of the man who ruled a nation where followers of Mohammed now outnumbered Jews.

"My government and I affirm even closer relations, particularly in our troubled times." Clark raised his eyes to look directly into Verdi's, "No matter who is chosen as the new Pope."

Verdi appreciated the diplomatic skills of Clark, who in one sentence had opened the door to discussion of *papabile*—cardinals who might be chosen Pope—and the American problems with the Youssef group. Concentration of power is always the goal for a politician, and no doubt Clark would rejoice if an American were chosen Pope instead of an Italian. Behind the scenes, Americans would be lobbying for his New York rival, Cardinal Muldowney, by calling in debts from cardinals whose religious freedoms existed largely because of U.S. insistence on human rights in their oppressed nations. Verdi guessed President Clark might have ten to fifteen votes already in his pocket, perhaps enough to swing an election. For centuries, papal elections have been theoretically free of political influences, but Verdi knew from experience that modern governments still try.

"I have said a Mass for the victims of the bombings," Verdi declared, peaking his fingers as if in prayer. "And I have instructed our people to report anything that could help identify the perpetrators."

"Thank you, Your Eminence. My hands are tied on this one, as you can appreciate. If I release Youssef and The Sheik, terrorist blackmail would never stop. But I anguish over the cost."

"Ah, the loneliness of power. Sometimes I feel it."

Clark studied him, about to ask something but changed his mind and peered into his goblet. In the brief silence, Verdi decided it was time to end this nonsense.

"*Dominus vobiscum*, peace be with you, Mr. President," Verdi pronounced as he scrawled the sign of the cross in the air in blessing. "Thank you again for coming, but please excuse me now. The Requiem Mass will begin shortly."

❋　❋　❋

"We are almost to St. Peter's" Ellison told them. Through the open sunroof of their limousine, Ellison could hear the clanging of the church bells that had begun anew, in earnest now as the hour of the Requiem grew near. Some bells struck a bass note that vibrated his innards, while others made a crystal high tone that made him want to listen to the beauty as it decayed and revealed its harmonic undertones. Veiled and dressed in black from head to toe, Miranda looked absolutely proper. Francois, deeply moved by the death of Hildebrandt III, sat in the jump seat across from him, where he led Miranda and Eduardo through a rosary, the silent ride broken only by the clicking of the beads as the three of them worked their way though the glorious mysteries and Hail Mary's. Eduardo sat resplendent in formal wear emblazoned with the Order of the Golden Spur, a golden medallion hanging from a thick golden chain. Outside, half a million faithful crammed themselves into St. Peter's Square, straining to see the pomp of entering dignitaries. Their limousine took its place in a long cue of black cars fluttering pendants, passed through the stony arches, and let them out to walk the short distance to the main door of St. Peter's.

Even before they could see the interior of the church, the ceremony sent sensory messages to them. Carried on the waves of music of a two hundred-voice choir, the scent of incense wafted out of the great basilica. Whenever he looked at their numbered and engraved invitation, Ellison felt a subdued excitement at the honor of being there. Just as they reached an iron gate, a Swiss Guard inspected Sir Eduardo's invitation, allowing him to pass, and doing the same with Francois. When it was Ellison's turn to present papers, the guard stiffened and moved a step to block him.

"You cannot enter, sir."

Though the body language was plain enough, the guard's heavily accented English made Ellison wonder if he had misunderstood.

"What? But this is an official invitation," he protested, pointing to the seal of Cardinal Lopez.

"It has been cancelled. My apologies. Please move out of the way. You, too, signora."

When Miranda gasped, Ellison turned in time to see a look of shock and humiliation sweep over her face. "Eduardo!" she called.

"What seems to be the problem?" Eduardo asked.

"We have orders not to permit the Ellisons to attend, sir. Please ask them to step aside."

Behind them Ellison could see a logjam developing; and though mortified, he knew that nothing he could do or say would sway the implacable guard. It was best not to worsen the already ugly scene. Bracing his shoulders, Ellison did his best to sound calm when he spoke to Eduardo and Francois. "We'll see you at the plane." Reluctantly, he took Miranda's elbow and did an about face.

"Verdi, the sonofabitch," he whispered in her ear.

"What do you expect, Todd?" He could see fire flashing in her eyes, that at once showed the hot blood of her Spaniard father and soon, he hoped, the wisdom of her Chinese mother. She was angry. "Look what you have gotten us into."

The click and whirr of cameras flashing intensified their embarrassment. Newscasters struggled toward them holding microphones out for sound bites, shouting questions in several languages.

Wading upstream against the arriving guests, with Miranda fuming beside him, Ellison tried to think of something to say to her. Photographs of them being turned away were sure to make the inside pages of the all-color tabloids. And though he felt deeply troubled by the scandal, he knew that whatever discomfort he felt paled next to her torment. Even before she knew him, she had been in *W Magazine* as Miss Philippines. The publisher had chosen her for her new world look, featuring her in a fifteen page spread with others from around the world who highlighted the beauty of offspring from mixed genes. Ellison knew her public image was of paramount importance because she was moving in the political arena, where controversial events can truncate a career overnight. A thousand questions would be asked about why they had been turned away. Most columnists would speculate on the details of some lurid tale of sexual infidelity, alleging that the Vatican had learned she was the secret concubine of the Sultan of Brunei. It wouldn't matter what they invented, it would sell magazines. Worse, if some persistent journalist serendipitously unearthed Ellison's theory of papal murder, all hell would break loose. The public humiliation was a terrible development for both of them.

"I am so sorry. Really, I am."

"This is the most embarrassing thing that has ever happened to me," she answered, already calmer. "I know that all of us have debated the problem here and, though we all have reservations, in the end were convinced by you, Todd. You had better be right, because I have been having a hard time supporting you, and this really hurt me."

Just yesterday Ellison had talked of his deepest fears with Francois, and today he felt the heat of the flames. If he had believed in magical thinking, he might have believed the one had somehow caused the other. He struggled to follow Francois' advice. He wanted to talk it out.

"Miranda, I..."

"Not now, Todd. You are the most precious person on earth to me; and it isn't wise for me to talk too much right now. Just give me a few minutes."

It was a long ride home to *Valkyrie One*, with Miranda refusing to look at him while they watched the funeral ceremony on the limousine's television. She muttered prayers and responses in cadence with the liturgy, and once, when he put his hand on her knee, she nearly brushed it away for the first time ever before she took his hand in hers. It had been a long time since Ellison had felt so low, or so filled with doubts about his own judgment.

❈   ❈   ❈

Twenty thousand jammed into seats near the altar, churchmen on the left, secular leaders on the right, all arrayed according to decreasing rank like wavelets from a stone dropped into still waters, as if their distance from the altar reflected their distance from Truth. As princes of the Church, Verdi and the other cardinals sat closest to the source.

Verdi loved Mozart's *Requiem Mass in D-Minor, K.626*, and still knew its Latin by rote from his years as a parish priest. It had always amazed him that Mozart had written the mass just a few months before he died, and that while ill with delirium, the composer imagined he was writing the mass for his own farewell ceremony. While the soaring voices of the choir moved from the *kyrie* to the *recordare, confutatis*, and *lacrymosa* and plunged into the deep sadness of the *sanctus* and *hosanna*, Verdi faced the altar and gazed on Hildebrandt III's smooth face, visible for the last time. The embalmers had done a better job than with Pius XII in 1958, when an experimental technique of leaving the intestines inside the deceased Pope had led to rapid putrefaction. Rapidly expanding gases had caused his corpse to thunder with unseemly farts and belches of such a foul odor that one member of the honor guard fainted. And, as a final symbolic proof of the corruptibility of human flesh, his nose had turned black and nearly fallen off before he was safely in his triple coffin.

This time, though, perfect orchestration by the Master of Liturgy smoothed Hildebrandt III's passage to the afterlife. A solemn panoply of cardinals in their finest vestments, followed by archbishops, bishops, and priests aimed to pay fitting honor to the fallen Vicar of Christ. In its holy magnificence, the pageant would close the book on Hildebrandt III's chapter in world history, and demonstrate that though even the most exalted of men end as dust, the institution of the Church itself would go on forever.

When the Mass ended, six pallbearers lifted Hildebrandt III's body from its catafalque and placed it inside the first of three coffins. In keeping with his final requests, he wore an ermine cape to keep him warm for his eternal journey, the triple tiara crown that symbolized his greatness as a man, and held a jewel studded crucifix against his stilled heart to protect him against evil. Coins minted during his brief tenure joined him in the lead coffin that would guard him from the damp, which was placed inside a coffin of cedar—as if he were a common man—and finally the heavy casket of bronze.

When the last lid closed into place, Verdi felt a wave of exultation. Nothing could unmask him now. Hildebrandt III's body would never be seen again by mortal men. When he watched the coffin be lowered into the grotto beneath St. Peter's altar, an immense peace settled over him. He felt a miracle of forgiveness from Christ that rendered him perfectly absolved of guilt for what he had done. Basking in the warm glow of his inner peace, he sensed the hand of God on his shoulder, with a message that he had done the Lord's will. God's hand tightened, and Verdi found himself in the grip of an experience that he had never had before. Piercing both ears with a penetrating force that could not be denied, he heard the Lord command him, "Approach the altar!"

Overcome with the influence of the Holy Spirit that compelled him to break every precedent, Verdi fell to his knees and crawled to the High Altar reserved for a Pope himself. Oblivious to the twenty thousand pairs of eyes staring at him in stunned silence, he raised his hands to heaven and scrawled the sign of the cross in the air. After making the cross a dozen times, each faster than before, he felt possessed by a formless demiurge. It invaded his body, occupying every aspect of his being with the ecstasy of communication with elemental truth. Overcome, with trembling arms outstretched in the shape of the True Cross, he fell forward on his face. Tears of rapture streamed from eyes that could see beyond this world, and he heard himself speaking a strange language.

How long he remained prostrate Verdi did not know, but when he crept back on all fours, the hushed crowd and all of the cardinals eyed him. If the scholastic Catholics in the audience disapproved of his emotional display, the charismatic segment of Catholics understood the power of the spirit and began a murmur of voices that swelled and grew until the basilica reverberated with cries of, "*Gloria in Excelsis Deo*, glory to God!"

Startled from his trance by the chant, Verdi controlled his mind enough to find his chair, with just enough awareness to recognize that for every person hailing his exalted piety, there was one who turned away in distaste. Amongst those he found the eyes of Eduardo Santiago, frowning and angry, but—to Verdi's immense satisfaction—Eduardo stood without his sister or Ellison at his side.

❈   ❈   ❈

"It was incredible!" Eduardo began as soon as he and Francois rejoined them on *Valkyrie One*. "Verdi spoke in tongues."

"Aramaic, the language of Jesus," Francois added. "I recognized the words. He was calling out the names of God and three times cried, 'Lord, take this cup from me.'"

Ellison grunted with disgust. "He's probably got a lot on his mind. He should have anyway after what he—"

"Stop it, Todd!" Miranda interrupted, still angry. "I wish I had been there to see such a thing."

"After the Mass, people could not stop talking about him," Eduardo continued. "Verdi has always been considered a superstar destined to go great places. How this will play out, no one knows."

"For him, there is only one place higher to go," Francois rasped.

Ellison frowned. "The Papacy. What a disaster that would be!"

"That's all I can take!" Miranda objected. "You are jumping to conclusions." She walked out of the conference room and gave the door an emphatic slam behind her.

Francois gave Ellison a "that's why I prefer men" shrug before he studied his fingernails.

"We should leave these two alone, right Francois?" Eduardo said, pushing his chair away from the table. "In my whole life I have never seen my sister so furious."

"So out of character for her," Francois mused. "Perhaps she is less angry than confused. Perhaps she confounds the man and the office. Conditioned to believe no clergyman can be evil, she experiences her tension as anger when you suspect a revered man. She is torn between your suspicions and her idea of a priest."

"Especially when she has been humiliated on global television," Eduardo sniffed.

"You should go to her, *monsieur*."

"Not yet," Ellison said, jumping up. He was unsure why he felt so desperate. Was it Miranda's criticism of him creating a male need to regain her approval? And how much came from his sense of injustice that a killer's star was ascending? "I just had another idea."

"What now?" Eduardo asked. "This obsession of your is really starting to interfere with your relationships. To hell with your ideas. Take care of Miranda."

Ellison stopped short. This whole situation was getting crazier by the hour. He put his hands to his temples, trying to collect his thoughts. "You're right, Eduardo. We'll meet here in a couple of hours. I'll tell all of you my thoughts then. Thanks, brother. And like you said, I'll mend my fences."

Miranda sat at her computer sending e-mail to her parents in Mindanao. She greeted Ellison coolly. He pulled up a chair so he could sit beside her and nuzzled her cheek, which she allowed without pulling away. He spoke softly. "You are more important to me than anything or anyone. What do you want me to do?"

"I was just writing to my father about the crisis here. Eduardo sends him encrypted notes every day, so Daddy knows the general outline of our problem."

Ellison had great respect for Miranda's father. In the tradition of many religions, Margarito Santiago had turned to preaching when he passed the stage of having any material needs in his life.

After visiting every village and *barrio* on the enormous island of Mindanao, he now had a flock of followers that reached into the thousands on days when he provided food and drink outside the rustic church he had built on Hacienda Teresita.

"What does he say?"

"To review every possible course of action with you, to reach a decision we can all support, and to pray to the Lord we do the right thing."

Generalizations like that seemed easier said than done to Ellison, but he knew it was the proper starting point for them to talk. For an hour they discussed Verdi, with Ellison martialing every argument he could think of to convince her that the man must be stopped. At the outset, in the style of a defense attorney, she vigorously argued that all of Ellison's theories were based on circumstantial evidence. After he went through his bits of evidence one by one, she finally acknowledged that if Hildebrandt III had been murdered, Verdi had to be a suspect, but just one of hundreds of potential killers. She simply did not share his sense of certainty that Verdi was the killer. Ultimately he was left with, "Trust me, Miranda, that's all I can ask."

"I know you are a special man and that you mean well," she said. She turned to wrap him in her arms. "It's so hard, Todd, but I love you."

"We'll try my last shot. That will be it. I promise."

When she smiled and said, "Why do I have trouble believing that?" they both broke out in happy laughter. It was wonderful to have a woman with a sense of humor. Even with both of them frightened by the stress on their marriage growing out of the struggle over how to react to the assassination, they could still whistle in the dark.

An hour later, they all fidgeted in the conference room with grave expressions on their faces. "Yes, *monsieur*," Francois began. "You are right. Pentasulfiram in the blood. The Pope was murdered for sure."

Miranda reminded them of the flaw in the logic immediately. "But how can we be sure it was the Pope's blood?"

"To be certain, of course," Zaharian nodded, "we would need a sample of Hildebrandt III's cells. In a way, we are back at our starting point. We need tissue from him, for poison and for DNA."

"Too late for that," Ellison grumbled. "He's buried."

"And you have worn out your welcome at the Holy See," Eduardo continued for him.

"He's advisin' you to forget it, pardner," Beecham added.

Ellison looked each one of his friends in the eyes. "Do you believe my theory or not, because I need to know."

"Why? What difference does it make whether we believe it?" Eduardo asked.

Instead of answering, Ellison looked across the tarmac at the soaring tail of *Air Force One*. On the outside, President Clark's aircraft looked nearly identical to *Valkyrie One*, though Ellison knew it was crammed with electronics his pilots and technicians had never heard of. He turned to Beecham with a teasing smile. "Say, General, you have friends on that plane, haven't you?"

"Sure, even the Big Boss hisself. Why?"

"Just thinking we haven't got much to lose."

"I hear that rattlesnake mind of yours breeding trouble for yours truly, pardner."

"Can you get me a meeting?"

"Probably. He knows about you for sure, ol' buddy."

Aboard *Air Force One* less than an hour later Ellison finished detailing his suspicions and evidence to President Clark, who tapped his fountain pen on a yellow legal pad filled with notes. He looked at them, waiting for more. "That's it?" he asked, arching an eyebrow. "That's all you've got?"

"Permission to speak freely, sir?" Beecham asked.

"A bit late to be asking that, isn't it, General? Think about it. Here I am dealing with Islamic terrorists going ape-shit and three thousand families making headlines in every newspaper saying I indirectly killed their kin. And now you bring in Dr. Ellison here to tell me a man who we figure has a fifty-fifty chance of being the next Pope is a killer. Permission to speak freely? Sure. What the hell else?"

"You know what I went through in the Philippines with him, sir. Basically, Todd here stopped a big war."

"I know. Go on."

"All's I'm sayin' is that what he just told you is a lot better than most of the crap CIA and military intelligence bring you."

Clark studied Ellison before speaking. "I have known Cardinal Verdi for several years, Doctor. Granted he has changed, used to be a lot less frenetic; but as for murder?"

"If I had Hildebrandt III's tissues, I could prove—"

"Nothing," Clark cut in. "All you could prove is that in response to an outrageous request, Verdi gave you hair from someone else. Before I ran for Congress I did criminal defense law, Doctor. You have not even proved a crime took place; and if by some stretch of the imagination you could prove Hildebrandt III was murdered, you could never get a conviction against Verdi."

While the President spoke, Ellison remembered the day he stood naked in front of his mirror, looked himself in the eyes, and vowed never to put himself or Miranda in harm's way. Accidents can happen to anyone, but to choose danger voluntarily means someone has plenty of deep soul searching to do. What am I doing here? he wondered. But he forced himself to concentrate on what Clark was saying.

"So, Dr. Ellison, despite the improbability of it all, my instincts tell me you might be on to something, and Beecham obviously takes this seriously."

"Thank you, Mr. President," Ellison said.

"But," Clark continued, "the American government absolutely cannot get involved." He paused, seeming to ponder some deep, invisible calculus before raising his eyebrows with a conspiratorial twitch. "At least not officially."

What did that mean? The skill leaders have with diplomatic double-speak amazed Ellison, but before he could ask for clarification, Clark ended the meeting.

"Thank you, Doctor, General. My secretary will escort you out."

"In summary, now what?" Aboard *Valkyrie One*, Ellison finished his report to Miranda, Eduardo, and Francois at the conference table.

"The President will talk with his people, but we'll never know what actions he takes, if any," Beecham said.

"At least he didn't revoke your citizenship," Miranda said, smiling.

"He couldn't do—"

"Half joking only," she said.

Ellison looked at Francois. "When will the election conclave begin?"

"By canon law, it must begin no sooner than nine but no later than fifteen days after the death of the Pope."

Once President Clark declined to put the United States Government behind him, Ellison knew his personal wheel of fortune had rotated back to the same number…2. There were only two choices he could identify. He could give up, or—

Ellison took a deep breath and made his announcement.

"For now anyway, since outside help seems out of the question, I am determined to do whatever I can to keep Verdi from being elected."

Eduardo shook his head. "Don't worry about him any more. According to rumor, Verdi has become too much of a loose cannon to get elected."

"Anything can happen, and until recently he was considered one of the favorites."

"Please, brother, don't go to the newspapers. We will all look like fools."

"Agreed. That's not my plan. The only hope left is for me to get into the conclave, and somehow find a way to prevent his election."

"Into the conclave?" Miranda said, in startled disbelief.

"Impossible," Eduardo snorted. "The conclave is the most secretive gathering on earth."

"But with your help, Sir Eduardo, there is one small chance I can get in."

"How?" Miranda asked.

"Francois gave me a book about the history of medicine in Vatican City and the Holy See. Listen to this," he said thumbing to a marked page in a thick book. "A cardinal may bring his personal physician into the conclave."

"You must be crazy," Francois said.

"Get me in as Cardinal Lopez's doctor." Eduardo's eyes went wide. "You can do it for me, Sir Eduardo."

CONCLAVE

With the unerring accuracy of salmon swimming home in response to an irresistible instinct, the one hundred forty-nine cardinals came from across wide oceans to satisfy their own inexorable call. But these men ranked with the rarest of species on earth, humans who have dedicated themselves to the spiritual life of man's soul, their own and others. The amount of good they had done during their lifetimes passed beyond all measure.

Several of the cardinals who had arrived in time to march ahead of Ellison as they paraded into the Sistine Chapel were *papabile*, potential Popes who harbored aspirations despite their many sins. According to Francois, more than half had violated their vows of celibacy, and if one took seriously the injunction against masturbation, perhaps ten percent could profess unstimulated genitalia since ordination. But Ellison knew no man is perfect, and these old men had diligently worked on themselves striving for, if not attaining, self-perfection. Ellison respected them, for in the name of their Christ, they had renounced much that most men want and need: the love of a woman, children, sex, grandchildren carrying on his genes. For a Darwinian, a celibate priest is a failed experiment in evolution, since like a sterile dog's, his genes die with him.

When Ellison had discussed that notion with Francois, he carefully adjusted the straps on his artificial legs for what seemed like a very long time before he responded. "On the contrary, *monsieur*, they believe that they have transmuted their sexual energy into the power of love for their flock. Instead of children, they propagate the faith in future generations. They believe they are the fathers of our civilization, like it or not."

Following the cardinals, Ellison kept his rehearsed position in the procession, grouped with four other physicians there to attend aging men. He marched next to Dr. Morra, who with Hildebrandt III beyond his realm now ministered to an Irish cardinal hobbled by a fulminate case of gout in his big toe so painful it rendered him barely able to think.

Almost breathless with excitement, yet simultaneously exhausted by eleven days of effort, obstacles, and stress, Ellison could see the doors of the Sistine Chapel just steps ahead. Verdi had tried everything to exclude him, but when five doctors certified that Cardinal Lopez's diabetes was wildly out of control, no one could block his statutory right to bring in the physician of his choice.

Cardinal Lopez was clearly ill, even to the untrained eye. He shuffled as he walked, with a festinating gait that proved his weakness. Ellison knew Lopez's blood chemistries were wildly out of control. A brave man, Ellison thought, someone who has put himself in danger for a cause. Of course no outsider knew that the Philippine cardinal had failed to take his insulin injections for five days in order to make his chemistry tests certifiably critical and in need of constant care.

Ellison dared to be there only because he felt driven by an obligation to discover some way to block Verdi's chances. Yet he knew an element of foolhardiness in himself played a role, as in the vanity of one individual taking on a mighty prince of the Catholic Church. Now, as he crossed the threshold into the conclave, he felt he had crossed the line between being an observer of events to being a player in them. Actually, he felt like an Assassin himself.

Vanguard of modern Islamic terrorists, the Muslim "hash-hash-ins," named after their drug of choice, sprang up as a secret society in response to the Crusaders taking Jerusalem and establishing Crusader Kingdoms throughout the Holy Lands. Trained to work alone, the Assassins infiltrated enemy headquarters, stayed dormant for months or years—often as trusted functionaries—then made suicide attacks on ministers and kings with knives, poisons, or strangling ropes. Richard the Lionhearted, determined to annihilate them when his scouts discovered the hidden valley the Assassins used for training, discovered how fanatically dedicated the Assassins were when he led his troops to attack. When their leader, The Old Man of the Mountains, rode out to confront Richard, he pointed to a rank of Assassins standing at the edge of a cliff. At a wave of The Old Man's hand, thirty Assassins leapt to their deaths. Far from his lines of supply, Richard decided the better part of knightly valor was to retreat.

And now, going directly into the lion's den to slay it, Ellison felt as dedicated as one of the Islamic warriors. Someone had to stop Verdi. Why him? In the end he decided no one else could do what he was going to do. In some far off corner of the world, or maybe just a block away, someone else might be working in his own way at stopping Verdi. Ellison had no way of knowing. No matter, for Ellison was sure of one thing: a unique moment sat on his own plate.

An unexpected chain of events had led him in the past two years from an indebted bachelor's life in San Francisco, one of hundreds of thousands of men as different from each other as cows in a herd, to a unique situation where the easiest and safest course in Vatican City would be to say he had done enough, already more than anyone could reasonably expect. His unexpected circumstances made him wonder anew about predestination, the notion that the gods script a man's entire life at the moment of birth, and he lives it out with the illusion he is in control of his own destiny. From the beginning of civilization there have been many who have concluded predestination to be a cosmic truth. Even Buddhist reincarnation carried a similar message. Ellison didn't buy into that. At most, he agreed with one homespun philosopher that destiny dealt you your cards for the poker game of life; and free will was how you played them. Crashing the conclave had not been an easy choice, but he had to choose between playing the game or leaving the field—and when Miranda and Eduardo backed him in the end—he became a solitary, probing fighter.

Cardinal Lopez, rebuffed by other cardinals when he floated the assassination rumor to friends, felt he could risk no more than help Ellison gain entrance. Like Ellison, he was a man torn by conflicts. He told them his own life story so they would understand why he had taken such a radical risk in joining them.

How unlike Eduardo's background Cardinal Lopez's life had been, and it surprised Ellison that two such different men could find themselves yoked in a dangerous undertaking. Eduardo had always lived a life like the Great Gatsby, full of shiny cars, loose women, and slick business deals. Cardinal Lopez sprang from a family of impoverished squatters who lived alongside an open sewer in Manila. When a Canadian philanthropist donated money to educate the brightest of the underprivileged waifs, Lopez was encouraged to give up his job begging for money from drivers stuck in traffic on the South Superhighway. Once in school, Lopez studied with the intensity of an athlete training for the Olympics. A priest who worked with child prostitutes in his neighborhood talked with Lopez and drew him toward the priesthood. Years later, when Lopez lived in his archbishop's palace, he never forgot the poor. In that he was like Eduardo. One born rich, one poor, but both fountains of generosity for the underprivileged. Whatever criticism one might have of Eduardo's zesty lifestyle, no one could say he lived only for himself.

Cardinal Lopez reported that after long prayerful consideration of Ellison's observations, he, too, believed Verdi was likely a killer. Ellison, by dint of the medical angle, became Lopez's ally, along with Eduardo, and—after the cardinal spoke at length with all of them and gave them room to maneuver in the context of their religious philosophy—Miranda, Francois, and Beecham announced they supported Ellison's plan. Already suspecting foul play when he brought the rumors about Hildebrandt III's precipitous decline to Sir Eduardo, developments since then, he said, particularly those reported by Ellison, had convinced him murder had taken place. He argued there could be several suspects, not just Verdi. Nevertheless, Lopez told Ellison that as a prince of the church, he felt obliged by the truth as he knew it to block Verdi's election. Neither he nor Ellison knew what they could or would do to stop Verdi in the conclave, Lopez just knew that he wanted and needed Ellison. However, he would not lie to get Ellison into the conclave. To him, lying would be too great a sin. Under the rules of the conclave, Lopez would suffer the penalty of self-excommunication from the Church forever, and would die a soul without a home. Ellison's mind reeled at the idea that a priest would have to ex-communicate himself, an act of spiritual suicide.

"Truly," Lopez had said, "I fear Verdi, as a grave danger to Christianity. For if Verdi is guilty, and I believe he is the most likely suspect, then having such a man at the helm could lead to shipwreck of the institution already weakened by flux. The Vatican is an institution that does not like change. After the Vatican II conference of all churchmen was concluded in the 1960's, there were such shocking modifications to the Church that thirty-eight thousand priests left the priesthood. Whether the Roman Catholic Church would continue to exist became a question for serious debate. Many argued that the changes wrought by Vatican II would lead to a drastic downsizing in Catholicism over the years because the new doctrine claimed less exclusionary ideals."

Unconsciously, Lopez wrung his hands with concern. "For us, a patricide Pope would be like Nero, the Roman Emperor who killed his mother for the throne. Once Nero felt threatened by a new sect, he burned Rome and blamed it on the Christians to create an outcry against them."

Lopez reminded them of several other times the Catholic Church almost came unglued, including the period of the Anti-Popes, and the fleeing to Avignon in France for two hundred years when Rome itself stank with unclean streets, plague, and roving gangs of thugs. Rome's population dropped from over a million to just seventeen thousand, a ninety-eight percent decline. When the Muslims controlled much of Europe, the Church had to retreat to the north, planting roots with the Celts and Teutons, where it thrived in the hardy climes. Yet when rebellions of Northern priests led by Martin Luther split the Church, hundreds of years of wars and mutual persecutions followed. Catholics and Protestants had never again been reconciled. Having seen such calamities take place in the past, Lopez knew what disaster would come from a murderer as Pope. For him the Church was eternal only so long as wise stewardship guided its pilgrimage through time, adapting to each new age as mankind advances, at least scientifically if not spiritually.

Indeed, Lopez feared for the very life of the Church. Across the chapel, Ellison could see it in Lopez's eyes. Ellison heard the doors of the Sistine Chapel slamming shut. With Michaelangelo's fresco of Judgment Day staring down at him, Ellison joined the others in unison in a mandatory oath.

"I swear," he read aloud from the manual that specifies behavior in a conclave, "by all that is holy that I will never reveal what I see or hear inside this conclave. I also swear that I will not support any group of people or individuals who might wish to interfere in the elections of the Roman Pontiff. Amen." I guess I have to live with that false oath-taking, Ellison thought. I'm operating outside the usual rules.

❋   ❋   ❋

Stifling a shiver of excitement, Verdi took the oath, though he had memorized its pledges and unlike the others had no need of a paper to remind him. His mind continued to race like a locomotive full of fuel and out of control, thundering first along one track before abruptly switching to another.

"*Extra omnes.* All but the electors out," the Master of Ceremonies ordered. Verdi frowned as Ellison filed out of the chapel with other support staff. Damn him! Yet what could Ellison do now? Still, seeing him in the sacred conclave, Verdi felt like a bull moose who scents the same wolf trailing him day after day. If Ellison came too close, he would crush him.

Finally facing each other alone in a conclave that might go on for months, the College of Cardinals quickly began the predetermined processes. Tradition called for a quick first vote, in case an overwhelming favorite could be elected by acclamation. Suspecting he ran a strong second to Muldowney, Verdi hoped that on the first vote many of the undecided cardinals would vote for their friends as gestures of great honor. After the first ballot, the election would begin in earnest.

Contrary to popular belief, the cardinals can elect whomsoever they wish, so long as he is a baptized male, or even a male willing to be baptized. With the new dormitories at *Domus Sanctae Marthae* just a few feet away, quality of life would be good enough for the cardinals to feel comfortable, to enjoy the great gathering, and to be in no particular hurry to end it. Verdi felt he could use the time for deep thinking if it came to an extended conclave. During one conclave that sat three and a half years, the cardinals wavered so long that the town's people finally tore off the roof of the building and put the cardinals on a diet of bread and water until they chose a Pope.

After the single vote on the afternoon of the first day of the conclave, the rules called for two ballots per day, and—with the new rule that after two weeks of unsuccessful voting, an absolute majority of the cardinals could suspend the rules and waive the two-thirds requirement for election—no future conclave will likely last more than a month. Verdi agreed with the cardinal consensus that lengthy conclaves stir confidence problems throughout the Church, and should be avoided.

The one hundred forty-nine took their places in front of canopied thrones for each prince. An atmosphere of great solemnity and import prevailed with crystal clarity, as all knew that this election, taking place in a closed conclave, always ranked as amongst the supreme events of man on earth. Verdi suspected he might be the only one not humbled by the experience, for he felt entitled to The Keys to Heaven.

Verdi knew each and every one of the cardinals from his world travels. And he knew that each of them, like him, knew the customs and regulations of the conclave to a scholarly depth. The prior agreement on strict rules made for a swift, almost silent procedure.

Three scrutineers selected by lot by the senior cardinal deacon took their places beside an altar with a golden chalice upon it. In just a few minutes, the ballots would be placed in the chalice, and the scrutineers would count them. Three revisers would do an immediate recount.

Even the infirm can vote. Three cardinals chosen as *infirmarii* would go to Cardinal Bezos' cubicle to help him vote. Bezos had to be supported during his determined procession from the ornate Pauline Chapel in the Apostolic Palace to the Sistine Chapel. Once through the sacred portals, Bezos staggered, stumbled and was unable to continue. Dr. Morra and Ellison had put him on a stretcher and carried him to his room, where by virtue of crossing the threshold qualifying as an elector, his vote would count, and Verdi expected to get it.

After prayers to invoke the Holy Spirit, voting began when Cardinal Lopez passed out ballots the size of business cards printed with *Eligo in summum pontificem,* I elect as supreme pontiff, one to each man. Verdi's hand trembled with excitement when he felt the ballot in his fingers, so small but so powerful. The tremor increased when he wrote his own name on the ballot—unseemly he knew—but this was no time to take chances. If he were to lose by a single vote...

One by one, in order of seniority, the cardinals processed to the altar. Verdi voted in ninety-sixth place, but by the time the seventh man cast his lot, he already felt irritated by the ponderous slowness of the balloting. Though he tried to control his feelings by watching the fervent but serene manner of his colleagues, his impatience verged on an anger that grew nearly uncontrollable. If his turn at the chalice had not arrived at just that moment he might have broken the pristine silence and said something he knew he would regret.

When the cardinal from Venezuela passed him, Verdi stood to go forward. Looking neither left nor right, all the while trying to observe the faces and body language of the cardinals as he passed by, Verdi took measured steps toward the altar, where he knelt in brief prayer before he spoke the ritual words each cardinal repeats while casting his ballot.

"I call as my witness Christ the Lord who will be my judge, that my vote is given to the one before God I think should be elected." Verdi spoke the words with complete conviction and pure confidence that he should be the one.

He placed his ballot on top of a golden plate, then tipped it into the chalice from high enough that all eyes could see only a single ballot fell. In some mystical way he sensed this was the most important moment of his life, this conclave, at least by far the most intense. Once back at his throne, Verdi's impatience to hear the count kept him agitated, but in ten minutes the scrutineers began their work in silence, triple counting the ballots while Verdi's mind felt like a racehorse gone wild, leaping over one idea after another.

Will it be me? Is this feeling inside me Christ at work? Can the world be saved from damnation? Repent! Repent! He struggled to rein in his mind without success. *Can the others see into me?* His pounding heart made rapid claps of thunder in his ears, and sweat dripped from him like drops of rain.

"The vote is as follows," Strizzi, by lot a scrutineer, intoned. "Cardinal Muldowney, thirty-eight. Cardinal Verdi, thirty-seven. Cardinal Righetti, twenty. Cardinal—"

Close to what I expected, Verdi mused. Righetti is Roman by birth and could emerge as a compromise victor. Twenty other cardinals received votes.

"We have no Pope," Strizzi declared.

A needle and thread made the ballots into a necklace, and after counting again to be sure all were bound, Strizzi took the ballots to a stove. There under the watchful eyes of the secretary of the conclave and the Master of Ceremonies, scrutineers burned the ballots with damp straw and manganese powder to make the smoke black. When it poured from the chimney of the chapel, more than a billion faithful around the world would know they had to continue to wait for their new leader.

In the coming morning, voting would begin in earnest. With the conclave finished for the first day, Verdi processed in silence across the manicured courtyards to his temporary room in the dormitory with the other cardinals. While others slept or prayed, Verdi paced his tiny room like a caged tiger anxious to devour votes. During the conclave dinner that evening, Verdi controlled his urge to promote himself. With Strizzi serving as his great elector, his main advocate, Verdi knew deals and explanations were being made on his behalf, just as the great electors for the other *papabile* worked the electors in the casual gatherings before the *angelus* prayers that marked the end of a long day with the commemoration of the Annunciation. Resigned to the knowledge that his moment to speak would come in due time, while others slept Verdi mulled over what to say; until just before dawn, unable to find precisely the right tone for his speech, he simply prayed that he would be open to inspiration by the Holy Spirit when his turn came.

UNEXPECTED

Ellison cleansed Cardinal Lopez's thin skin with an alcohol swab before slipping the needle into his flabby belly for the first insulin injection of the new day.

"As we discussed, Doctor," Lopez said with a grimace of pain, "why do you care so much about this problem? Have you asked yourself that?"

They were alone in a makeshift clinic adjacent to the tiny room crammed with beds for the doctors. Despite the minimal privacy, Ellison felt a sense of timeless isolation inside the conclave. No news from outside could come in, and in the many hours of waiting, Ellison had been asking himself the same question without reaching a completely satisfactory answer.

He knew it sounded like a cliché when he answered Lopez. "How can I ignore such evil and still be a man? Several times I wanted to walk away, to say this is not my problem, but something inside forces me on."

"Ah, so you are a religious man."

"More of a humanist, I think, at least since I turned twenty. I grew up Protestant in America, but after university courses in philosophy and comparative religion I stopped believing that whatever god exists takes any interest in human affairs."

Lopez eyed him, both eyebrows raised in surprise. "Really? You can believe in an emotionless Prime Mover? How empty. I believe that through his son, God sacrificed himself for mankind." He took Ellison by the arm and led him out of the room toward a small chapel. "I pray that God in his wisdom grants you the ability to see the wonders of his actions on earth."

"Sure, I can see the cosmic beauty of it all, but look around us—war, cruelty, death. If God is all powerful, then he is not all good."

Lopez completed the famous Renaissance conundrum for him. "Yes, and if he is all good, then evil on earth means God is not all powerful. Spoken like a true rationalist, Doctor."

"I am a scientist, Your Eminence."

"A swashbuckling one, my son. Just remember that God is ineffable and that you cannot understand his ways. You cannot know, you can only feel, and perhaps God is working through you now. Have faith."

"Either you have faith or you don't," Ellison responded, "and if you have it, there is no way to explain it to someone who doesn't."

As Lopez eyed him, Ellison changed the subject, more interested in events than speculations he had mulled over for years. "What will happen today?"

"Speeches and two more votes if necessary. In discussions at the dormitory last night, Muldowney seems the clear favorite, but his supporters need to sway the undecided."

"And Verdi?"

"Strong, though many worry about his stability of late. He rarely sleeps and has taken on an air of otherworldliness. Sometimes he rambles, as if transported by the Holy Spirit."

"I doubt that's what inspires him," Ellison grunted.

❄   ❄   ❄

After the first vote of the day, while listening to the reading of the tally by the first set of scrutineers for the day, Verdi struggled to contain his agitation. The results made him feel both distress and relief: distress that Muldowney's total soared to sixty-three, still thirty-seven votes short, damn him, and relief that votes for Verdi climbed to fifty, up thirteen.

In the time scheduled for reflection before the day's second vote, Verdi fell to his knees. He felt God calling him to do great things, offering him a covenant for all mankind if Verdi would do His will on earth. When the deliberations resumed, Verdi felt outside of himself, as if listening and watching life through a curtain of fine lace. Following three others, Verdi saw the American cardinal rise to speak.

"My Brothers in Christ," Muldowney began. His fame as a historian and scholar attracted every cardinal's rapt attention. "I will be brief. What man wants this burden of becoming Pope, especially in our time? Our Church, worldwide but particularly in the advanced nations like mine, must undergo radical change to adapt to our new transnational world."

"In the past century, Rome has exploited the use of new technologies to centralize the power of the Holy See in unprecedented ways. More than ever in history, a Pope has absolute control."

Muldowney looked at the assembly with friendly eyes. "But with all respect, I believe no man should have such unbridled power.

"Our doctrine of Papal Infallibility is relatively new in Church history, as it passed the College of Cardinals only in 1846 and then only by a few votes. It is the Church herself, through the four thousand bishops of the world, that is central, not the one of us who becomes our leader. In America we believe in checks and balances on the power of any one man, lest he become a despot.

"Therefore," Muldowney continued, "I believe a Pope must share power with the bishops, especially in political matters in their nations. In my diocese, for example, we allow women to be almost equal to priests, and I see no reason to perpetuate a centuries-old myth that women are unclean and incapable of doing what we priests do. Most important, with the world overflowing with our species, we must not condemn birth control, a technical ability God has allowed our civilization to discover. This should be obvious to any thinking person. Since you want to know, I do not favor abortion but I wonder what God thinks is right for a young woman raped by a cruel, criminal moron.

"This is the culture in which I live. Why must I support Roman policies that I believe are wrong?

"Also, I believe we need to reach out to the other great religious traditions, to carry on the ecumenical theme of John Paul II, not to convince non-Catholics of the damning errors of their beliefs, but to search together for the ultimate truth that could unite us, not divide us. Unless we do that, endless conflict darkens all mankind's horizons.

"As you know, I am a direct man. There has been only one non-Italian Pope in the past five centuries. Why is this? Does it make sense in our modern world? I ask not for myself, as truly I am not worthy to be elected, but I ask for the centuries to come. Many of you from the far corners of the earth are better suited than I to be the Servant of the Servants of God, are holier than I; and I believe that in recognition of the new world realities we must make the Chair of St. Peter open to all.

"Perhaps my liberal ideas offend some of you," Muldowney concluded, folding his hands in prayer; "but in this solemn moment I have spoken the truth as I see it. And whomsoever we elect, may God have mercy on him."

After Muldowney finished it was Verdi's turn. During Muldowney's speech, he had heard grunts of disapproval, especially from the Italian cardinals, but most heads nodded in agreement. While he realized much of what Muldowney said rang true, Verdi sensed he now must speak the truth as he could see it himself; for if God were with him, Verdi would say the right things.

Looking from one cardinal to the next, he began with words from the Mass, sure to induce respectful attention. *"Misureatur nostri omnipotens Deus et, dimissis peccatis nostris, perducat nos ad vitam aeternam.* May almighty God have mercy on us, forgive us our sins, and bring us to everlasting life."

"Amen," they murmured out of reflex. But Verdi knew he already had them.

"As Vatican Secretary of State I have met with the leaders of the world, political and religious. With great respect and esteem for Cardinal Muldowney, I must say that my experiences lead me to different conclusions about the future of the Church."

Verdi knew that mentioning an opponent by name would raise hackles in some, but he felt that controversy worked in his favor. "For me, the centralization of power made possible by technical advances opens the door for us to complete what Jesus Christ charged us to do. He told Peter to bring the word to all. To do this we must not allow fragmentation of Vatican control, but rather should work toward even more consolidation to improve our worldly force. The Pope is God's Vicar on Earth, no one else. Blessed though all bishops may be, Christ gave St. Peter the Keys to Heaven, no one else."

He wanted to continue this train of thought, but a new topic jolted him off track.

"Amongst you are some who secretly favor the end of priestly celibacy. You want to change the rules so priests can have sex with women. We cannot be like St. Augustine, saying, 'Lord give me celibacy, but not yet.' This idea of redefining the priesthood flows from our own human weaknesses in a corrupt world and is promoted by lay groups that secretly desire to see themselves equal to us, trouble-makers like *Opus Spiritus*. They do not understand that through celibacy we priests have been initiated into the deepest mysteries of our faith, accomplished by a transmutation of finer energies they simply cannot share with us. All of us know that. Therefore I stand firm in our historical belief that just as Jesus himself was celibate, so must we keep ourselves holy."

He hesitated, looking at the electors for a reaction. "Our priesthood needs reinforcement of our sacred tradition, not reformation."

Verdi paused, confused. Perhaps it was the heat? Why was he suddenly drenched with sweat? He could feel himself losing control of his mind in the strength of God's grip, as at the Requiem Mass, beginning to say words part of his mind knew he should not utter.

"As for working with other faiths, remember that God sometimes comes as the Lamb, at other times as *Sabaoth*, the warrior. Across the world Muslims bomb our cities, destroy our aircraft, infiltrate our societies and attack the very foundations of our culture. All of you know that centuries ago they invaded Rome and even desecrated St. Peter's. They defiled the tombs of St. Peter and

St. Paul then, and now they wish to come again. I can feel it! Christ spoke to me at the altar two weeks ago, I tell you. Now is the time to fight them, not to seek ways to co-exist in peace with their foul religion. For if we do not, if we allow the weak to lead us, in a hundred years there will be thousands of turbaned believers on their hands and knees in St. Peter's, but bowing toward Mecca instead of the Cross. God shows me the future as it will be if we do not repent for our sinful weakness.

"Repent! Repent, I say in the name of Christ, who speaks through me. Kneel to praise Him, then rise to pick up a holy sword! The Day of Judgment is at hand!" At that, Verdi slumped to the ground, overcome by religious fervor.

When he rose, how much later he was unsure, a buzz of disapproval still reverberated in the room. "Madness! He claims Christ speaks through him," he heard a cardinal say. "Heresy!" shouted another.

Verdi took his seat beneath his canopy and heard himself mumbling. More than ever he felt loss of control, yet he felt euphoric, almost omniscient, a god amongst mere men. "Thy will be done," he prayed aloud.

Cardinal Righetti, angered and embarrassed by Verdi's display, took the floor facing Verdi. "I disavow the words of Cardinal Verdi, who no longer seems to be the holy man I once knew, a man who would never say such things. His God is the god of old, not the Redeemer of our New Testament. Is there now a cardinal among you who stands for him? Let us vote again, Brothers in Christ. We have heard enough for this day."

A roar of assent swept around the room. What had happened? Verdi wondered. How could he have so completely destroyed his years of work and plotting? What was it that had possessed him?

While he berated himself, a trio of swiftly chosen scrutineers seated themselves beside the altar. The *infirmarii* sought the vote of Cardinal Bezos, still too weak to take his seat. Fresh ballots were distributed. As he struggled to regain control of himself, the most senior cardinals clustered around Verdi, either frowning at him or wearing looks of utter scorn.

It would be Muldowney, he was sure. Verdi knew he had lost, and felt a crashing desolation that he could have been so wrong. How could he have misinterpreted the signs? He felt certain God meant for him to be Pope. How could it be Muldowney?

Just as the first cardinal pledged, "My vote is given to the one—" a furious pounding on the door began, and shouting, "Let us in! You must be told! Jerusalem is destroyed!"

❈   ❈   ❈

Ellison stood amazed as a swarm of cardinals raced past the medical clinic and out of the Sistine Chapel, with Cardinal Lopez in the rear.

"What's going on?" Ellison asked.

"The Holy Sepulchre has been bombed!" Lopez exclaimed as he shuffled past Ellison. Ellison took him by the arm while the old man continued. "Muldowney is about to be elected. Verdi is finished. There is no doubt. The conclave is suspended for two hours while we learn the facts about the Holy Land."

Stunned, Ellison followed the cardinals into the Apostolic Palace, where he found a phalanx of cardinals and reporters glued to a big screen tuned to Fox News, bright with an atomic flash and a famous reporter reading network news.

"With this flash, the unimaginable became reality in Jerusalem. For all of us it is something painful to acknowledge, but we have confirmed the following to be true. At four p.m. Jerusalem time, this fiery mushroom cloud appeared over the city. We have little camera footage yet of this first terrorist use of a nuclear weapon, but early word is that tens of thousands are dead or wounded. There are reliable reports that Muslim terrorists seeking the release of Ramzi Ahmed Youssef have claimed responsibility, just as they did for the airliner bombings last month. Stay tuned as we bring you breaking developments. Now this."

So, it had finally happened. For years, U.S. State Department's counterterrorism experts had been cautioning that it was only a matter of time before some bad guys got hold of atomic weapons. Most of the people of the world had learned to deal with the possibility by using simple denial as a defense mechanism, since there was nothing they could individually do about the danger anyway. But everyone would have to think about it now. It would strain the world in a way that had never happened before. Ellison guessed that launch codes were being updated on hundreds of missiles around the world, from America, to Russia, to England and France, to India, to Israel herself. If there was anywhere on earth that a bombing could lead to worse consequences than Jerusalem, Ellison couldn't imagine where it would be. Religions have long memories. Now there would be trouble for a thousand years, if anyone on earth was still alive in a few days.

By the time a lithe actress shilling pantyhose finished prancing across the screen, Ellison already knew he had to get to *Valkyrie One*. Rescue Team International, *his* team, would be needed now more than ever; and conflicted though he was about leaving the conclave, Lopez's reassuring words that Muldowney would be elected Pope set Ellison free of his vow. During his hours in the conclave he had discovered no way he could intervene anyway, especially since but a hint of disruptive behavior would have led to his immediate expulsion. It wasn't the ending to his venture into the conclave that Ellison had expected, but the result was what he had hoped for. Relieved that Verdi's bid had failed, Ellison felt he would be more useful performing a mission for which he was trained than standing by to observe, like some favored tourist, the rest of the conclave after Muldowney was announced.

He was about to leave when Verdi stormed toward him. Before Ellison could reach the door, Verdi grabbed his arms in a steel grip. His body movements as rapid and jerky as his words, his face pale and damp, Verdi shoved his face so close that his nose brushed Ellison's. "You!" Verdi screamed. "You caused this!"

"What? How could I..." None of what was happening made any sense to Ellison.

"Armageddon is come. *The Seventh Seal* shall be broken!"

Verdi's eyes rolled wildly and he shouted at an auctioneer's clip. "You shall be crucified and damned!" Pushing Ellison against a wall, Verdi gave him a last hateful glance, then swept away without looking back.

Ellison knew he had to turn to walk away before his urge to tackle and throttle Verdi became uncontrollable. A man out of his mind, Ellison decided. No doubt about it. Murderer and whatever else Verdi might be, to a medical man, Verdi was insane.

Stuck in traffic after leaving the Vatican, Ellison pondered Verdi's bizarre behavior. He wanted to describe his observations to Francois, to get his medical opinion. In less than an hour he was aboard *Valkyrie One*, where after a lingering kiss from Miranda, he found General Beecham drumming a tattoo on his ostrich cowboy boots while he waited for Ellison's orders. Francois had both of his legs off and was doing push-ups on the cabin floor.

"Status report, General?"

"The whole world is on hair trigger. Every air force on earth is on patrol. Same with navies. Tanks are moving and troops are ordered back to base. Let's saddle up, Commando Doc, 'cause the herd's in a stampede. I've got us clearance to fly over Jerusalem, and *Valkyrie Two* along with everyone else is on the way from California as we speak."

"Any more news?"

"America sent a reconnaissance plane from Incirlik, Turkey that can sniff radioactive dust to identify what kind of weapon went off. Pakistani for sure. Low yield but Jerusalem is history anyway."

"Was it a missile?" Miranda asked.

"Radar says, no way. Unfortunately, honey, some ranch hand could jes' mosey hisself into Jerusalem, probably in a van. Then it was the last roundup."

"Military responses?" Ellison asked.

"Everyone is ready to kick the shit out of the blackhats, but who knows where the hell they are? It was the Youssef gang, though. They called NATO one minute before the barbecue."

"Is everyone ready?"

"Time to stop jawin' and ride, pardner."

"While you were in the conclave I prayed for you, *monsieur*," Francois said as he log-rolled unto his back and used his mighty arms to lift himself into his wheelchair. "Somehow your courage almost made me believe again. And I missed you."

At that, Miranda gave Francois a friendly punch on one brawny shoulder and wrapped her arms protectively around Ellison's waist. "He's mine, Francois. Forever."

"Yes, yes, Little Sister, we all know that," Eduardo said. "What we do not know is Todd's experiences in the conclave."

"As his wife, I can tell by the look on his face it was stressful. Tell us, my darling."

Ellison began to describe the conclave and to relive his encounter with Verdi, so that by the time *Valkyrie One* waddled to the runway for takeoff, Ellison and all the others wondered if they lived in a world gone irrevocably mad.

❋   ❋   ❋

Verdi sat in his Sistine pew, nearly oblivious of the activities going on around him. A knife-like pain of disappointment threatened to carve his heart out, and as he sought to escape its attack, he plunged through a wide spectrum of emotions—from fear to exultation, from ecstasy to despair, from confusion to perfect confidence—with his whole state of being changing with great speed. He could barely comprehend the conversations of the other cardinals above the roaring of several voices in his head.

"I suggest we recess the conclave for several days," began the senior cardinal. "There are precedents."

"Yes," Righetti the Roman agreed. "The College of Cardinals can rule in the interim."

"No!" came a voice like a whip. Cardinal Strizzi, his great elector, rose to speak. "I say that we should vote now. With destruction around us, the world needs a Pope now more than ever. Don't we all know there is one among us touched by the Holy Spirit?" He pointed to Verdi. "That man! What he spoke was the truth. A prophet in our midst!"

"He's insane!" shouted a cardinal from Canada.

"No, he is the prophet who must be Pope!" Strizzi shouted back. "Take off your blinders, brothers. Do not forget the Holy Sepulchre is gone. Our most sacred relics destroyed. It is just as Cardinal Verdi says. Look into yourselves and acknowledge that in these conditions we must fight."

All eyes turned to Verdi, who sat as if pole-axed by a divine revelation that had already transported him beyond mortal existence. He could barely comprehend their words but he could feel their veneration for him. He prayed that his moment had come.

"Let the vote begin," came a chorus of voices. "No delays."

"No heretics!" shouted another.

JERUSALEM

By the time they entered Israeli air space, Ellison's mood had grown more tense. Massive traffic came over *Valkyrie One's* on-board communications gear, which Beecham had upgraded after Tokyo and now could monitor any transmission except those from America's nuclear submarine force. In the name of national defense, clamp-downs on civil rights were taking place as they flew. Huge groups of Jewish demonstrators in New York and Washington were screaming they had learned in Germany not to be silent, that they would not tolerate this latest holocaust. Everyone was horrified, no matter what their religion, but the government had to preserve order, and large numbers of Washington D.C. police took to the streets around the White House and Congress hosing down surging protesters of all faiths. When the mob swelled with Georgetown University students, some of the boisterous youth attempted to scale the fence nearest President Clark's

Oval Office. Ellison watched television footage of billy-clubs cracking open scalps and paddy wagons being filled with hand-cuffed students. He had seen it before in photos of the riots in 1968, when the Vietnam War and the assassinations of Kennedy and King led to tanks in the streets of Berkeley. In the wake of the Jerusalem bombing, worldwide rioting threatened to plunge the planet into chaos.

Francois took a break from his almost constant exercises to brief everyone on the history of Jerusalem. "A sacred city for three religions with common roots—Jewish, Christian, and Muslim—mankind has fought over Jerusalem for thousands of years. Why?"

He usually had a professorial manner when it came to the history of religion, so sincere and open that Ellison gladly assumed the role of pupil. When teaching, Francois always seemed more like a parochial school priest than a doctor. This time, though, he was gloomy. Ellison had been thinking about Jerusalem for hours. "Tell us, *padre*."

"It's not as simple as you might think." Hands clasped behind his back, Francois hobbled the entire width of the jumbo jet, his mechanical knees creaking with every step. "To begin, for the Jews the city is the capitol of their civilization, the site where King Solomon built the Temple to house the Ark of the Covenant. By then, the Jews were already age-old descendants of Abraham, already escaped from Egypt, already bearing the Ten Commandments from Moses. They believed that they were building the Temple on the Rock of Mount Mariah, the source of the Deluge that floated Noah from this watery navel of the universe. Then and now they believe that from that Jerusalem rock, God will open the gateway on Judgment Day. Though the Jews first built it more than three thousand years ago, they have been unable to maintain control of their city. They have been thrown out or captured again and again. From the moment Jerusalem fell to King Nebuchadnezzar of Babylon, they have yearned for eternal control of Jerusalem, the home of their holy of holies. In fact, the Jews have regained and lost it three or four times over history. They've wrested control from the Palestinians since the Second World War."

"I cannot believe this explosion is true until I see it with my own eyes," Eduardo said, standing. "I've been in Jerusalem several times. Just last month *Opus Spiritus* held our quarterly meeting at the King David Hotel. Right in the Old City."

"What a loss," Miranda sighed. "I was there, too, once when I was just a girl. A group of young people came from Manila."

"For Christians," Francois continued, "Jerusalem is the city in which their savior preached, suffered death by crucifixion, and rose again from the dead. In the Church of the Holy Sepulchre, you can see the stone where Mary and Mary Magdalene washed Jesus' body."

"Used to be able to see," Beecham corrected. "It's gone now."

"What about for Islam?" Ellison asked. "I think Jerusalem is the third holiest city for them, after Mecca and Medina."

"It is hard to believe Muslims are responsible," Miranda added.

"Oh, they are, ma'am," Beecham drawled. "No doubt about it."

"I recall some other occasions when America blamed the wrong people," Miranda parried. "And I know Jerusalem is very sacred to Islam."

"Agreed. It is the site of Mohammed's famous *Night Journey*," Francois nodded. "Todd's right. For Muslims it is the third most holy city. Though Prophet Mohammed never visited Jerusalem, he dreamed that he was conveyed miraculously from Mecca to the Jerusalem Temple Mount by Archangel Gabriel. Astride his heavenly white steed with the face of a woman, the noble Buruq, he galloped through the seven heavens to Paradise to meet with his god, Allah himself. It was the only time Mohammed ever met Allah face to face. Allah told him to teach Muslims to face Jerusalem when they prayed."

"But they pray facing Mecca," Miranda objected.

"That came later, after he got angry at the Jews," Francois answered. "For the next twenty-two years Mohammed taught and dictated the Koran while he was in spiritual trances. Faced with fierce opposition to his new religion, he had to become a warrior to save his followers. His armies flourished until his death in 632 A.D., and grew even stronger once he was gone. Just five years after he died, Muslim armies were camping outside Jerusalem's walls. At that time, Jerusalem was a Christian city in the Eastern Roman Empire. To avoid slaughter, Patriarch Sophronius rode out to greet and open the gates for Caliph Omar, who sauntered into Jerusalem on a white camel at the van of a victorious army.

Caliph Omar found the Temple Mount reeking with filth, which he ordered be cleaned away so he could build a great mosque. Anyway, the Muslims held Jerusalem until the First Crusade in 1099, or more than four hundred fifty years. For comparison, my American friend, your nation has existed about half of that time."

"I see what you mean," Ellison said. He often forced himself to remember that just as he and all of his friends were living in the now and believing themselves to be at the hub of history, so too did men of earlier times. He tried to imagine how his descendants would feel if an invader came two hundred years from now to evict Americans and Canadians from their great lands.

"If that first changeover was without violence, five centuries later the Crusaders arrived after their year-long walk from Paris and it was slaughter. They took off their armor and walked naked around the city seven times before they prayed at Gethsemane. This so befuddled the Muslims that they missed their opportunity to take the field to slaughter the taunting but momentarily defenseless Crusaders. After the Crusaders built battle towers that allowed them over the walls, they rampaged from wall to wall inside the city, swinging their weapons until the streets ran ankle deep in blood and they had killed every man, woman, and child in Jerusalem. In a few hours, the Crusaders converted each mosque into a church. Implementing the plan of an occupying army, they established a defense that held for almost a hundred years by fighting off every counterattack, until Saladdin annihilated them in 1186 and made the churches back into mosques."

"That started the crusades again, right?" Ellison asked.

"Yes, many crusades, but none succeeded in recapturing Jerusalem. The Muslims held Jerusalem for eight centuries this time."

"That's four times as long as the history of America."

"Correct, *monsieur*. The Muslims held the city from Saladdin to the day in 1967 when Moshe Dayan led the Jewish Defense Force in triumphant passage through the Lion's Gate, where General Dayan said Jerusalem will be Jewish forever."

Beecham pointed beyond the left wingtip. "Who will care now, ranch hands? Look over yonder."

As they approached, Ellison strained to see the city in the low hills thirty-five miles from the Mediterranean coastline.

"My God," Miranda murmured. "Look at that, Todd."

"It's just a huge plate of smoking black glass."

"Radioactive glass, pardner."

At the periphery of the city, a few buildings stood as useless rubble, but nothing more than three feet high remained in the center.

"All the religions lost here," Ellison blurted out.

"Look down there, folks. That sight sure as hell isn't going to promote peace," Beecham said. "I'll tell the pilot to go around again."

"The pilot says there is something you need to see, brother," Eduardo interrupted, reaching for a remote control and snapping on the big screen.

Its telephoto images relayed by the satellites circling the globe, a camera panned into a close-up of the chimney atop the Sistine Chapel. White smoke poured out.

"We have a Pope!" Eduardo announced, eagerness in his voice.

"Keep your fingers crossed," Miranda added.

While newsmen engaged in several minutes of wild speculation, Ellison struggled to contain his own churning emotions.

"That it is Cardinal Muldowney, *monsieur*, let us pray to the Lord," Francois said as he held his hands aloft in a gesture of prayer.

A thin figure appeared on the balcony above the main door of St. Peter's, where the new Pope emerged to give his *Urbi et Orbi* speech, to the city and the world.

The camera went to high power as the figure turned slowly and majestically, and at each quadrant of his turn made a stately sign of the cross to the billions watching around the globe.

"*Oremus*," the white-clad figure said, just as his face became visible. "Let us pray."

"No!" Ellison shouted at the screen. "Oh no!"

Verdi barely heard the dean of the college of cardinals asking him, "*Tu es papa?* Do you accept your canonical election as supreme pontiff?" Sudden tears of joy steamed down his face when he nodded assent.

"*Accepto*."

After a dreamlike experience of being taken to a side room to be dressed in the pure white vestments of a Pontiff, Verdi took his place on the papal throne, where one by one the cardinals came to kiss his foot and his hand in the ancient ritual of fealty.

"What shall you be called?" the dean asked him.

"Pius XIII," Verdi answered without hesitation. During one of his long night vigils, Verdi had pondered what he would call himself when the time came. Should he keep his own name? The last pope to do that was Marcellus II in 1555. How did the strange tradition of renaming, symbolic of being reborn as the Vicar of Christ, begin? For the first six centuries of the papacy, men kept their given names, but when a pope with the given name of Mercury won election, he changed his name from a pagan god to Christian by taking John II. And when a man named Peter was elected in 983, he refused to exalt himself to par with St. Peter by naming himself Peter II, and so chose John XIV. For the last thousand years, almost every man has taken a new name.

Now, as Pius XIII, he gazed out over the mass of humanity below him. Two hundred thousand crossed themselves and stared at him with rapturous gazes that carried a radiant energy that added to Verdi's own. Before them, he stood convinced that he was more than any previous successor to the Chair of St. Peter, more than the simple Vicar of Christ on earth. Try as he might to avoid the logical conclusion, he believed the only reasonable explanation for the miracle of his life was that he himself was Christ incarnated again, come to judge the quick and the dead. But this time, he vowed, there would be no crucifixion. The armies of God would rule triumphant!

He prayed and opened his mind to receive Divine Inspiration of what he should say to the crowd. During and after his ascent to the Secretary of State position, he had given more than two thousand speeches. He had concelebrated Mass in a stadium packed with enthusiastic American teenagers. He wanted to give his heart for them all, to lead them to a better life. Verdi had to admit how good it felt now to be Pius XIII, Ecstatic that his moment had come, Pius XIII took a deep breath before telling the crowd the content of his deepest revelations. "Repent!" he cried out. "The Kingdom of Heaven is upon us. Cast aside your empty lives and follow me to reclaim the Holy Lands! *Deus Vult!* God wills it!" He had memorized the words of the Pope who had called for the First

Crusade.

"I pledge to use the wealth of the Holy Roman Catholic Church to plant Christ's flag, my flag, in Jerusalem, where it shall wave until the end of time. Take up the Cross! If you kill our enemies in Christ's name, you shall be forgiven. And if you die in His name, you will surely enjoy everlasting life at the right hand of God the Father Almighty."

He sensed they were with him. "Can you read the signs around us? Of course you can. Follow me to Christ's victory over the infidels.

"*Vigilate fratres!* Be on your watch, brothers and sisters! Our times are dangerous. In the name of the Father, and of the Son, and of the Holy Spirit."

He signed the cross over the multitude, and heard them respond, "Amen."

For an instant after, silence reigned, before a few cheers broke the ice and turned into a swelling, deafening roar that almost drove him back from his balcony. "Papa! Papa!" they chanted in unison.

He felt a breeze make whipping waves in his flowing robes, and his hair blew until it swept back in two horns. A wide smile spread across his face. Pius XIII raised his arms in holy benediction, an otherworldly statue floating over the vast crowd.

✳   ✳   ✳

"He's calling for holy war!" Ellison exclaimed in disbelief.

Francois clutched the arms of his chair, the huge veins in his arms standing out. '*Deus Vult!*' Those were the words of Pope Urban II in 1096. Verdi...I mean, Pius XIII—is calling for a Crusade."

Suddenly filled with regret over his decision to leave the conclave, Ellison paced the floor. "Verdi is insane. Now I'm sure of it."

"From the way you described him at the conclave, I've wondered if he might have a thought process disorder. Paranoid schizophrenics often make mystical utterances like that," Francois said.

"No, he's not schizophrenic," Ellison mused. "He reminds me of a patient I once had with true mania."

"*Diagnostic and Statistical Manual, Number 296.40?*" Francois said. "That one?"

"Almost, my friend. What an incredible memory you have. To be exact, I think he has *296.44*, recurring episodes of fulminate true mania. Pius XIII is sick and out of control. That's why he has lost so much weight and Cardinal Lopez says Pius XIII almost never sleeps."

"A crazed bull is a dangerous bull, guys," Beecham interjected, "but as for a Crusade? Forget it? He's all hat and no cattle. I mean, how much has he got, Eduardo? Reassure doc, here. Pius XIII sure as hell doesn't have any army."

"Maybe two billion dollars in cash in the Vatican Bank, a fortune in real estate that would take years to sell, surely some big money from believers who will contribute," Eduardo answered.

"See, doc? Don't worry about this guy."

Miranda kneaded the kinks in Ellison's neck. "I know Verdi's election sickens you, but put it behind you. Don't we have other things to do?"

Francois waved his arm toward a porthole. "Look at the fringes of Jerusalem. There must be thousands of injured people we can help. That's something on our scale."

"After everything you tried, Todd, Verdi got elected anyway," Eduardo added. "I agree with Miranda. We should stick to doing what we can do."

Beecham reassured Ellison with a pat on the back. "Pius doesn't have enough money to conquer Cuba, much less drive out the Jews."

A knot in his stomach warned Ellison there was something missing from Beecham's calculations. The gold! Pius XIII had tens of billions of dollars worth of gold bullion under his sovereign control now. Probably not enough by itself to succeed in a Crusade, but enough to spark wildfires that could make big armies roll. In dozens of places from Russia to Indonesia, from the Philippines to China, probably even in America, dry tinder awaited ignition.

"Pius won't be satisfied with Jerusalem," Ellison groaned. "He wants the whole world."

— Plato
Protagoras

CRUSADE

No one dared interrupt Pius XIII during his morning prayers in the private chapel beside his bedroom suite, where he had spent the past seven hours on his knees communing with God the Father.

Too excited to eat when he finally forced himself to his ornately carved desk—still covered with stacks of documents he planned to speed read when he felt the need—Pius XIII telephoned Cardinal Strizzi, his appointee as new Secretary of State.

"Can you come up to our apartments?" Now Pius XIII used the royal *'we'* when referring to himself.

"Are you well, Holiness? Have you forgotten? Your coronation begins this afternoon. I have been waiting for hours."

"When the Lord speaks with me I lose all sense of time."

Minutes later Strizzi strode in, frowning and carrying a stack of newspapers. "Look at this, Your Holiness. The New York Times headline says, ***Pope Sparks Riots***. They go on to call you *an unfor-tunate selection* and *a menace.*"

"Bah!" Pius XIII felt himself flush with anger and used the last of his energy to listen attentively.

"*Le Figaro* in Paris reports riots by ten thousand Muslim students in the Latin Quarter. In New York City, huge Islamic gangs burned cars and blocked traffic in protest of what they call provocations from the Vatican. Muslim Turks are throwing fire-bombs in Berlin, according to *Stern*, and look—more of the same in Amsterdam, Madrid—." He placed one front page after another before Pius XIII. "It's the same everywhere. All in all, not good press for you, Holiness."

"Jews," Pius XIII snorted. "Jews in control of the media. Just think. There are one billion eight hundred million Christians on earth—two thirds of them Catholic—and one billion two hundred million Muslims, but only fifteen million Jews. We Catholics outnumber the Jews a thousand to one." He waved his hands with a gesture of irritation. "They must all be bankers, doctors or media owners. Worse, it was the Jews who crucified me under Pontius Pilate."

Pius XIII sprang up to pace his office, hardly glancing at the headlines. "The dogs bark but the caravan moves on. Forget them." He waved dismissively and fixed Strizzi with a stare. "What do the faithful say?"

"In honor of your coronation today, and as you commanded, every priest on earth read your letter aloud to his flock at Mass yesterday. When you commanded them to join your crusade, the collection baskets overflowed with money and pledges for more. Plazas thronged with men chanting that they will close their shops, leave their families, and march with you."

"Good. As it is written, the Holy Spirit begins to fill the world."

"No one else on earth can deliver a message that carries the power of your order, Holiness."

"I am God on earth."

"And I am your servant. What now?"

"Last night, when I tried to sleep, God came to me. 'Holy Fire,' He said, and in my dreams I saw flames sweep away the world, burning away the chaff, until only the Church Triumphant remained."

Strizzi genuflected. "Yes, Your Holiness, the cleansing power of fire."

"We will use our wealth to put weapons in the hands of our crusaders, the most fiery kind of all if we can buy them. Do you remember the *Gospel of St. Luke*?"

Strizzi nodded. "Which chapter and verse?"

"Where Jesus says, 'I have come to set the earth on fire. Suppose ye that I am come to give peace on earth? I tell you, Nay; but rather division.'"

"*Luke 12*," Strizzi mumbled. He gave Pius XIII a questioning look and mounted a mild objection. "But Jesus meant the fire of spiritual transformation, not the fire of destruction."

"Wrong!" Pius shouted. "He didn't mean that kind of psychological rubbish! He meant the flames of his religion should burn away all false beliefs. Tell me! Can we obtain the fire or not? The same as they just used in Jerusalem!"

Strizzi paused too long for Pius XIII to contain himself. Transported by his apocalyptic vision, he grabbed Strizzi by the collar. "Can you do it or not? Tell me now, so I can find someone who will succeed if you choose to fail."

"Possibly. Once we have committed to this course, we should gather all of the power we can. It is only prudent."

Satisfied, Pius XIII sighed and turned away. "Once the flames begin, all nations will be forced to choose sides."

Fanned by the giant ostrich feathers of his escorts, Verdi rode into his coronation in his chair, the *sedia gestatoria*. The choir sang *Tu Es Petrus*, Thou Art Peter, while they carried him down the main aisle to St. Peter's altar behind the Master of Ceremonies. Three times the procession stopped to burn a wisp of flax on a silver tray. As the flax blazed from flames to ashes, the Master of Ceremonies cried aloud, "*Sancte Pater, sic transit Gloria mundis.* Remember, Father, thus passes the glory of the world."

After hours of posturing and solemnity, the great moment came for Pius XIII when the Master of Ceremonies placed a triple-tiered crown on his head. "Wear this crown to remind you thou art father of princes and kings, the ruler of the world, the Vicar of Jesus Christ, Our Savior, on Earth. Amen."

Pius XIII felt confirmed in what he had already known.

❋ ❋ ❋

Valkyrie One, Jerusalem Airbase

It seemed incongruous that they could forget the world outside them, but Ellison and Miranda wanted each other. When they finished making love, Miranda stretched her long legs before cuddling Ellison again. "I missed my period, darling."

A child. The thought speared into Ellison. He would have to be a more responsible man once he had a child. He remembered holding each of his little brothers merely hours after they were born, still wrinkled and red. Caring for all four of them had been a big part of his life, something he recalled as happy times. A wide smile spread across his face, matching hers. "Really? That's so wonderful, Miranda. I will always love you."

Turning pensive, Ellison stared out the window toward a tent city springing up near the airport perimeter. With their main hospital tents already crammed with patients screaming with pain from their burns, a secondary hospital cobbled together in the open air had more than a hundred cots full of overflow patients. Looking like a long column of wretched beggars, thousands of survivors formed lines to receive doses of iodine that would protect their thyroid glands from radioactivity.

"You really should not be here," he said, "especially with the baby so tiny now. This is a critical time for the child, and we are absorbing a lot of radiation, even staying inside."

"But I don't want to leave you, Todd. How long do you plan to stay?"

"There's more work here than anyone can possibly do."

With Rescue Team International operating at the outskirts of what used to be Jerusalem, he had a view of mangled corpses stacked like cordwood about to be bulldozed into mass graves. Unsure what religions the victims professed, groups of rabbis, priests, and *imams* prayed for all of them. Some, the ones vaporized in the blast, would be found no more. The clerics blessed the universe and prayed for their atomized spirits. The spiritual leaders eyed one another nervously, hardly conversing.

Ellison knew that despite heroic efforts by his huge team of doctors, acting in concert with a swelling international relief effort, the graveyards would be busy for weeks. Most of the survivors had received enough gamma radiation to cause fatal radiation sickness, with its indolent course of bone marrow destruction, infection once the immune system fails, and death. Approximately the yield of the Hiroshima widow-maker that ended World War II, the Pakistani bomb was a dirty one, and more than one hundred thousand were dead or missing.

Ellison had seen more than a dozen Israeli Kefir fighters take off on what Beecham said would be a retaliatory strike. Now, when they returned hours later, an ashen Beecham rushed in to summon Ellison, "Fucking A...they used hydrogen bombs on 'em."

"Oh, shit." Ellison muttered. "Well, I guess I'm not completely surprised."

"Just the second time in history warfare's gone nuclear."

"It won't be the last."

"I'll tell you something, though, pardner. They made damn sure them Pakistanis are out of it for twenty years."

"Without some level of Pakistani government conspiracy, no one could have obtained that Jerusalem bomb."

Eduardo and Francois joined them."The Israelis have always believed in swift, multiplied, punishment," Francois said.

After the Karachi broadcasters beamed pictures of mushroom clouds over Pakistani weapons depots, Beecham told them the whole world waited for more retaliation from one side or another. General war plans were dusted off from the Kremlin to Tokyo and Beijing. Troops started on the move. Though he ordered American forces to highest readiness, President Clark steadfastly refused to release Youssef and the Sheik, while behind the scenes every intelligence agency on earth rounded up suspects for severe interrogation.

"Why can't the three religions co-exist in peace?" Ellison asked. "Christianity and Islam both developed from Judaism, and all three believe in the same god. What do all of you think?"

Francois answered without hesitation. "Remember when I lived with Akhmed? Under his influence, I made the following vow before an *imam: I believe in the one God, Allah; and Mohammed is the seal of his prophets.* To become a Muslim, that is all you have to say. After I converted to Islam with that act, Akhmed took me to Mecca for the Haj, the holy pilgrimage at the holiest time of the year. *The Koran* urges every Moslem to perform the

Haj at least once in a lifetime. Outside of Mecca in Saudi Arabia, we camped with a caravan of Bedouins from his native Algeria. All of us put all of our belongings in safekeeping and exchanged our clothing for an Identification Card and a simple white robe. From the edge of town, we walked in a trickle of a crowd that grew to be a great river of humanity flowing toward the *Kabaa*, the Holy Stone. Stripped of every badge of earthly power, the uniformity of the crowd symbolizes every man is equal before Allah. I saw the *Kabaa*, I felt the numinance of Allah. I learned that all men are equal before God."

Ellison felt unsatisfied. "If all are equal, why do the religions fight?"

"The human tendency to exclusivity," Francois answered, pointing his finger at his own chest. "People say, '*My* town is better than *your* town. *My* political system is better than *yours*,' and so on. A group creates stature for itself by claiming superiority over others."

Eduardo thumbed his well-worn Bible and read from it, "'He that believeth in Christ and is baptized shall be saved; but he that believeth not shall be damned.' Not much room for Jews or Muslims under that tent."

"He that believeth not shall be damned," Miranda repeated. "And when you have the Jews staunchly claiming they are the Chosen People, while the Muslims believe that Mohammed is the *Seal of the Prophets* and deny the divinity of Jesus, some irreconcilable differences exist." She was a preacher's daughter who had struggled with the issues of Islam and Christianity all of her life in Zamboanga City, a major interface of the two religions. The Moros held most of the seven thousand islands of the Philippines when the Spaniards arrived. The Christians pushed south, trying to drive the Moros back to Indonesia, from whence they had come. Over the centuries it had proven impossible to eradicate them, and a moving frontier of hostilities and control had developed in place of a decisive result. Zamboanga City was the frontier, half Christian, half Moslem. Miranda had seen the resulting turmoil all her life.

"Yet the beliefs of the three religions are otherwise nearly identical," Francois continued. "One God, an emphasis on love and good works, belief in the same ancestors, for example Abraham and other prophets."

"I did my masters thesis on the history of fighting between each of the religions," Eduardo said. "At University of Santo Tomas in Manila. Older than Harvard."

"I remember," Miranda said. "I knew you wrote it because of seeing Muslims and Christians fight all of our lives in Mindanao."

Ellison had the kind of mind that felt most intellectually satisfied when it was understanding the origin of things, elucidating first principles. His father had always told him, "If you want to know the future, look at the past." He patted Eduardo on the shoulder. "Right now your master's topic fascinates me. When did it all begin?"

"Yes, I can tell you. I wrote on the first fighting between these religions. Until recently it has been Christian dogma that Jewish fighting against Christians began with the crucifixion of Jesus himself. In fact, for several centuries Christians always blamed the Jews for the crucifixion, though official dogma in our time holds the Jews innocent. Nowadays people might date the first mortal conflict to the martyrdom of St. Stephen, when he was filled with arrows for refusing to recant his beliefs. That took place in Jerusalem shortly after Jesus."

"I don't call that kind of crap fighting," Beecham interrupted. "What about organized armies? Commando Doc and I know that's where the rubber meets the road."

"Right, General," Eduardo agreed. "You could say that early Christians fought with Jews, but just as simple individuals or small groups and not as a state-supported army. That changed after the Roman Empire itself converted from pagan worship to the new religion. Emperor Constantine the Great, the first Christian emperor, began his reign by sending out his huge army and slaughtering nearly every Jew who would not convert and repent the killing of the messiah. That was 336 A.D."

"Which pair fought next?" Miranda asked.

"Of course there weren't any Muslims that early. It was three more centuries before the Muslims and the Jews fought," Eduardo continued. "Their first battle came not because of or in Jerusalem but in a Jewish settlement in distant Saudi Arabia, where Jews fleeing Roman persecution had established a small community in the Arab city of Medina. Hundreds of miles away in Mecca, after Mohammed founded Islam and it began to grow, believers in the old gods of the desert and oasis concluded Mohammed posed a threat to their civilization. The Arabs believed in many gods, but Mohammed's radical vision saw only Allah, and to eliminate dispute the Arab elders vowed to exterminate Mohammed. In an effort to save his followers from certain death, Mohammed led his people from Mecca far across the desert to the city of Medina. There, Mohammed became friendly with the many Jews living in the settlement, who taught him much about their religion. Their ideas and religion deeply influenced him, particularly as Mohammed himself was not a profoundly educated man. Whole sections of Mohammed's philosophy come directly from the Old Testament. It was his first contact with the Jews, and though it began well, its result was disastrous.

When enemies from Mecca pursued Mohammed to Medina, he prepared to fight. In an inexplicable act of betrayal, the Jews opened the gates of the city and allowed the foe to attack Mohammed's Muslim forces. Miraculously, Mohammed defeated the invaders despite the complicity of the Jews, but the next night The Prophet slaughtered all one thousand five hundred of them in the city."

"Not a good beginning," Beecham drawled.

"The first fight between the remaining pairing of religions, the Christian and Muslim, occurred soon after the slaughter of the Jews. It began as Francois said, over Jerusalem itself, for Jerusalem had been a Christian city for more than two centuries. When Mohammed died suddenly, Caliph Omar, his successor, spurred his white camel far and wide spreading the word of the Prophet. Within a hundred years Islam's armies conquered much of the world. Never has there been such a rapid expansion of a religion, despite a harsh political system in which rivals murdered four of the first seven rulers."

"It is that expansion that frightens people," Miranda said. She looked at Ellison. "But, Todd, you haven't told us what you think is the real reason the three religions constantly fight."

"Yes, *monsieur*. What is it then?" Francois asked.

"In my analysis I basically follow you, Francois."

"Deeper if you can, Todd. Unless mankind can reach an answer to this question of religious war, I foresee a planet populated by mutant insects, with five headed monsters looking for food amongst the ruins of a dead world."

"Not a pleasant prospect," Ellison sighed, with a glance at Miranda. He wanted his children to grow up in a world of beauty and joy. "Okay. It's deep, at least for me with my limited intelligence, and it starts with this: You can take everything away from a man but his ability to decide whether or not he believes in a divine power outside of himself. That you cannot take away."

"His political freedom, for instance, or all of his worldly goods," Eduardo said.

"Yes, but not his ability to decide about God. You may torture a man to death, but in his heart he can believe what he wishes, even as he screams his last breath. His decision on that is central to his being, and he must choose. All the way in, all the way out, or try to make a balance of belief and non-belief. Because the decision is so personal, and particularly because doubt exists for the rational mind, a man must *believe* he is right." He looked at each of them to see if he sounded too weird. They urged him to continue. "All of us want to feel that we know what is right. The problem comes from this: unable to accept cultural determinants of the local religious beliefs, beyond a certain deviance, our man, or woman, decides the others must be wrong because he is certain he is right."

"And once he perceives them as wrong," Eduardo interposed, making a fist, "he is duty-bound to make them right."

"This is too abstract," Ellison said, putting his palms down on the table to signal closure for him. He wanted to talk about what was bothering him right then, something he could keep secret no longer. Ellison glanced out the airplane window before he turned to face Miranda. "I am really in agony, Miranda."

"Yes, it's an unspeakable disaster out there. And I know you have to stay, but to protect the baby, I'll visit my parents until you come."

"That's not it, though. I'm not talking about you and the baby, or us, or all of that outside." He hesitated. "I've got to try to stop Pius XIII."

"No, Todd! What can you do now? He is already the Pope."

"A madman now in control of the Vatican Gold. You saw the

treasure with your own eyes. He has a trainload to turn into cash."

"Eduardo says no one can sell that much metal on the world market."

"I don't believe that. When it comes to gold, especially in an unstable world, someone will pay. Like it or not, and no matter what economists and politicians say, in times of trouble the world reverts to a gold standard. The price of gold is up fifty percent today and headed higher. Pius XIII has a fortune multiplying in the Vatican. With that amount of money, he can buy arms and men. He can buy a war."

"What can you do about it?" There was dismay in her voice. She looked at the others in the room, appealing to them. "Can you people believe this?"

Ellison stood beside her and took her arm. "Remember I told you how I felt like an Assassin in the conclave, and I told you the story of King Richard the Lionhearted? For some reason I've been thinking about Richard, how he was captured by Saladin and ransomed. I simply could not get that story out of my mind."

"I know that story, but—"

"Then the connection came to me."

"What connection, Todd?"

"Why my unconscious would not let me stop thinking about him. Suddenly I understood that it was like a dream trying to tell me something. Out of the blue I remembered that when Richard returned to England, he forgave Robin Hood."

"Yes, but I don't understand you."

"It's one of the great archetypes of our culture. Robin Hood and a small following took on the ruler of all England. The story gave me the idea for a new plan. Like Robin Hood, I wonder if we could steal the gold to keep it away from Verdi. It would be like taking the fangs out of a snake. Crazy, I know, but that is it in a nutshell."

Miranda stared at him. "Gentlemen, my husband and I need to talk alone."

Almost before they closed the door of their stateroom, Miranda turned to face Ellison, concern twisting her normal smile. "Crazy? Worse than crazy. First of all, it is impossible. Second, you would wind up in jail just trying. And finally, I am pregnant. Does that not mean something to you? Sorry to be so blunt, but I believe you should get this idea out of your head right away. Is this something Francois thinks is a cute idea? Does he know?"

"If I—we—can steal the gold, we might be able to stop Pius XIII, or at least weaken him."

"I am sick of crusades, Pius XIII's or yours," she said, turning away from him. "When you talk like this, I want to go home to San Francisco to live a quiet life. And maybe even to Zamboanga."

"But I need your help persuading Eduardo and Beecham," he said. "I know we would be risking everything—"

"Including our lives!" she interrupted angrily. "And our baby's life. What has happened to you?"

He didn't know what was happening to him, things were happening so fast. Swept up in events, he knew major changes were going on inside of him, but at too fast a pace to really understand. It was an unpleasant feeling for him to acknowledge had had lost control of his peace-oriented life. "Look out there," he answered, taking her face in his hands and turning her to the window. A fresh truckload of corpses was dumping its cargo in a lime pit. "Don't I have to try?"

She grew quiet, pensive. He needed her. Without her support, he would be lost. Even with it, he would likely lose. Her eyes smoldered with mysterious calculations that Ellison believed women do better than men. To him, she was like a fortune-teller, possessed of unusual powers. Miranda had a youthful, broad face, unlined except for the first traces of crow's feet at the corners of her eyes. Her skin was tan, with slim hips, pert breasts, and long silken legs. Her body fat was so low that Ellison could see the muscles move in her strong body. When she stood, she had absolute commitment in her eyes, a blazing intensity that he suspected must exceed any he had ever seen. "He did it," she said. "I just know it."

※　　※　　※

"Another miracle," Pius XIII announced to Strizzi. "Now we have more than a trillion dollars."

"The Lord works in wondrous ways, Holiness."

After Pius XIII galvanized the myriad of Vatican businesses and surrogates into financial action around the globe, world gold traders noticed a sudden increase in offers to sell. Anxious to make their one-fourth percent commission for brokering a deal, the traders made international phone and fax lines hum with unprecedented activity. Though the total volume of metal offered should have depressed the world price for gold, the wave of religious unrest sweeping the planet forced anxious Saudi princes, Asian tycoons, and Western portfolio managers out of their stock markets and into hard assets. Flawless diamonds soared to fifty thousand dollars per carat, and when jittery stock markets crashed in free fall, the price of gold rose beyond the thousand dollar per ounce level, previously believed unattainable.

"In two days," Cardinal Strizzi continued, "we can begin to ship the gold to Kloten, Switzerland."

"Good. The Swiss bankers will take care of the rest."

ROBIN HOOD

Valkyrie One, Rome

After gathering his team, Ellison presented his reasoning on Pius XIII step by step. "I believe he will try to move the gold," Ellison finished. "Because issuing bonds or gold certificates takes months, selling the bullion is the fastest way he can convert the gold into cash. As Miranda points out, since we do not know when Pius XIII will relocate the gold, we need to plan and act fast, right?"

"You are one wild motherfucker," Beecham began, catching himself. "Pardon, ma'am. Your husband—"

"My husband and I have talked for hours," she interrupted. "I am with him."

"As am I," Eduardo said. "The question is—"

"Can we do it?" Ellison cut in. "Can we really do it, General? I need your best military opinion."

"It will take detailed planning, but that's what we specialize in doing in a hurry. Once we collect and analyze our intelligence, I can give you a solid opinion."

"But what's your gut feeling, General? Can we get in?"

"Is the Pope Catholic? Of course we can get in. And likely we can get away using that crazy railroad scheme of yours, but there's no guarantees in this business. Especially when it comes to the biggest train robbery in history." Beecham gave Ellison a fraternal wink. "I like it. Definitely out of the ordinary."

Beecham, too, was definitely out of the ordinary for a soldier, especially one previously at such a high rank. Close enough to the book to get through West Point, he had fought in Desert Storm, Bosnia, and the Philippines. It was his role in getting American control over a large chunk of the Yamashita Gold that had caused his unprecedented jump from major to general. He was in favor in Washington D.C. and could have become Chairman of the Joint Chiefs of Staff with a few years of persistence, if he continued to use the Texan's charm that made everyone like him. Always in the right place at the right time, Beecham's single star seemed destined to be joined by several more. It had surprised everyone when he resigned to go to work for Ellison.

Eduardo pushed his chair back from the conference table. "Don't you need more time to plan, General?"

"Our guys are ex-Delta Force, all two hundred of them. We've got some work to do, but we can be ready tomorrow night. I'll give President Clark a heads-up. America will turn a blind eye."

"But what about the Italians?" Eduardo pressed.

"We've got some black boxes that will make their Intel chips go blind. The Italians would rather fuck than fight, but they won't even know we're here."

"Providing we can silence the Vatican security," Ellison added. "Disabling Vatican security is the key."

"You and I will mosey over to the Vatican and scout that rail line and decide how to get in undetected, if possible," Beecham added.

He had been lucky enough to escape from the morgue using Beecham's plans, Ellison thought. Maybe they could make it work. "What about the ships, Eduardo?"

"I know where I can buy two, top of the line and plenty big enough as ferries go. Beecham tells me the special electronics can be operational in minutes."

"That's it, then," Ellison said. "When do we go, General?"

"We'll spend all of today and most of tonight gathering information and making a plan. Tomorrow we review and prepare, get a little rest. Tomorrow night we'll hit."

"Shall we cancel my birthday party tonight?" Eduardo asked. "It doesn't seem very important right now."

"No," Beecham answered without hesitation. "If you've got the luxury of choosing when to fight, a little distraction on the night before never hurts. But afterward, we need to walk through the operation. It's going to begin late. Oh—three hundred. Three in the morning."

"When the human body is least vigilant," Ellison added. "Gives Miranda time to pack for the flight to New York."

She interrupted him. "You have got to be kidding, Todd. I'm in this all the way. If you will be in danger, I have to be there."

"No way, Miranda, not in your condition!" he protested. "I'm not going to let you—"

"I am coming, and that is final."

Ellison knew there would be no way he could change her mind. She was the finest example of womanhood, brave and resourceful. She had encouraged him to write poetry, and he had a few times, sonnets he knew were no good. They sometimes laughed together at how corny his love expressions could be. Ellison was many things, but not a poet.

He quoted one of his lines he knew she would remember. "You are my wife, my lover, and my best friend," he said, relieved actually that she would be with him.

She smiled at him. "Stay by my side and cover my back," he said. She had done it before.

Before Eduardo's party, they scattered to complete their assignments. Francois vowed he would locate the schematics and operations manuals for the *Corpo de Vigilanza*, whose insignia emblazoned the uniforms of the guards Ellison had seen in the treasury. Miranda studied every legal scenario she could imagine, from Italian law on robbery, to trespassing, to homicide. It would be foolish to embark on such a desperate course without having a plan in the event of their capture and imprisonment. Ellison asked her to identify all nations that eschewed extradition treaties with the Vatican State and Italy. Living in any of the backwater countries she found would be unpleasant, but better than jail. With luck and with her family's power in the Philippines, they could probably live in splendid exile on Hacienda Teresita. Still, in the modern world, law enforcement will eventually get you.

Muttering at Ellison's side, the bow-legged Beecham walked the entire stretch of track from Vatican City to the main railroad terminal in Rome, Termini Stazione—a soaring glass hall built in modern style by Mussolini, *Il Duce*, during the 1930's. For a few years the Fascists amazed the population by making Italian trains run on schedule for the first and only time in Italian history.

An unused double track swept out of the main terminal toward Stazione Vaticani, a tiny building located just inside the forty foot high walls built to protect Vatican City from Muslim hordes. The rails probed the thick walls at a single location, marked by an arch blocked by a gate made of two steel bars that could be swung open in the rare event that a special train came to pick up the Pontiff and his entourage. Just inside the wall, a short spur track split from the main line and appeared to end against the face of Vatican Hill.

The moment Ellison had seen that spur track, his plan had crystallized into complete form. Though hidden from frontal view by the massive basilica at its base, Vatican Hill actually rises two hundred fifty-six feet above St. Peter's Square. Ellison knew the bumper at the end of the railroad spur must have marked a false ending of the track against a carefully manicured hillside garden. Beneath that soil, a short distance he hoped, an entrance to the cavern holding the Vatican treasure lay hidden. The gold train had entered that way more than half a century ago; and like a long snake emerging from hibernation, he planned to bring it out the same way.

"Okay, pardner," Beecham said, once they decided they had seen everything critical to their attack. "I've got to download these photos so we can digitize the operation for tomorrow."

Ellison shook hands with Beecham, someone he considered a real man. "Thanks. You know you don't have to do this."

"Sure I don't. Ain't a bit of sense in it." He ground his jaw. "Tonight I think I'll tell you why I'm doin' it."

"I'd like to hear that. See you at the party."

By the time the evening rush hour of motorbikes carrying young lovers in pairs had dwindled, Ellison and the others celebrating Eduardo's birthday were finishing their *antipasti* course at the rooftop restaurant of the Hassler Hotel. An unexpected fashion show of the greatest designers of Europe was unfolding beneath them, where a crowd of rich, tanned fashion fanatics watched slim models slink down the Spanish Steps in the latest Valentino, Chanel, Ermengilda Zegna, and Armani designs. Several styles appeared so comical to Ellison that he was sure no one but an exhibitionist would wear the creations. Whenever he went home to North Dakota and told his family about the places he'd been and the wonders he'd seen, even before he met Miranda, his mother cautioned him, "You can take the boy out of North Dakota, but you can't take North Dakota out of the boy. When you see the high and mighty, remember your roots." In contrast, Miranda always told him to consider fashion and extravagance in the light of mankind exploring its potential. "There is a playfulness in our species. Squelch it and boredom seeps in." He supposed Miranda was right, particularly since his family was famous for its phlegmatic opinion of luxuries. Once, after he had taken his father to the best steakhouse in Omaha, while Ellison was smacking his lips over a fine T-bone, his father made a statement he could never forget. It was crude and unrefined, yet it captured part of the brutishness of life.

"Good food, eh, Dad?"

"Makes a turd, son."

As Eduardo's party went on, Ellison fought to keep his mind off violent memories of the cycle of life in the American wilds. On the prairie, life could be as violent as the African veldt. Outside his Dakota bedroom window, coyotes had bloodied their faces in jackrabbits too slow to save themselves. The city kids seemed to have less comprehension of the realities of life than the country children, used to birth and death they had to touch with their own hands.

Why was he thinking such bleak thoughts now? Ellison shook his head, trying to clear away the somber mood. It was Eduardo's twenty-fifth birthday, a quarter of a century, perhaps a third of his life if he didn't lose it tomorrow. Ellison wished he felt like celebrating, but he did not. Hoping to lighten his mood, he took

Miranda's hand and asked her to dance. Sexy in a new outfit that fit her like a glove, she pressed against him for a slow rhumba. At the gentlest pressure from his hand, she followed his lead and made a slow turn all the way around him, arriving before him in perfect time for them to slide into the basic step with practiced grace. He enjoyed dancing with her so much that he'd agreed to take dance classes with her. It was fun, but he could see she felt as distracted as he did. When he held her close after a deep dip, he whispered to her, "There's no other woman on earth like you." She smiled and led him back to the table, hand in hand.

After a few brief efforts at frivolity, everyone grew more subdued, troubled. Ellison knew that they, like he, were face to face with a fear that tomorrow would bring inevitable change to their lives, probably not for the better.

Questions swirled in Ellison's mind. What was Eduardo doing here? Eduardo had always considered himself a high-profile man who enjoyed the limelight. His family had expected him to be a great success reaping the profits of the hacienda, but he had chosen a rarer road, the way of the adventurer. Rebellious by nature, the strict life of a first-born son straight-jacketed him from the time he developed awareness of himself. During what turned out to be his final piano lesson, the teacher rapped his knuckles with a wooden ruler. Without a word, Eduardo climbed out the window and scampered up a giant acacia tree, where he came face to face with a thick black snake. He jumped and broke his arm. At age thirteen he found himself in the orthodontist's office, with a stainless-steel device on its way to his oral cavity. Before they could force it in, Eduardo jumped out of the third-floor window and was knocked unconscious when he landed on a Chevrolet sedan parked below. He did well in school due to his innate brilliance rather than any concerted efforts. Exasperated by his lackadaisical approach to studies, the Santiago family enrolled him at the exclusive Hill School near Philadelphia, where for three years he chafed beneath the mandatory coat and tie. After graduation, he enrolled at Oxford, Magdalene College, home of roasted chestnuts and cream tea and eight-man shells racing along the river. Though he enjoyed the nightlife on his weekends in London, academic life bored him.

To no one's surprise, Eduardo didn't like the religious life either, which in his own mind came to an abrupt end during an argument he had with Monsignor Perez, the Zamboanga City priest. Already skeptical after noticing no spiritual jolt from swallowing the body of Christ during communion, he demanded to know the precise monetary level at which theft passed from being a venial sin, which is pardonable and does not estrange the soul from the grace of God, to a mortal sin, which leads to damnation. He had told Ellison the story at least four times, three times recently.

"Father Perez, if I steal four dollars from the market, is that a mortal sin?"

"No, Eduardo."

"A thousand dollars?"

"Yes, that would be a mortal sin."

"How about eight dollars?"

"Yes, a mortal sin."

"Four dollars and fifty cents?"

Cornered by Eduardo's relentless questioning, Father Perez reluctantly opined that theft of five dollars would be a mortal sin, but $4.99 would be a venial sin. His opinion led to an eight-year apostasy of Eduardo, which ended only after he found the gold, and then by coincidence.

After childhood experiences unearthing shards of ancient pottery and a few pieces of Pre-Columbian gold, death masks of the primitive tribes of Mindanao, Eduardo developed an abiding and relentless interest in treasure. He quit school for a year and SCUBA dived on wrecked galleons at five different sites in the Philippines. Seeing the beautiful co-eds at Zamboanga State University lured him back to the classroom, where he performed well enough to gain admission to the University of Santo Tomas in Manila for graduate school. As soon as he finished there, he sought treasure maniacally. Three years later, before even a quarter of his take in the Yamashita Gold had been counted, Eduardo became the most successful treasure hunter in history.

Now, over bananas flambé, Eduardo told them how he had come to realize that limitless wealth was not the most important thing in life. He had returned to religion, and dedicated himself to *Opus Spiritus*.

"Same for me," Francois remarked.

Ellison noticed a new tone in Francois' voice. "What do you mean?"

"After much prayer, I have decided to return to training for the priesthood at the conclusion of our campaign against Pius XIII. Maybe I feel the need to expiate my wrongdoing against the rules of the Catholic Church. I knew it on the day I saw you risk yourself entering the morgue, *monsieur*. It has been nearly ten years since I lost my legs. At the end of my struggles to break away from my old religion, I find myself back at the beginning, a sinner in need of help. I failed my test the first time, but I humbly wish reconciliation with the Lord. I hope you all will pray for me."

"If that ain't the derndest thing" Beecham snorted. "Shit, since we're all talkin', I might as well say my piece." He stood to make himself appear larger, something he invariably did whenever he spoke. "When it comes to religion, I'm just a cowboy who remembers damn few words from the Bible. The daddy who adopted me was readin' around the campfire one night when we was campin' along the Arkansas River. I can still repeat part of what he read, something from Psalms or somethin' which just rolled the whole of the endless Texas night into one beautiful line. 'The heavens declare the glory of God, and the firmament showeth his handiwork.' Good a man as he was, I never felt like I had a family, until I met you folks." He choked, fighting back tears, sheepish. "I don't feel comfortable talkin' about such things, but that's why I'm with you instead of in the Pentagon. Y'all are my kin." He wiped his cheek with the back of his hand. "Shucks, look at me now. You'll hear no more from me."

Everyone sat in silence, stunned by Francois' announcement and Beecham's uncharacteristic openness.

"Come to the priesthood with me, Eduardo and General Beecham," Francois finally said. "You are single men. Let us change this hoary institution."

"Not me, pardner. I've got too much killin' under my belt."

Eduardo laughed nervously. "Can't do it. I miss her so much."

"You've got love in your eyes now, Eduardo," Miranda said, "but you will never be faithful to one woman."

"Just watch me, Little Sister. Karina is nineteen. Young, I know, but from a fine family. Her damn chaperone follows us everywhere. I offered to send my pilot for her tonight, but her father refused permission. When we're done, I want to marry her."

A round of congratulations followed Eduardo's announcement. "If something happens to me, I want you to take care of her," Eduardo said.

"Agreed," Miranda said. "But let's not get pessimistic."

"Unusually prudent is all. Love is doing it to me."

"Anyone else got something to say?" Ellison asked. "If not, we need to get back to work."

"A soldier's last request," Eduardo said. "Francois, as my birthday present, will you sing for me?"

"Yes," Miranda agreed. "We've never really heard you sing."

"Jes' a lot of hummin'," Beecham said. "I learned to do that to keep herds of cattle calm at night. Hum to a cow, he's generally happy."

Francois clapped Beecham on the shoulder. "Though I swore I would never sing again, tonight it will be my honor, Sir Eduardo." Francois rattled across the terrazzo courtyard to where the orchestra was taking a break from their first set entertaining the growing dinner crowd. When he returned with a classical guitar cradled in his arm, Ellison realized he had no idea what to expect, beyond certainty that Francois would shake the walls.

Francois bent his ear to the guitar and tuned it to his exacting taste. "A Ramirez," he said appreciatively after reading the guitarmaker's name inside the rosette. "Brazilian rosewood body, and Yugoslavian fir for the soundboard. The best, like Andres Segovia used to play."

He smiled to himself, reminiscing. "I took Master Classes in guitar at the Sorbonne. The curves of a guitar are like the curves of a woman." After he plucked the harmonics, which only a master can do with such ease, he smiled at them and launched into a flamenco scale, mournful in its minor intervals, fiery and wild as he added a second voice to the first. By adjusting his fingers, Francois made one voice rich and sonorous, the second brilliant and piercing. It seemed there were two guitars playing. As amazed as the others, Ellison recognized the love song from Giuseppe Verdi's opera, *Aida*, an aria the hero sings as he is about to die, never to see his true love again. But still, Francois did not make a sound. His hands flew across the guitar in four-finger chords over a pulsing, Gypsy rhythmic base. Ellison couldn't take his eyes off Francois' hands, which were creating music of such melancholy beauty that Ellison felt a hurt deep in his chest. What a musician! He froze when Francois inhaled a great breath.

His song began with but a whisper of sound, yet its sweetness caught Ellison's attention. The note was deep and low, a baritone D-sharp that swelled from nothingness to concert-hall presence along the line of a single note, animated by the throbbing of his guitar. He sang in perfect Italian of astonishing beauty. When he played through the aria, faultlessly, his voice and manner seemed to Ellison the equal of the finest opera singers of Europe. He had tremolo, range, and perfect pitch that pleased the ear. Though it might not have been noticed by the others, Ellison could see Francois be carried away by the music, relaxing in a way that allowed his voice to grow stronger, louder, more confident. His song flew over the walls of the restaurant, and landed gently on the shoulders of the crowd watching the fashion show. Ellison could see their faces turn upward, searching for the source of such hypnotic music. Looking at his friends, he could see even Beecham had silent tears on his cheeks. He might not know the music, but Beecham knows the feeling of loneliness Francois is singing about. Too quickly, Francois raced into a final scale, a staircase of reverberating notes that echoed his voice across the Spanish Steps, and ended his guitar playing with a rasguedo strum. It was finished.

"If anything happens to any of you tomorrow," he said, "I will never sing again."

— John Bunyan
Pilgrim's Progress

THE TRAIN

The half moon cast a warm glow over the nocturnal revelers in the Piazza Navonna, a vast ellipse used by the Caesars for chariot races. The happy plaza was now graced by Renaissance fountains and bordered by pastel buildings five stories high, architectural masterpieces of an earlier age. Jugglers and street artists entertained the modern Romans and tourists sipping espresso or Chianti in the outdoor restaurants that rimmed the cobble-stoned plaza. Billowing clouds scudded in front of the moon, making shapes like happy lambs ambling home without a care in the world.

Too much light, Ellison thought nervously, forcing himself not to stare at the dozens of thick-necked men scattered in casual groups. Dressed in loose warm-up suits that matched their black sports equipment bags, the young studs looked like Olympic athletes relaxing after a hard workout; but Ellison knew their events were about to begin.

The technical capabilities of Beecham and his men flabbergasted Ellison. Much of the equipment they showed him he hardly knew existed, especially the stealth equipment and the command and control devices. By noon before their assault, every one of the two hundred men had played a high-resolution video game of the entire operation that included scenarios for fighting various opposition forces they might encounter. The men most likely to have to fight the guards received special training in holographic helmets in which they could decide which way to dive and fire with maximum effect. They had maps and plans of remarkable detail, considering the short period for preparation. America has most of the planet digitized with coordinates so accurate that admirals can decide which window of an enemy's headquarters to fly through with his missile. Ellison reminded himself again and again that without Beecham, this Vatican robbery would be impossible.

"Let's rock and roll, pardner. Ma'am," Beecham whispered.

"Right, General." Ellison glanced at his Constantine Vachon wristwatch, a thirty-two thousand dollar birthday present from Miranda given in honor of his thirty-second birthday. "It's two o'clock in the morning." Accustomed to being up all night in emergency surgery, he felt fully alert, but beside him Miranda stifled a yawn despite their excitement. But he knew he could count on her when the time came.

Out of the corner of his eye, Ellison noticed groups of four or five of his men blending with sleepy Romans strolling casually toward the different exits from the plaza. All of them knew their assignments to perfection and in forty-five minutes would be at various locations throughout Rome, ready for action if Beecham's daring strike overcame the first obstacle, by metaphorically gouging out the eyes of Rome.

After a brief taxi ride, they stepped out at the railway terminal. Though late at night, dozens of long trains destined for or arriving from Venice, Milan, or European capitols rumbled in and out of the station along twenty tracks. Slumbering in their comfortable rolling beds, one trainload of unsuspecting passengers was about to encounter an unexpected delay.

Ellison planned to hijack a diesel locomotive outside Stazione Termini for a hell-for-leather run to Vatican City and the gold.

"Those," Ellison whispered, recognizing the silhouette of D341 diesels, a pair of flat-faced locomotives in tandem at the head end of a *Ferrovie dello Stato* passenger train bound for Florence. Years ago, when he had worked on the Great Northern Railroad as a college student supplementing his scholarship, he never guessed that the wonderful romance of the rails as a brakeman and switchman would become useful so far from home. He glanced at a schematic and operator's manual printed from the World Wide Web that afternoon. Not much different from an American General Motors diesel he had driven half a dozen times years ago, before medical school. Scotty, the engineer on Ellison's North Dakota to Montana crew, regularly took LSD and a handful of other hallucinogens before the long haul.

"I'm dropping some acid" he'd shout over the din of the motors, and on several occasions Ellison had to take the controls when Scotty's concerns became too cosmic to care much about an insignificant ten thousand ton machine roaring across the Great Plains at close to a hundred miles an hour. Now, thanks to Scotty's dissipations, Ellison felt sure he would be able to handle the Italian diesels.

His scheme to use the railroad, once conceived, had been confirmed by eliminating all other options one by one. Eduardo's research had verified that the normal approaches to the Vatican Gold consisted of impregnable bastions scattered at choke points in an incomprehensible labyrinth. Facing those obstacles, a stealth attack by night paratroopers could never succeed. To overcome them, an armored division similar to the security guarding most of America's gold at Fort Knox, Kentucky would have been necessary for the frontal assault on the Vatican. Fort Knox was built during World War I and, in the center of its 33,000 acres, houses gold in a subterranean vault built below a bombproof steel and concrete warehouse completed in 1937. The vault itself rests on solid rock deep underground and its hundred foot by hundred foot interior has walls of steel several feet thick, all wired with sensors for sound, light, heat, vibration, electromagnetic radiation, chemicals, and most gases. During World War II, this safest place in the world became home to such treasures as *the Declaration of Independence* and the British Crown Jewels. Beecham told them that the base commander had once observed that, "the whole fucking *Wermacht* of the Third Reich could never have reduced Fort Knox. We have more firepower here than all of the armies of World War II combined." While the Vatican defenses were much softer than the armored cavalry of hundreds of Abrams A1M2 Main Battle Tanks at the very home of America's heavy armor school, the Italians had enough to make an undisguised assault by Beecham's limited force impossible. Considering higher technology options, though Beecham reported it might be possible for him to purloin one of America's most secret munitions, use of an Area Denial Weapon on a friendly nation would exterminate every living thing in Vatican City, insure that they would all spend the remainder of their lives in solitary confinement, and was therefore an option beyond further consideration. In the end, the old railroad spur line that had allowed Hitler's train into the vault was the only weakness in Vatican defenses vulnerable enough to exploit.

The railroad strategy had its own problems. First, most of the *Ferrovie della Stata* right of way underwent electrification before 1980, which reduced Ellison's options when it came to locomotive power. He needed to have a diesel engine because electrical wires necessary for any electric motor did not extend into the Vatican vault. Diesels were rare, but he had to have one, preferably a pair. He remembered that the locomotive already on the gold train in the Vatican vault was an oil-fired steam engine. However, since it had not been fired up for years, it would take hours to build up enough of a head of steam to move. There would not be enough time for that. Ellison would have to pull the German engines in the gold drag—assuming they could manage to escape Stazione Termini with the D341 diesels.

Miranda fidgeted beside him. Actually, once she had forced her way into the mission, he had felt a sense of relief. After all of her years living on the Wild West island of Mindanao, Miranda possessed an uncanny radar for danger, as if she had eyes in the back of her head.

Ellison glanced at his watch again. Two forty. "Let's go."

Beecham and Miranda followed him along the quay, acting as if they were passengers hurrying to take their seats in the sleeping car nearest the engines. Just as the throaty rumble of the locomotives increased, six athletic figures emerged from the shadow of a billboard advertising Alpha Romeo convertibles.

At precisely two forty-three, all electric power to the terminal vanished, plunging it into total darkness.

"Now!" Ellison ordered, his voice husky and dry.

Beecham and two of his men raced to the cab of the first locomotive and climbed the ladder, bursting in on the unsuspecting engineer and his assistant. Seconds later, Ellison saw two unconscious figures slung over the shoulder of one of the Delta Force men, then three bursts from Beecham's laser pointer, signaling him.

"All clear, Miranda. Climb aboard."

After a mountain of a man beside Ellison handed him a set of night vision goggles, Ellison jumped from the quay to the track below, between the second locomotive and the first sleeping car. By the surreal green light of the night optics, in ten seconds he had opened the couples and turned closed the stopcock on the airbrakes. On a train, all of the cars are connected by a continuous air hose to a huge air compressor on the locomotive. The air pressure pushes the brake shoes away from the steel wheels, which allows the train to roll. He knew that without sealing the airbrake system the locomotives would come to an emergency stop as soon as the air blasted out of the open hoses, and their run for the Vatican would stop after less than ten feet.

After a strong hand helped him vault back to the quay, he and his burly helper ran for the locomotive and climbed the ladder. Beecham greeted him.

"No killing, just like you said," Beecham reported, grinning with enthusiasm. "They'll wake up in an hour, not that they'll remember much."

Ellison gave the throttle a test pull that resulted in a satisfying crescendo. Pulsating vibrations shook the ground, as two sets of sixteen-inch cylinders, almost eight thousand horsepower in all, revved up in perfect synchrony. When he tugged on what he thought to be the brake lever, a deafening blast from the locomotive's horns resulted, startling him and everyone else.

"No, Todd! The other one!" Miranda gasped with a nervous look out the window.

When he tested a second lever and hissing air told him he had the correct control. Excited to a fever pitch, Ellison gave the universal cry of railroad men ready to move. "Highball!" he shouted above the rumble of the motors, but his voice was smothered by the diesel roar.

He yanked back on the throttle, causing the locomotives to lurch ahead with a shudder and screech of the wheels. Nearly thrown from the engineer's seat, he eased off to allow the wheels to get a purchase on the slick tracks. He felt a wave of euphoria as the roaring motors propelled them forward.

Ahead, through the eerie green of his goggles, Ellison spied two squad members working feverishly to throw the switches that would shunt his train from the main line to Florence to the short line to Vatican City. Just before reaching the first man, Ellison saw the switch points slide into position for a short run down a connecting track. But to Ellison's horror, an oncoming passenger train swept around a curve just as they changed rails, running toward them on the same track. In just seconds both trains would derail in a mangling collision. Though half-blinded by the train's headlight, Ellison could see it was already too late, but there was no turning back.

When the oncoming engineer realized imminent death lay just ahead of him, he slammed on his brakes. The wheels began glowing red from the friction. As Ellison raced toward the switch that would put them safely out of harm's way, he held his breath, while Miranda covered her eyes in fear.

"Goose it, pardner!" Beecham yelled.

Ellison's hands, wet with perspiration, almost slipped from the throttle when he pulled back with all his might. The roaring motors, the screeching of the oncoming train, and the smell of hot metal nearly unnerved him.

Ahead, a second soldier hesitated at his switch, confused by the unexpected complication. At the last moment, he threw the switch that could save them by sending them hurtling down the Vatican track. Ellison knew it would be close. Remorse pierced him as he took a last look at his wife.

He wished there were some final desperate act, something that could save them. Expecting to die, Ellison pulled the rope and the horn blasted a steady, resonant low E Flat. The light from the passenger train was now so close that he could feel its heat. He imagined he could hear the screams of the Italian train crew, doomed men he had destroyed with his foolish obsession, and imagined passengers thrown violently from their seats as their train decelerated at a killing rate. Out of the corner of his eye, he saw the Italian engineer leap out of his cab and roll across the gravelly ground, a desperate effort to save himself, while Beecham, Miranda and the Delta Force men bellowed in helpless terror.

With just inches spare, Ellison's first locomotive flashed in front of the driverless engine screeching toward his side. Half a second after Ellison's first locomotive passed, the Italian E402 electric plowed into Ellison's trailing second engine with a deafening, grinding shriek of metal on metal. A wrenching snap threw them all to the floor. In a mirror he could see his second engine as it reared on its side, lifted off its wheels, and was ripped away like an animal being disarticulated.

Alive, side by side with Miranda on the metal floor, for one glorious moment Ellison felt the sheer joy of survival, the euphoria of escape. A heartbeat later he stiffened as he sensed his remaining locomotive's brakes applying with a vengeance. They were coming to a stop!

"The air hose!" he shouted, struggling to his feet. "We were in sequence with the second engine. We've lost our air!"

While his engine screeched to a halt, Ellison clambered down the ladder with the speed of a fireman sliding down a pole, raced to the rear of his remaining engine, and found the dangling air hose venting the last of his pressure. After a quick twist of the stopcock, Ellison sprinted back to the cab.

The inbound train had miraculously escaped derailment and stood hissing on the rails. Uniformed porters had already thrown open doors to find out what had happened. Standing before him like a black and white photograph in the night, three Italian trainmen shouted and shook their fists at him.

Onboard his remaining D341 diesel, Ellison felt the brakes pump up and release. After an initial creep, the monstrous engine surged forward as powerfully as an ox under the lash. Would it have enough power to do the job alone? Without an option in any case, Ellison threw the throttle wide open. They were rolling toward Vatican City again.

ELEGY

Rome lay dark ahead of them, blacked-out by small detonations of C4 plastic explosives at twelve sites in and around the sprawling metropolis. Without diversion and confusion, no plan would have a chance. He knew hundreds of *carbinieri* from Rome's police stations would be converging on the railway station, where a contingent of Delta Force would attempt to baffle them by wrecking the control center. They expected to make Ellison's location on the tracks invisible to the Italian traffic control computers, which normally know the exact position of every train in Italy. Again optimistic, Ellison shouted above the din of the motors. "Nice work, General."

"Piece of cake so far."

That didn't seem to be the proper description to Ellison, but he had experienced battle only once, and perhaps Beecham had a more objective view of what they had just gone through. With their searchlight probing the Roman night ahead, they rumbled toward the Vatican ramparts, now less than half a mile away, just around a bend.

"There!" Miranda pointed. "The arch in the Vatican wall."

"And my boys've got the barnyard gate open," Beecham drawled with pride.

Eduardo and Francois headed the main crew, almost two hundred Delta Force doing the heavy work of clearing the track by blasting into the Vatican vault with micro-ordnances that delivered great force with nearly inaudible explosions. Precision timing usually hallmarked a Delta Force operation, Ellison knew, but this mission overflowed with uncertainties. When Ellison roared through the breach in Vatican City ramparts, his heart sank.

The tunnel to the gold remained unopened.

❊   ❊   ❊

Pius XIII knelt before his private altar, in a near trance while he received divine messages specifically for him as the reincarnation of Christ, moreover as the second coming himself. He hardly noticed the lights of the Apostolic Palace flicker, then die. Consumed with his mystical experience, his body felt transfigured into a finer, magical material now, as if he had undergone a preparation to ascend to heaven to resume his rightful place for eternity.

A muffled boom ruffled him enough to make him rise from his prayers for a glance out of his chapel window. Rome dark again, he thought. No wonder Italians yearn for the old Fascist times.

Another soft explosion comforted him. Before he could move the gold train to Switzerland, the tunnel from the vault to the outside had to be re-opened. The workmen were getting an early start, he concluded, probably because they feared the power failure would impede their scheduled reopening of the vault. By evening his Vatican Gold would be in Switzerland. But so unlike a Roman to care enough about anything to go to work early. Should he investigate? Before he could answer himself, a fresh round of revelations transported him away from earthly concerns. And why worry? He felt so powerful that he could open the tunnel with a wave of his divine hand.

※   ※   ※

With the overburden of soil blasted away, Ellison could see the formidable concrete plug filling an arched tunnel into Vatican Hill behind and beneath St. Peter's. Eduardo and Francois stood with him beside the rumbling locomotive, anxiety written on their damp, blackened faces. After leaving Piazza Navonna, they and their men had converged from all quadrants of the compass to begin the demolition. Gesturing at the men working as silently as ants to prepare more charges, Eduardo gritted his teeth. "Shit, brother, we are too slow."

"This should do it," Beecham reassured him, with a nod to a soldier holding a transmitter. "Watch out."

A rapid fire series of six explosions shook the earth, sending shock waves against Ellison's chest. "The guards inside must hear those," he said, shaken.

"Too bad for them, pardner. My guys are ready for 'em."

When the dust settled, a yawning rent in the concrete gaped before them. Ellison crawled aboard the engine and snapped on its headlight so that its beam probed into the darkness ahead.

"We're in!" he shouted.

Miranda smiled in response to his jubilant hug. While his two hundred warriors cleared the rubble from the track, Ellison revved the diesel and edged into the vault. The rail led straight to the gold train.

Once again dazzled by the rows of golden chalices and altars stretched upward to the ceiling of the vault, Ellison fought against distraction, against fears for himself, Miranda, and his crew. Too deep to retreat from their plan now, they were long past acting on any second thoughts. They would have to perform as they had planned.

"I'm going to couple up with the German engine and connect the air hoses, Ellison said. "Eduardo, can you get onboard the steam engine and release the handbrake? Turn it to the left."

"You bet."

"And ask Beecham to have men check every boxcar for hand-brakes."

"Got it."

"As soon as we get enough air pressure in the lines, we can pull out. That is, if we can handle such a heavy train with one engine," Ellison muttered, almost to himself.

As they rumbled toward the gold train, Ellison eased his locomotive slower until he felt a soft clank against the couples of the German steam engine. After he threw his locomotive into reverse, he felt a satisfying tug of resistance.

"Got her," he said.

While Beecham ordered the soldiers to take up defensive positions inside and outside the vault, Francois, unable to contain his desire to venerate the True Cross, picked his way across the rubble toward the chambers of relics.

"Francois!" Ellison leaned out the window of the cab and shouted, worried at seeing his friend stray. "Stay here!" But deafened by the explosions and the din of the locomotive, Francois continued his jerky scramble without looking back.

Ellison clambered down and chased Francois across the chamber until he got a big hand on his shoulder. "Francois," he shouted again, almost in his ear. "Come back!"

Just as Francois turned to hobble back, a guard burst through the vault door. Ellison stood directly in his line of fire. Their eyes met, and the guard's Uzi began blazing even as he brought it up to firing position. There was no way he could miss Ellison at such close range.

"*Monsieur!*" Francois screamed. Putting the ultimate effort into his stumps and metal, he threw himself between the guard and Ellison. As he moved, he tripped over the uneven floor and began to fall. Thudding impacts changed his fall to a jerky death dance. It was already too late when one of Ellison's soldiers electrocuted the Vatican guard into unconsciousness with a Taser gun. Before anyone had time to think, two more guards rushed in, their eyes widening with surprise before they, too, were felled by electricity. A hundred Delta Force men took the offensive by racing along predetermined routes, where they could silence other guards unawares.

Ellison rushed to his fallen comrade. The room stilled.

"I'm hurt bad, *monsieur*," Francois gurgled, blood flowing from his mouth.

Chest wounds, Ellison could see. And no way to stop the bleeding. "Medic!" he yelled cradling Francois in his arms, Francois' blood soaking him. "Hang on, my friend."

When Beecham rushed over with a medic, he turned away with a gasp. "Shit!"

"Start an intravenous and give him fifteen milligrams of morphine stat," Ellison ordered the medic. He felt desperate but knew he had to keep control if Francois were to have any chance to live. "Have you got blood?"

"Yessir."

"Hextend?"

"No, sir, just Ringer's lactate."

"Give him six bags of blood and two bags of fluid as fast as you can. We have to get Francois to a hospital, and right now." It was the only hope, but what made Ellison feel worse, Francois looked beyond recovery.

Eduardo and Miranda gathered round, crossing themselves when they saw Francois' wounds, now exposed after the medic cut away Francois' shirt. "Hospital?" Eduardo asked, confused. "What about all this?"

"Eduardo?" Francois gasped.

"Yes, my friend." Eduardo's eyes were shut with pain. In the months Eduardo had known Francois, he, too, had come to consider Francois like a brother.

"You are like a priest," Francois rasped, fading. "Give me Last Rites."

Eduardo fell to his knees. "I will do the best I can." He made the sign of the cross over the fallen comrade and mumbled while he rubbed a speck of dirt on Francois' forehead. *"Perducat nos ad vitam aeternam.* God, bring us to everlasting life." Eduardo intoned, tears streaming down his cheeks.

For Ellison, though accustomed to witnessing death, the scene in front of him threatened to rip his guts out. While Eduardo chanted the prayers, Francois struggled to tell Ellison something.

"Closer," he rasped, pulling Ellison's ear to his lips. "I see the stars. I hear the rolling thunder." He opened his eyes wide, seeing something beyond Ellison's shoulder, exhaled a death rattle and breathed no more.

Ellison started mouth-to-mouth resuscitation and motioned for the medic to press over Francois' heart in cadence with him. For three minutes they tried. When Miranda touched Ellison's shoulder, he knew she was telling him it was time to stop.

"It's unbelievable. He's dead," Ellison moaned, feeling tears slide down his cheeks while Miranda wept silently against his chest, shaking with sobs. What had he gotten them into? No doubt about it, Francois had died trying to save him. Remorse pierced his heart like cold steel.

"Git ahold of yerself, doc," Beecham growled. "Let's finish this. For him."

He knew Beecham was right. It was what Francois would have wanted. Feeling as if his own body were made of lead, Ellison forced himself to stand, "Okay. For Francois."

"Put him in the old engine," Beecham barked to a squad of men.

"And treat him with the respect due a hero," Ellison added.

While everyone rushed toward the train, Ellison forced his mind back into gear. If they didn't move, and fast, others might join Francois. No more guards had arrived on the scene, but it was just a matter of time.

Once aboard, Ellison glanced back at his train. Soldiers piled into the pried-open boxcars, ready to ride shotgun across Italy to the sea. Ellison eased back on the throttle, expecting to move forward, but the steel wheels simply spun in place, making the engine jump wildly up and down as it strained to pull the heavy train into motion.

"Sand," he yelled. "What's Italian for sand?" He looked at a wall of switches for the one that would spray sand on the rails just in front of the driving wheels. Sand would increase the friction between the wheels and the rails, and perhaps, just perhaps, let him yank the boxcars into motion. "I'll try this one."

When Ellison threw the switch, he heard the welcome hiss of sand spraying on the tracks. With a jolt, then a shudder, he felt the engine move ahead. Its wheels spinning and screeching, the engine gave a mighty tug and the gold train began to roll.

Two minutes later they were on the rail line to the coast. Except for helicopter searchlights orbiting around the Presidential Palace, Rome dithered in total darkness. Until the unconscious and drugged guards awoke in a few hours, perhaps no one would connect the blackout with the renegade locomotives.

Once on the main line, they thundered toward their destination. The Italian night was warm and scented with oranges and plowed fields. Almost an hour behind schedule, Ellison thought, looking at his map. Sixty miles from Rome, on the Adriatic coast, the Tiber River empties into the sea at the ancient port of Ostia, the opening. The ships were there. Physically ill with grief, Ellison studied his wristwatch, dismayed to see the hands indicate four-thirty in the morning. Just seventy minutes before first light.

Once they were beyond the blackout, all of them gazed at the village lights as they flashed by. Cleaving to the course of the Tiber River, the rail line passed first through industrial towns, which gave way to quaint villages where everyone slept unaware of the bandits racing through their warm night.

For an hour people hardly spoke, each contemplating the loss of Francois. Coupled with Ellison's worries about dangers ahead, his grief made for the longest hour of Ellison's life. But Beecham's advance men had completed their assignments, setting switches in proper positions before Ellison thundered through. Now, at seventy miles an hour, it would take the million pound serpent two miles to brake to a stop.

"Do y'all realize this is the biggest heist in the history of the world? Bar none?" Beecham asked.

"It doesn't mean a thing compared to Francois' life," Eduardo said.

"Hey, Eduardo, this gold isn't for us," Ellison objected.

"I wasn't accusing you. Of course it's not for us, but—"

"There it is, just ahead," Miranda said, interrupting them and pointing.

Ellison eased off on the throttle, felt ten small thuds as the heavy boxcars ran in against the slack of the stretched out couples, and then applied the brakes with a gentle hand. Stopping too fast could create so much heat that steel wheels would crystallize, crumble, and cause them to jump the tracks and plunge into the river beside them. Now in full control and at ease with all the levers and switches, Ellison slowed the train to a crawl for the last quarter mile. At the end of the track, a wharf pointed like an index finger at a looming gray vessel riding at anchor, where a clutch of tugboats chugged to keep its stern flush with the end of the railroad tracks.

There was the cool smell of the sea about the place. A rosy dawn cast a blush on placid seas, creating the illusion that a pink mirror extended as far as the horizon. A small switching yard with five tracks sat empty in front of the gaping rear door of the towering ferry, as large as most cruise liners, which resembled a great whale ready to take Jonah into its maw.

"International waters out there, my man," Beecham crowed.

"We're going to make it," Miranda whispered, as if she were praying in church.

With a final screech, the gold train came to a stop. "Turn the air cock on the Nazi engine like I showed you, Eduardo, then pull the uncoupler on the first boxcar. We have to shove the steam engine into one of the other rails, run around the train on that far siding, then push the boxcars onboard—three on the right rail, four in the middle, three on the left." The ferry had three rails inside, enough to swallow the whole train.

"Got it."

With help from the soldiers now sealing off the wharf, Ellison did a neat bit of switching and in minutes had shoved the boxcars into place inside the ferry's cavernous hold. Soldiers fastened thick steel chains to the boxcars and chocked their wheels after tightening the handbrakes. In rolling seas, rogue waves could shift the boxcars enough to capsize the vessel despite its size.

Just as an orange sun rose in the direction of distant Rome, Ellison, on the bridge of the ship with all the others, watched the ferry door winch closed.

"Anchors aweigh, my boys, anchors aweigh," Beecham sang.

"Heading?" the grizzly bearded Captain Kouros asked.

"Straits of Gibraltar," Ellison answered.

While their decoy ferry set sail toward the opposite end of the Mediterranean, Ellison, aboard the gold-laden *Aphrodite*, raced toward Gibraltar and the open seas of the Atlantic.

ESCAPE

In the middle of his morning *angelus*, Pius XIII heard the hue and cry of Secretary of State Strizzi bursting into his chapel.

"The gold is gone!" Strizzi shouted as soon as he entered the room.

"What? Who?"

"Eduardo Santiago and that meddling brother in law. One of the guards recognized Santiago."

Pius XIII shivered. *"How?* Where are they now?"

"We've been able to trace their movements. Hijacked a locomotive in Rome, blasted into the vault, and somehow pulled Hitler's train to a railway ferry in Ostia."

"Get the Italian Navy to stop them."

"I have already notified them, Your Holiness. Eyewitnesses at Ostia report two ships, but according to the Navy, only one shows up on radar."

"Incompetents!"

"They will interdict that vessel, of course, which they say is sailing toward Greece."

Frantically trying to fathom what to do next, Pius felt an explosion of frustration in his mind. Coming to his rescue, God immediately spoke to Pius XIII, his beloved son, with divine counsel suggesting proper punishment. "I excommunicate them! Pius growled. "Deny them the sacraments. Sinners! I will send them all to hell!"

Mankind might have other punishments for them, but Pius XIII preferred to be endless, infinite, and swift.

More collected after condemning Ellison and the others, Pius XIII forced himself to consider the vast organization at his sovereign whim. "Notify every nuncio, cardinal, bishop and priest you can to look for them. I will offer the ultimate reward for their capture. I will elevate the finder directly to a state of perpetual grace, forgive any act, forgive any sins. The fate of the world depends on that gold."

"Yes, Holiness."

"Also, call every head of state on earth. Tell them thieves have plundered our relics."

"Excellent."

"And send a crew from Radio Veritas to me." He would tell the whole world his version of the truth via his fifty thousand watt pulpit.

❈   ❈   ❈

By sundown, Captain Kouros reported they had made almost half the distance to the Atlantic. To Ellison's relief, Beecham's electronics reported no obvious pursuit. With Apollo's Chariot of a sun setting in the direction of the Rock of Gibraltar, Ellison felt a renewed confidence. At least they should make it through the twelve mile strait that separates Spain from Africa by the following dawn, steam northwest into the open seas of the North Atlantic, and be much safer from detection. Only eight hundred miles from shore to shore and two thousand miles from end to end, in the age of modern electronics the Mediterranean felt too much like a lake for Ellison. Though no one had discovered them yet, he knew that in such confines it was just a matter of time. Night, he thought, is our only ally.

He stood on the bridge with Miranda and the others, enjoying the salty spray from mounting seas driven by the new storm on the horizon. The atmospheric disturbance had come out of Africa, a kind of reverse hurricane. The clouds swirled in ugly, forbidding shapes that suggested danger. In just the past few minutes, Ellison had noticed the wind blowing harder on his face.

A wiry man with deep squint lines from years at sea, Captain Kouros rubbed his salt-and-pepper beard while he studied a sheaf of navigation charts. He spoke with a thick, Greek accent. "Do you mind telling me our port of destination? What I was told before no longer makes sense, eh?"

Ellison glanced at the others for consent before answering.

"I think it is okay now," Miranda said.

"Sure, why not?" Beecham added to Eduardo's nodded assent.

"Well then, we are headed for Norway, specifically a place called Nordfjordeid."

Kouros removed his captain's hat to scratch his bald head. "Three days to Norway, by the normal channels. Why there?"

"A place to hide. Because my great grandfather came from Nordfjordeid, I qualified for a Foreign Student scholarship in Norway and was lucky enough to visit cousins there. We paddled our sea kayaks far down the fjord one day, and they showed me where great uncle Elias pulled his ferry away from the pier just as a busload of Nazi soldiers was being loaded aboard. Uncle Elias drowned them all and got executed for it. Two miles from the wharf we saw a huge cavern carved into a cliff. German submarines used to hide there, in what they called a U-boat pen, with two thousand feet of mountain protecting them from above. I remember it being large enough to hide us."

"And at least Norwegians are Protestants," Beecham added. "Besides, where else could we go?"

At that, they all fell silent. Criminals now, how could they find any safe haven?

"Yup, doc, like a rustler not knowin' if he can get the herd to Mexico."

Eduardo had the same kind of gallows humor, "Like a pirate not knowing if he can sail home."

"That is my husband," Miranda said, not really joining their joking. "One of a kind, you are, and like Francois used to tell me, if I didn't hang on to you, he would gladly take my place."

Francois! A hollow feeling surged in the pit of Ellison's stomach. His friend's corpse lay in the meat locker below decks, amongst the mountains of provisions for more than two hundred men, beside beef halves and headless turkeys hanging by their legs. All traces of enthusiasm rushed out of Ellison like electricity going to ground. He looked helplessly at Miranda, desperately wishing she had some magic that could bring Francois back. He needed time alone to talk with her. But before she could say anything, a man dressed in battle fatigues rushed toward them.

"Our radar man says a patrol of two jets is vectored our way, General. Italian, sir, from their transponders."

"E.T.A.?"

"Ten minutes, unless they go to afterburners."

"Battle stations!" Beecham barked into the intercom. "I don't think they can see us on radar, but if they pass close enough for visual contact, who knows what they'll do."

So far their anti-radar devices had made the *Aphrodite* almost stealthy, as the classified electronics sensed incoming pulses, combined the incoming with opposite wavelength, and ate the pulses like anti-matter devouring matter. Before Beecham took them into action, he told Ellison he'd had a long talk with President Clark. Clark had authorized Beecham to requisition equipment from the Sixth Fleet Headquarters at Naples on an emergency basis. With the classified equipment, he said their four hundred foot vessel appeared the size of a speedboat to everyone except an American station; and while President Clark probably knew where they were to a six inch accuracy, unless Clark ordered the intelligence shared, no one else could know.

Barely visible until the last rays of the sun glinted off their wings five miles above, a pair of F-15 jet fighters angled toward them. They made contrails more than twenty miles away but not on a course to intercept the ship.

Ellison held his breath, hoping the pilots would miss them. With the sun in their eyes, the sea below the pilots might appear black as night. But to Ellison's horror, they banked in formation and streaked toward them in six hundred knot per hour dives. In less than a minute, both jets screamed overhead, the noise so loud that everyone covered their ears.

Flown by the cream of Italy's pilots, the fighters looped in a seven G turn and then came straight for the ship, nose cannons blazing. Two hundred yards ahead of the *Aphrodite*, their weapons churned the sea to frothy white foam: a shot across the bow commanding the vessel to stop.

"Let's test 'em," Beecham shouted. "Fire at will!"

"No!" Ellison protested.

"Trust me, doc."

Both planes flew in a racetrack pattern three miles out, no doubt waiting to see if the ferry would stop while they radioed news of their discovery.

Ellison watched a soldier hoist a shoulder-fired rocket. In one smooth move he aimed and fired, red flame and smoke erupting. Too fast for the eye to see, the modified Stinger missile almost never missed. With just seconds to live, the pilots—having seen the flash and heard the threat message screaming in their headsets—ejected before the closest aircraft disintegrated in a rose-colored explosion. Like a ghost ship, the second plane flew empty for five pilot-less seconds, before it, too, was detonated in mid-air by another Stinger.

"Now we're fucked," Ellison grunted.

"We weren't before?" Beecham countered.

Miranda trained binoculars on the two parachutes. "At least we can pick them up."

"Sure, ma'am, we'll get right to them," Beecham motioned a crewman to prepare a rescue boat. "Well, doc, now what?"

"How long have we got?"

"Less than an hour. I imagine they already have more aircraft on the way, and we could encounter hostile ships at any time."

"They won't sink us because of the gold," Ellison mused, hoping it were true.

Captain Kouros fiddled with a computer program that gave a digital image of the ocean bottom below them. He had lost his physical bearing of a captain, and had turned nervous, even if Eduardo had been clear about the risks when he signed the contract. "The water is twelve thousand feet deep here."

Ellison studied Miranda, her face grim with tension and fear.

If boarded by the Italian Navy, they would all spend the rest of their lives in prison. Perhaps he would never see Miranda again, never see his unborn child. But if they tried to fight it out with a cruiser, they would surely die. He had to choose the lesser of two evils.

"Scuttle the ship," he said. "Get everyone in the lifeboats."

"But that storm on the horizon—" Kouros protested.

"Sink this ship, dammit!" Ellison shouted. He memorized their Global Positioning System coordinates, smashed the display screen before anyone could have recorded their position, and tore the last five pages out of the ship's log. No one else would know their location within several miles.

Beecham eyed him appreciatively before giving the order. "Abandon ship! Man the lifeboats!"

After lowering a dozen strong wooden lifeboats into the rolling seas, more than two hundred men and one woman piled in. They had brought the entire army they needed to protect the gold in Norway. Just before they pulled away from *Aphrodite*, Ellison remembered Francois' body cooling in the galley's meat locker. But Eduardo was already racing across the sloping deck; and in a minute, he returned lugging Francois' shrouded, stiff corpse.

Already the torrent of water rushing through open valves made a deafening roar, as minute by minute *Aphrodite* settled lower in the waves. When the diesel motors of the twelve lifeboats coughed to life, the boats jack-hammered their way into the deepening gloom.

From a short distance, all eyes turned back to *Aphrodite*. Her stern heavy with gold, *Aphrodite's* bow began to angle skyward, until, with a grinding, unexpected shriek, the boxcars inside the ship ripped loose from their moorings, smashed open the ferry doors, and plunged, one by one, heavier than any rock, in a final dive to the sea bottom two miles down. *Aphrodite*, now vertically poised like a sea serpent rearing its head for a goodbye survey of its domain, gave a final shudder, and sank beneath the waves in a bubbling roil.

"What can be lonelier than this?" Ellison wondered aloud.

"Todd, so much open sea frightens me," Miranda said.

"Helmsman," Beechman ordered, "Steer for the pilots."

While they made way for the downed men bobbing in tiny

rafts, Ellison peered through the near darkness at the heaving seas over the grave of the Vatican Gold. "Mission accomplished, I guess."

"Pius XIII will find it, you know," Eduardo said. "Titanic sank in waters this deep and submersibles found her."

Ellison shook his head in disagreement. "I doubt it, Eduardo. These are international waters and the Holy See has no legitimate claim. I don't think the Vatican wants to explain how it held Nazi Gold for sixty years."

"Listen, pardner," Beecham argued. "If they can explain a virgin birth, they can certainly come up with something at least that plausible for any other topic."

"Maybe. But even if Pius XIII can mount a salvage operation, it will take years to recover the bullion. More likely, legal wrangling will go on until he's long dead."

"Ever the optimist," Miranda said. "Maybe you created the new Atlantis down there. It might never be found."

"So much gold," Eduardo muttered. "I can't help feeling sad that it is gone."

"There," Miranda pointed. "One of the pilots."

In minutes both pilots were hauled aboard. A quick examination satisfied Ellison that they were shaken but unharmed. After they edged away from the shrouded body beside him, the pilots joined him in looking at the rising clouds rapidly converting the sea into a pitch-black endlessness.

INFINITY

Pius XIII received the communiqué verifying the ferry sighting with satisfaction, one of several favorable reports of the day. What had begun as an inauspicious morning with the theft of the gold had turned opportune with the broadcast of the world news.

In response to riots by Turkish workers in Vienna, the Austrian parliament had voted to deport Muslim Turks. Better yet, with Pakistan racked by another coup after the Israeli retaliation pulled Islamabad's atomic teeth, India's powerful military was mobilizing to settle old scores in Kashmir and Jammu. Indonesians from Timor and Celebes were joining their Muslim brothers in Mindanao to fight the Christian Filipinos, whose wholehearted crackdown in response to Pius XIII's encyclical was brutal and swift. And perhaps best of all, the four and a half million Muslims in America were demonstrating at all the universities, vandalizing businesses, setting fire to cars, and defacing Christian churches and Jewish synagogues.

Yes, he thought, Christ's work is proceeding well, hindered only by the loss of his gold. With such tinder everywhere, the fires he could start with the money from the gold would sweep the planet.

And was he not Christ himself? He had no doubt, despite grumblings by timid cardinals unable to fathom the celestial beauty of his plan.

"You should rest, Holiness," Cardinal Strizzi urged. "How many days since you have really slept?"

"Stay awake, I tell you, for the Lord is come. I am come to judge the quick and the dead."

"What, Holiness?"

"And while there remains much to be done, I can do it. When Jesus prayed, did he sleep?"

❈   ❈   ❈

Around them a howling wind from Africa flayed peaks off twenty-foot swells that moved them three stories up and down every eleven seconds. His belly long since emptied by constant retching, Ellison lay next to Miranda, fearful that the next dizzying slide down the face of a wave would be their last.

Except for the faint light of stars, all was black without even a flash of light from beacons on the other lifeboats. Though long since blown away, they sent crackling radio messages that they, too, were in danger of sinking in the fierce gale.

As a teenager, Ellison loved the surf at Santa Cruz beach, just an hour from the Stanford Campus. On sunny weekend days he used to paddle his big surfboard out to sea, fight through the breakers to the open ocean beyond, and then sit astride his board to study the oncoming swells like a hunter watching for big game. The waves came in sets of seven or nine: a couple of smaller ones, followed by two or three getting bigger, until—if he was lucky— a monster began to hump up in the distance, racing toward him like a freight train carrying a load of youthful pleasure. An eight foot wave gave him a lesson proving the power of the Pacific; for once an eight footer picked you up, once you were balancing atop your board sliding down the face of the wave, ducking beneath the curl into a tunnel of cool green water, the force of the sea was entirely in control. Ellison remembered the first time he had felt the exhilaration of riding a force of nature.

But the Mediterranean storm made chaotic waves as big as buildings, a thousand times more massive than he had ridden as a youth. Instead of joy, he felt utter, piercing fear—for himself, true enough, but especially for his wife, his friends, and for the two hundred others put at risk when he ordered *Aphrodite* sunk. He wasn't sure the heavily laden *Aphrodite* wouldn't have sunk in this storm anyway.

Counting the two Italian pilots and Francois, fourteen people shared the lifeboat with Ellison, all wearing orange life preservers with snap lines attached to the gunwales to prevent anyone from being swept overboard. Through a small hole in the clouds, Ellison could see the planet Jupiter on the ecliptic, its bright light almost straight overhead. Suddenly, a looming dark shape obscured Jupiter's twinkle. In a stomach-churning ascent, they felt themselves being swept upward by a rogue wave that felt a hundred feet high. Ellison snapped on his flashlight, aiming it into the roiling trough far below them.

"I can't stand it!" Eduardo screamed. "We are going to die!"

They plunged on a watery sleigh ride, feeling weightless, until the lifeboat crashed sideways into the trough, almost overturned, and in righting itself took on hundreds of gallons of water. "Start bailing!" Ellison shouted above the wind. "Everyone!"

But Eduardo, his mind lost to fear, continued to scream, louder and louder, hysterical. When another voice joined Eduardo's terrified screams, Ellison felt he had to help Eduardo get control of himself, to slap his face and stun him out of his panic. He judged the distance to Eduardo, unsnapped his safety line, and threw himself across the boat. Yet instead of landing next to Eduardo, he felt an unexpected wave hit him, lift him in a flying somersault away from the boat, and plunge him head-first into the sea.

While flying through the air, Ellison instinctively took a deep breath. Once he hit the water, he waited for the life vest to indicate which direction to the surface. When he felt he was rising, he took two powerful strokes to reach air.

Breaching like a whale, he coughed and struggled to find the lifeboat. Flashlight beams probed the darkness, and he heard Miranda's shout above the wind. "Todd! Over here!"

Swimming with his head up with a lifeguard's technique, Ellison took four fast strokes toward the lifeboat. But suddenly it was six stories above him, then gone. He caught sight of Miranda's flashlight a minute later, already far away.

After that, he was alone.

Pius XIII smashed a porcelain statue of the Virgin when Strizzi told him *Aphrodite* had gone down in a freak storm.

"I am crucified," he cried, spreading his arms.

"A terrible turn of events, Your Holiness; but the Holy See must go on, yes?"

"I am the sword that bringeth the truth!" Pius XIII babbled, unable to accept this test from God. He felt himself losing his mind in an uncontrollable swirling kaleidoscope of ideas that swept him first one way, then another, almost random except he knew they led him toward godhead knowledge. And how could anyone choose to oppose him? He heard Strizzi as if from a great distance.

"And after that, you have an audience with the French Premier."

"Send him away!"

"But—"

"Instead of talking about politics, peace and love to men without the ears to hear, I now prefer to talk about them to God alone."

"Your Holiness!"

"I feel myself transfigured into divine, pure being. Enough of this! I must pray," he said as he dismissed the Secretary of State with an imperious wave. Pius XIII saw the confused look on Strizzi's face as he departed and knew that no mere mortal could understand him.

When another wave washed over him, Ellison wondered what will it be like to die? Will it be an eternal darkness like this night? If there is an afterlife, will I be in heaven or hell, and will I see Miranda again?

As the waves tossed him about, helpless, Ellison recalled the American Indian myth of the warrior's last dance. At the moment of death, just as the warrior passes from life, he pauses for one last dance. Then he dances his accomplishments, his loves, his children, his ancestors—and the more he has done as a warrior, the longer is that last dance before he passes to the Happy Hunting Ground.

Once the cold water drained away all fear or hope, once Ellison abandoned the constant struggle to live that—like Sisyphus pushing the boulder uphill every day—had been his life, he danced his last dance. He danced his carefree life as a child, when warm skies and wildflowers made life miraculous; he danced his teenage years with their hints of the challenges and conflicts that would face him as he became a man; he danced his friendships and loves; he danced of Francois, and of his work and play; but mostly he danced of Miranda and the child he would never see.

Ellison, a man in the flower of manhood, danced long, as he had strived to live well according to an unnamed inner compass that told him right from wrong. And just as the darkness of night turned the faintest gray, he felt himself slipping away. Like Francois, he heard the rolling thunder.

At the end he imagined a great barge coming for him to carry him across the River Styx. But when it sailed past without stopping, he felt judged, condemned to eternal suffering. Hope sprang up again when angels fluttered their wings above him, so painfully noisy they must surely have been sent by Satan to claim his soul, and lifted him out of his body and away into a limitless darkness.

❊   ❊   ❊

Around him, Pius XIII heard voices beseeching him, for what he cared not, as for him the world had ceased to exist. Transfigured, he dwelt on the plane of the gods, concerning himself only with the immutable laws of the universe. Briefly he remembered his role as Supreme Pontiff and his mission to cleanse the earth for

Christ; but he believed it had been done. Pius XIII, now completely God, lived in a continual state of joyous ecstasy.

ATTACK

Ellison felt soft pressure against his lips, so sweet and tender he imagined a kiss from an angel before he faded back into oblivion, where he rested in a steady, rumbling vibration all around him. Finally, as dreamily as a patient emerging from deep anesthesia, Ellison recognized voices. Frightened and confused by his heavenly hallucination, he believed he saw Miranda grim-faced staring down at him. Shaking his head to clear his mind quickly, he realized an oxygen mask bathed his nose in cold, dry air and he could see an intravenous fluid pouring at full bore into a vein in his arm. Unless eternal life takes place in a gray-walled infirmary, I have somehow survived. Those mountainous waves. *What? How?*

He tore the mask from his face and stared around him. "Miranda," he croaked, "Where am I?"

Beecham answered with a military clip, "*USS Harry Truman*, in the Mediterranean Sea near Malta."

USS Harry Truman. Ellison struggled to make his mind work. Yes, an American aircraft carrier. "But how?"

While Miranda massaged his head, Ellison listened to Eduardo and Beecham take turns telling the story.

"After you went overboard because of me, my heart nearly stopped," Eduardo began. "We looked for you but never saw a trace."

"You can imagine how I felt," Miranda said as she massaged his still cold hands.

"Yeah, the little cowgirl was a certified mess. 'Course she bounced back and held us together," Beecham said, "but damnit let me tell you what really happened."

"Since we are on your turf, General—" Eduardo said with a novice salute.

"So we rode that bucking bronco of a storm all night, 'til it let up just before daybreak, when steamin' west we saw a half dozen destroyers and guided missile cruisers."

"I fired off flares the moment I saw the ships," Eduardo cut in. "None of us cared if they were Italian or not. By then we all agreed a life in jail would be better than another minute lost at sea."

"But they were flyin' Old Glory."

"And we saw flares from several directions," Miranda added. All of them showed their relief to see Ellison alive. "We were just sure the flares came from our other lifeboats."

"But did the battle group stop at our corral? Hell no! They steamed by us, hell-bent for somewhere, until we saw this here big gray hulk of a *Harry Truman* cutting our way. Rescue helicopters picked us up and dropped us off on the flight deck, right above this infirmary."

"It wasn't quite as simple as he makes it sound, Todd. The ropes were so tight I could hardly breathe."

"Francois went to the morgue, and the rest of us to this medical clinic, where they checked us over before we were confined to quarters," Eduardo added.

"But the Admiral recognized me from Pentagon Joint Services meetings, and after I talked with him, he put in a call to President Clark. While we remain technically under arrest, we've been granted the run of the ship. Surprises me that we aren't in irons, but he's been on the horn with President Clark several times already, and I guess he's following orders."

"One doctor told me that counting the men on *Harry Truman* and all the other vessels, every single one of our men made it," Eduardo added.

"And you are last, but not least, my darling."

"Yup, a big Sea Stallion helicopter brought you aboard an hour or so ago. Unconscious as a steer in a Texas blizzard."

"Severe hypothermia, according to the doctor,"Miranda murmured. "Your body temperature was so low he feared it could be incompatible with life. Until he saw how strong you are, he wasn't optimistic you would survive."

"But hell, look at you now, pardner. A shave, some fresh duds, and you could go line dancin'"

Like a man gasping for air from the mouthpiece of his SCUBA partner, Ellison pulled Miranda to him and kissed her hungrily. That he was seeing her again seemed like the greatest miracle of his life, and with everyone else safe as well, he felt reborn.

He wanted to go on with their joyful reunion, made so intense by knowledge they had already lost one of their own when Francois died. He was about to hold Miranda closer to him, to feel her body against him from his ankles to the fronts of his thighs, to enjoy the pressure of her breasts against his chest and a gentle pressure from her hips; but before he could enfold her, klaxon horns blared, followed by the order, "Battle stations!"

"Battle stations?" Shocked by the unwelcome intrusion, Ellison started. What's going on?"

"This here posse is going to bomb the hell out of Libya. The guys who nuked Jerusalem are holed up a couple of hundred miles south of Tripoli, hiding out in the desert. In a minute I'll tell you how we located them. From what the Admiral says, his fleet is just part of what's going to hit 'em."

Visions of the Eiffel Tower's plunge, the disintegration of the airliner, and Jerusalem flat and smoking flooded into Ellison's mind. He felt a searing anger at the men who had committed such atrocities.

After forcing himself out of his hospital bed, Ellison tested his strength and stood to inspect his body. Wrinkled and pale from so many hours in salt water, his skin seemed to be the main problem.

Without further hesitation he pulled the intravenous needle out of his arm. When he tried to walk, he experienced a jolt of dizziness, and had to sit back down on the hospital bed.

"How can they be sure the terrorists are here?" Ellison asked, shaking his head.

"In war, intelligence is crucial, and we are the best at gathering it," Beecham began. "Later I might know exactly how we found them, but I can tell you our standard procedures."

Ellison flexed his arms and legs, and encouraged Beecham to continue. "Tell us."

"First we'd print up a couple of hundred million matchbooks that offer a ten million dollar reward to anyone whose information leads to the arrest of the Jerusalem bombers. In forty-eight hours, every raghead who lights up a cigarette from Casablanca to Calcutta will start wondering to himself, 'Should I or shouldn't I?' Informers usually decide to move fast, because they know someone else will if they don't. So we get leads that way, unless it's just a three-man cell, all of them sworn never to talk."

"So low tech, but I can see how it would work," Eduardo said.

"We've got the high tech working, too. Over in Houston they would turn on the Carnivore Computer and listen to every electromagnetic transmission on earth. First they might just ask it to scan for the word, 'Jerusalem,' but they might get millions of hits, so they would have to fine tune, to use filters, for instance scanning for, 'Jerusalem *and* travel.'" They'd add in certain Arabic words for other filters, and usually we get something. In this case I understand they isolated a transmission. Now we're gonna round 'em up."

"To go to war, we must have more than that," Ellison said.

"As soon as we got that intercept, we'd start steering satellites over the area, probably send up several to keep the bad guys under continuous vision. In close, we use drone planes the size of mockingbirds that are invisible to men on the ground. We circle fifty or sixty of them over the area that look down with their cameras and send real-time pictures to their operators. Some of them can scan for electrons that only spark out of nuclear weapons. That's how we can be sure they've got at least one more nuke in Libya."

"The terrorists have another bomb! Any guess what we'll do?"

"Hurt 'em bad, pardner. The decision will come from the

highest level and could range from dropping our own nuclear weapon to doing what looks like is going on here, a joint services attack. We're probably going to root them out, kill 'em all and be sure we recover the nukes."

"Miranda, can you find me some dry clothes?" At her nod, Ellison turned back to Beecham. "And, General, can you try something for me?"

"What's that?"

"Get me a seat on one of those planes headed for Libya. I want to see the terrorists get finished off." Ellison knew it was crazy, but somehow he felt personally involved and wanted to witness the final chapter firsthand.

Beecham snorted. "Some things are impossible, pardner, even for you. Hitching a ride in an F-18 Tomcat raid is one of 'em." He paused. "But I'll see what I can do."

"Anything on the Vatican?" Ellison asked.

Miranda and Eduardo both shook their heads, "Not a word," Eduardo replied.

"Upstairs I heard the Italian flyboys are screaming to get to talk to their headquarters, but no dice," Beecham said. "My guess is that right now everyone believes the gold and all hands were lost at sea in the storm." Preparing to march out the door, he gave Ellison a comradely punch on the shoulder, "Get some exercise, pardner, I'll talk with the Admiral."

When Ellison tried to walk again, his knees buckled under him. Catching him by each shoulder, Eduardo and Miranda helped him walk about the ward, with Miranda putting her strong arm under his. "My fighter pilot, indeed," she laughed.

Before Ellison completed five circumambulations of the room, Beecham burst through the door, grinning beneath his black ten-gallon cowboy hat.

"The Admiral gave permission for us to observe in the Combat Decision Center, so long as we stay out of the way. It's going to be big war, ranch hands!" Beecham's excitement about violence struck Ellison as incongruous, but he felt his own heart rate tick upward.

By now able to walk unaided, Ellison led the others in file behind Beecham through an endless maze of gray painted corridors and hatches, passing through a vast hangar below the main deck. Above them they could hear the screams of jets blasting into the air off steam catapults, while elevators as big as home lots lifted more jets up to the flight deck. Counting everyone on board, more than five thousand men worked in trained unison, hardly needing to speak into their headsets. Hand signals like railroad men, Ellison noted with pleasure, while Beecham led them to a passenger elevator that whisked them further down to the vault-like Combat Decision Center.

Admiral Warren Littleton, only the second African American to command a nuclear carrier, gave them a perfunctory greeting. "Doctor, ma'am, please sit in the back row of observation chairs, which I assure you is very special treatment. *Balls* Beecham here and I grew up together in West Texas. His ma was the only woman poorer than mine."

"Thank you, Admiral," Ellison said.

"You people have a friend in the White House. I know, because President Clark told me the whole, and I mean whole, story."

What that meant, Ellison was unsure. He knew he would never know everything. Great conflicts occur on a foggy ocean of unknowing, where everyone must act though great sea dragons may lurk just out of view.

They were in a room the size of an elementary school classroom that glowed with hundreds of display panels, some flashing numerical readouts, others rotating graphic images—of what, Ellison could not tell—except three that were obviously maps of Libya at varying degrees of resolution.

"Is that red diamond on the screen our ship?" he whispered to Beecham.

"Sure is. Looks like about a hundred fifty miles to shore, give or take."

Ellison recognized the outlines of the Gulf of Siddra, where three times in the past twenty years American warplanes had fired in anger. He knew the area to be one of the most dangerous on earth. "But why are we so close to the coast?" Libyan fighters going supersonic could be on them in minutes.

"Risky," Beecham agreed. "We could hit them with cruise missiles from two thousand miles, and these carrier planes have long legs. Might mean the Marines are going in."

"Putting troops ashore in Libya?" Ellison said, astonished. "Why, that will look like America is doing Pius XIII's work against the Muslims. That would be a disaster."

"Nothin' you or I say is going to stop the U.S. Navy, pardner. Watch the big video screens. I'll try to tell you what's going on."

Four jumbotron screens flickered to life displaying live broadcast satellite camera images of the same desert terrain in different powers of magnification, ranging from the way something looks from an airplane to a close-up where Ellison could see a terrorist lounging under a date palm reading an English language newspaper, *The International Herald Tribune's* banner clearly visible. The intermediate screens showed a military camp with six low buildings in a lush oasis, an unpaved airstrip with three twin-engine propeller planes, and a dozen sixteen-wheeler trucks parked in the shade. Ellison estimated fifty to one hundred men strolled about the camp. In unison, they rolled out prayer rugs and knelt to face Mecca.

"They're at Khadaffi's *Great Underground River*," Beecham said, "a three hundred mile system he built beneath the desert to bring water from the mountains to the populated coastline. It also has a warren of side tunnels for military purposes. What we can see above ground is just part of this camp."

"Does this mean Khadaffi is behind the terrorists?"

"They're in his country, ain't they?"

"But I thought he turned cautious after Ronald Reagan nearly killed him in the '86 bombing raid on his tent in Tripoli. He even turned over the bombers of Pan Am 103 for trial."

"Hey, Khadaffi ain't like your average Muslim leader. Most of them could sit around the campfire with us, peaceful and friendly as could be."

"Right," Ellison agreed. "A Muslim can be the kindest, gentlest person alive. The *Holy Koran* commands it. But if they believe injustice is taking place, they also believe Allah requires them to fight it."

"Read Khadaffi's *Green Book*, the one he patterned after Chairman Mao's *Red Book*. Brother Moamar Khadaffi believes he is the new prophet to interpret the *Koran* for our times. Much to his chagrin, there is hardly a religious Muslim who reads the *Green Book* without disgust at Brother Khadaffi's interpretation of the

Holy Koran."

They were conversing in whispers, while fifty sailors in the room went about their tasks with calm precision.

"Admiral, four bogies coming from Tripoli."

"Splash them."

What? Ellison wondered. No warning, no talk about International Waters or Freedom of the Seas. Just "Splash them?" This was war indeed, muscle coming to overpower and implacably kill, the human race at its most focused activity.

The Muslim fighters had just finished their prayers and stood about chatting when seventy-five blips appeared on an enormous radar screen. Like a shrinking compass rose, the images converged on the Muslim camp.

"Cruise missiles," Beecham explained. "Tomahawks just popping up from a hundred feet altitude to five thousand for their impact run. See that clock up there?"

Ellison looked up to see a digital clock with six numbers to the right of the decimal clicking at a furious rate.

"Accurate to a billionth of a second per year. All the weapons are synchronized to it. Watch. With our new guidance systems, the Tomahawks can hit the hole on a golf course putting green. This also means we can fly one right through anyone's front door."

"I see more incomings converging on a different location," Ellison said.

Beecham gave a low whistle. "This is big time, really big time. We're hitting dozens of airbases and radar installations, all at the same time. Khadaffi better be underground, 'cause that formation is headed for Tripoli."

Admiral Littleton strode in to take his reserved seat behind the Tactical Officer in charge of "fighting the ship." Only Admiral Littleton or the Captain of the *USS Harry Truman* could override the Tactical Officer's orders. "All planes up. Launch the helos." In response, the Flight Officer machine-gunned a stacatto series of commands.

Even below decks, the roar of helicopters crammed with Marines shook them. Dozens more soared from *Kearsage* class aircraft carriers that plowed through seas a few miles from the *Harry Truman.* "Things are happening fast now!" Beecham exclaimed.

On the display screen, Ellison could see a jumble of green, yellow and red dots moving across the sea toward the Libyan shore.

"A protective envelope of air cover for the Marines," Beecham explained. "With that much air superiority, they're as safe as babies in their prams strolling in Central Park."

"Bullshit, General." Ellison said.

"Well—"

Before Beecham could finish his sentence, the video screen flashed and flickered with a brilliant white light. On the lower magnification screen, Ellison could see an area one mile on a side erupt in fire and dust. Nothing above ground could survive such violence.

"Hot damn!" Beecham crowed. "And look at that," he exulted, pointing. "Remember those radar sites the Libyan's had to control their surface to air missiles?"

"Yes," Ellison answered.

"They're all gone!"

"But we didn't see any radar traces near them."

Beecham winked. "We didn't know what to look for. Could have been F/A-18s from this carrier loaded with AGM-154 Joint Standoff Weapons. Them big bombs are guided to their targets by global positioning satellites and can fly fifty miles after the F/A-18 pilot drops them. 'Course on the other hand it could have been Stealth fighter-bombers, probably from Aviano Airbase in Italy. F-117s. First we jam their radar to degrade their ability to see, like blinding Cyclops, then we use attack planes that they couldn't have seen anyway. We attack like this because America does not want to lose any of her boys."

Miranda leaned forward in her chair. "I'm familiar with all the rules of the Geneva Convention on warfare. This is according to the book, but it seems so one-sided."

"When the Marines hit the ground it won't be, ma'am. Some of them boys will probably die in this mission."

While they sat silent, gazing at where the terrorist camp used to be, a fresh round of even bigger explosions carpeted the base. "B-2s, the big stealth bombers all the way from Kansas and right on time. Can you imagine, doc, almost eight thousand miles?"

"Why them?"

"Big bombs. The kind that penetrate ten stories underground

before they go off. They're aircraft too large for carrier planes. We might even see some B-52 action, since it looks like the Commander in Chief decided to dump the whole load. Probably used our secret weapon, too," he said with a sly wink.

"Secret weapon?"

"It won't be after today, so I'll tell you. Every military depends on computers for command and control, right?"

"In the modern world, I suppose so."

"We've got a transmitter that wrecks their microprocessors. Forever. After we fly over them with the secret ray turned on, they're back in the Stone Age. Can't see us, can't talk to each other, their planes won't fly, their tanks can't aim, you name it."

"Incredible."

"Not really. We invented electronics, didn't we? A war with America, no matter who is the enemy, will be over in minutes."

"Can we go on deck?" Miranda asked. "I'm feeling faint."

Pregnancy, Ellison thought. "If it's okay, General, I'll take her up."

At Beecham's nod, they followed a sailor to a catwalk above the flight deck. The stiff breeze felt good, and the seas, rolling but much smaller than when he'd been adrift, hardly moved the massive man of war. Below them, flight operations continued at a furious pace, with tankers and fighter-bombers streaking on and off the deck every minute or two like honey bees swarming to the hive, depositing their pollen, and zooming off again.

Arrayed in a fifteen-mile circle around *Harry Truman*, Ellison could see smaller ships sending salvos of cruise missiles into the sky, and twice he saw an eruption of compressed air from beneath the sea, out of which came a missile launched by a submarine invisible beneath the waves.

When America struck Osama bin Laden's camp in Afghanistan, fifty weapons were used. It was like a slap on the wrist for destroying two American embassies and killing almost a thousand people. Bin Laden, a known collaborator with Ramzi Ahmed Youssef in Philippine terrorism, had lived to cause troubles for years after the strike against him. It was a lesson President Clark had chosen to learn. This attack on Libya carried full force.

While Ellison and Miranda observed the carrier's operations, a cook brought them mugs of strong coffee and a tray of sweet rolls.

"How incredibly strange," he said to Miranda.

Her almond eyes turned to him, heavy with fatigue despite the frenzied activity around them. "I mean, here we are, Miranda, as if we were in a coffee house in San Francisco, but we are on a ship at war. The images are like dozens of movies we've seen. It all seems so sterile. The best way, I guess."

"For our side, anyway. Everyone at that camp must be dead. And I'm dead tired, Todd. I have to sleep."

Once Miranda was tucked into a firm bunk, Ellison followed their guard back to the Operations Center, where Beecham and Eduardo sat in rapt attention.

"The Marines landed at the camp five minutes ago, commando doc. Early reports indicate fierce resistance from the *Underground River,* even after all the bombing. The Marines are going to clean them out."

While the Marine landing of fifteen hundred men went on, barrages of missiles and bombs pounded dozens of Libyan strongholds. If they were deaf and blind, as Beecham predicted, Ellison doubted if the Libyans knew the object of the attack. In fact, Ellison felt confused himself, as the operation looked more like "payback time for Khadaffi" than an "exterminate the terrorists" mission. But he, too, felt sinking waves of fatigue draining him; until, finally, he retreated to the wardroom, cuddled against Miranda's back, and fell into the sleep of a dead man.

❋　　❋　　❋

In Vatican City, Pius XIII rejoiced when news of an American attack in progress came to him. In the close confines of the Mediterranean, the military of every nation could see that a major offensive was underway.

"Now my crusade has truly begun," he told Strizzi. "My Christian soldiers of my Christian America will sweep away every non-believer. When infidels taste my sword, they will believe in the Redeemer."

Ideas popped into in his mind like camera flashes, bits of cosmic illumination too profound to put into mere words for mere mortals. While Strizzi bowed his way out of Pius XIII's chamber, Pius XIII threw open his window and shouted to passersby in the great square below the Apostolic Palace.

"Jesus lied when he said 'The meek shall inherit the earth.' He was a false prophet, I tell you. The strong must rule. God in all his power and glory is among you."

Pius XIII barely noticed the confused looks on the faces of a cluster of nuns leading Italian fifth graders on a tour of St. Peter's. The children turned toward him, fresh smiling faces so filled with instinctive reverence and joy at seeing the Pontiff. They waved to him with delight, but Pius XIII regarded them as if they were meaningless insects, ciphers in his heavenly scheme.

"Repent little sinners!" he screamed at them. "The hour of your death is near."

❋　❋　❋

"Get this, pardner," Beecham said as he shook Ellison awake. "The Marines captured the leader of the bombers, a little Palestinian fuck with curly hair."

Ellison snapped alert. "Are they sure?"

"You're gonna see him for yourself, doc. He's on his way to this here hospital ward, a little shot up, I guess."

Minutes later, four strapping Marines charged through the door carrying an Arab handcuffed to the litter. He was wide awake with eyes as defiant as a guard dog. Except for purplish bruises on his right temple, no doubt from a gunstock blow delivered with enough force to knock him out, the wiry man's only obvious injury was some bleeding from a leg wound.

"This is better than when we got Noriega down in Panama," Beecham boasted. "Abdullah Musa, according to his Jordanian passport. Probably false."

Ellison followed into a treatment room, where Abdullah Musa was spitting and snarling at his captors. Ellison shouldered in to get a good look at such a man.

"*Assalam Alleykum,*" Ellison said to him. "Peace be with you," the prescribed greeting by Muhammed.

Abdullah Musa eyed him with suspicion before answering grudgingly, "*Walekum Assalam.*"

"Do you speak English?"

"Of course."

"Why did you do it? Why Jerusalem and everything else?" When stony silence prevailed, Ellison prodded him further. "It doesn't matter now. You should tell someone."

Turning his head away, the prisoner's eyes filled with tears. He bit his trembling lower lip before answering, his voice choked with pain. "Shatila," he hissed.

"I don't know what he means," Ellison said.

"Shatila," Beecham repeated. "A refugee camp near Beirut, supposedly under the protection of the Jewish Defense Force after they invaded Lebanon. When the Christian militia attacked the camp, the Jews didn't defend the Muslims, though they were unarmed civilians. Almost a thousand men, women and children were massacred."

"I watched from beneath my father's body," Abdullah Musa groaned. "After I saw them gang-rape my mother and ten year old sister, the Christians slit their throats. Though I was just a child, at that moment I dedicated my life to revenge—Jews, Christians, anyone."

Ellison saw the same psychotic look in Abdullah Musa's eyes he had seen in Pius XIII's. Another maniac. After what Ellison had seen, he felt no inclination to countenance Abdullah Musa's hideous actions, regardless of what childhood horrors and injustices had been visited on him.

Quick as a mongoose Ellison grabbed Abdullah Musa's face in his big hands and forced Musa to look him in the eyes. "You are an animal," he said in hard, even tones.

Abdullah Musa spat at Ellison and, with a feral growl, he tried to bite Ellison's hand.

"Muzzle him," Ellison ordered, so at home in a medical clinic that assuming control came automatically. A leather helmet soon clamped the Palestinian's jaws tightly shut. When orderlies cut his tan shirt and trousers away, they found a money belt circling his waist. A corpsman unzipped it, removing a parchment map.

"What's this?" Beecham asked, peering over the corpsman's shoulder. "Next target, I bet. Intelligence will have to tell us where it is."

"Can I see?" Ellison asked.

"Sure." Beecham handed him the map. "Wherever it is, they're damn lucky. He had another nuke with him in the Great Man-made River."

When Ellison studied the map, his eyes grew wide. "Incredible!" he gasped.

"What?" Miranda asked.

"His target was Vatican City."

INQUISITION

With his mind flitting from one idea to the next like a nervous
bird, Pius XIII found it tiresome to concentrate on what the seven
men in red repeatedly asked him.

"Holy Father, do you believe you are Christ Incarnate?" They
were from the Congregation for the Doctrine of Faith, the modern Universal Inquisition, the notorious force first unleashed in
1542 to deal with heresy. These cardinals were charged with maintaining the doctrinal purity of the Church.

Pius XIII could see the confused, worried looks on their faces,
which surely arose from their inability to comprehend the incomprehensible. "Again, Your Holiness, do you maintain, as you have
in seventeen papal audiences this week, that you are the Risen
Christ?"

"What little faith you have," Pius answered, weary of their
questions. "Cleanse yourself and seek forgiveness for your sins,

that you might see me in all my glory."

Pius heard them mutter, "heresy," and "rite of exorcism." About to open the Seventh Seal with his mind, Pius XIII paid little attention, and retreated into his prayerful communion with God.

After the inquisitors walked out, shaking their heads and breaking into twos and threes for intense discussions, Cardinal Strizzi joined Pius XIII in private.

"The Church needs you to lead, Vincente. What is wrong with you?" He pleaded with the Pontiff. "Even documented threats against Vatican City itself elicit no interest from you."

"Bah!"

"No, old friend. You cannot say that now. The College of Cardinals meets in an unprecedented plenary session to discuss you."

"Hollow meetings where they pour from the empty into the void."

Strizzi continued to press him. "Though your call for a Crusade has backfired in many ways, especially where Church properties now lay in ruin, at least no one blames you for the loss of the gold."

"Christ's Gold," Pius XIII corrected him, "and no matter where it may be right now, at the bottom of the sea or on Mars, I will recover it at my will."

"The gold is gone, Holiness. Take hold of yourself, or I fear for you."

A loud, unexpected knock on Pius XIII's door startled the two men. Strizzi opened the door enough to allow Pius XIII to see five cardinals and Archbishop Bono of Venice. As the most accomplished exorcist in the entire Catholic Church, Bono had become the official exorcist of the Bishopric of Rome, the diocese of the Pope.

The Master of Ceremonies spoke first. "At the order of the College of Cardinals and the Congregation for the Doctrine of Faith, we come to minister to His Holiness. May we come in?"

"Of course, Your Eminence," Strizzi answered.

"I do not need you!" Pius XIII shouted, seeing an enemy in the face he recognized as the Exorcist. "Vex me not!" Years ago, he and Cardinal Bono had worked together on the revision of the Rite of Exorcism, which had not been changed since its last revision in 1614. When *De Exorcismis et Supplicationibus Quibusdam* was released in its ninety page leather volume in 1999, Pius XIII himself had authored many of the provisions. As a member of the Congregation for Divine Worship, he pushed for the recognition of the reality of diabolical possession. Weaker thinkers like Cardinal Muldowney of New York favored interpretation of evil through the lens of popular psychology. The right wing prevailed. The guide specifically reaffirmed something many contemporary Catholics find hard to accept—the idea of Satan as a living, thinking being. "The Devil," the document said, "goes around like a roaring lion looking for souls to devour." Unlike its predecessor, *De Exorcismis* warns against confusing possession by the devil with mental illness. Among the signs of demonic possession are "speaking in unknown tongues, discerning distant or hidden things, and displaying a physical strength that is at odds with the possessed person's age or state of health." Exorcism is fundamentally a prolonged Mass, during which each and every saint and angel is called upon by name and beseeched to convince God to drive Satan from the sufferer's soul. Little changed from four centuries ago, exorcism has been increasing in usage in reaction to the inexplicable horrors of modern life. Pius XIII felt more offended than frightened by Bono's presence.

Once inside the papal apartments, the men, including Strizzi, dropped to their knees at a nod from Bono. Pius XIII knew Bono would already have gone to Confession and implored God's help with fervent prayers before attempting such an historic exorcism, the first in history of a Pope. Dressed in surplice and purple stole, Bono approached Pius XIII behind a young priest fogging the air with expensive incense. From the outer chamber, a choir sent hymns of supplication soaring skyward.

How much do they know? It surprised Pius XIII to see the Exorcist, but he adjusted to the situation and decided the best way to rid himself of them was to play along. Knowing they would bind him hand and foot if he fought them, Pius XIII moved to a throne, where he sat staring straight ahead, keeping his face impassive. Bono traced the sign of the cross over him, over himself, and the bystanders, then sprinkled them all with holy water.

Bono began the Rite of Exorcism. *"Lord have mercy."*

All responded, "Lord, have mercy."

"Holy Mary, pray for us."

"Have mercy on us," the assemblage droned.

Bono continued by praying to each of the more than 200 saints of the Catholic Church.

"St. Michael."

"Pray for us," the others responded.

"St. Gabriel."

"Pray for us."

Pius XIII struggled to maintain composure while the interminable list continued with the droning of Bono and the cardinals responding in solemn cadence. They went on and on, and would not stop. The fools believed he had a demon inside him. Perhaps a demon for good, he snorted. Once finished with the saints, Bono read words from Psalm 53, *"God, by your name save me, and by your might defend my cause."*

The cardinals murmured, *"God, hear my prayer; hearken to the words of my mouth."*

"Save your servant," Bono chanted, making the cross again and again, as the cardinals murmured.

"Who trusts in you, my God."

Bono pressed his hands on Pius XIII's temples. "Let the enemy have no power over him."

"And the son of iniquity be powerless to harm him," the audience responded.

Bono drew himself up to his most powerful posture. *"Strike terror, Lord, into the beast now laying waste your vineyard. Fill your servants with the courage to fight manfully against that reprobate dragon."*

"Amen," they said.

Pius XIII knew that the preliminaries would soon end with the exorcism proper, done by adjuration, an urgent demand rendered solemn and powerful by linking it with the name of God. Adjuration requires compliance under penalty of divine visitation or rupture of sacred ties of reverence and love.

Bono began to command the demon, *"I command you, unclean spirit, whoever you are, along with all your minions now attacking this servant of God, by the mysteries of the incarnation, passion, resurrection, and ascension of our Lord Jesus Christ, that you tell me by some sign your name, and the day and hour of your departure. I com-*

mand you to obey me to the letter, I who am a minister of God despite my unworthiness."

He moved closer to Pius XIII and lay his hand on him again. Pius XIII shrank back at his words, *"They shall lay their hands upon the sick and all will be well with them."*

Bono made the sign of the cross over himself and Pius XIII, put one end of his ermine stole on Pius XIII's neck, and after putting his hand on Pius XIII's head, he spoke in a voice filled with faith and confidence. *"See the cross of the Lord!"* he shouted, *"Begone, you hostile powers!"*

Bono had hardly begun his adjuration when Pius XIII felt a welling up in him that made him yowl and gnash his teeth. He held his head in his hands and covered his ears against the chanting of the Exorcist.

Bono seemed huge and powerful beside him, his voice almost deafening. *"I cast you out, unclean spirit, along with every Satanic power of the enemy, every spectre from hell, and all your fell companions, in the name of our Lord Jesus Christ."*

Pius XIII noticed a foul scent fill the air, seeping from his body, like corrupted flesh kept ice-cold. Just as the Exorcist reached his climax with, *"Begone and stay far from this creature of God,"* Pius XIII felt a ripping in his chest and belly as something tried to tear its way out of him. A great fatigue came over him, when the Exorcist prayed, *"Amen,"* and led the cardinals out. Pius XIII was alone.

He drifted into a trance wondrously like sleep. When he came to his senses, Strizzi was sitting beside him. Pius XIII felt his mind revving up like a massive dynamo generating electricity from a waterfall. For a single piercing moment, he remembered poisoning Hildebrandt III during Holy Confession. Briefly shocked by sudden remorse, he crossed himself six times while taking deep breaths.

Strizzi faced him. "Are you ill, Holiness?" His voice was kind, caring.

"Satan tempts me to worldly concerns. Leave me now."

For hours after Strizzi bowed out, Pius XIII's painful recollection kept him on his knees in his chapel, wrestling with Satan, the fallen angel intent on bringing him down. Finally, long past midnight, his face drenched with perspiration and his body shaking with ague, Pius XIII stood triumphant over Beelzebub. Now is the hour of my ascension, he thought.

While two sleepy Swiss Guards followed him, Pius XIII wandered the Apostolic Palace, unsure where or why God was leading him, like blind Diogenes looking for another honest man. At last, after pacing the perimeter of Vatican City's walls, he felt transported by a mysterious force into the main basilica, where he found himself at the altar of St. Peter's.

Above him the interior of the dome looked like heaven itself, with its six-foot high letters saying,

"TU ES PETRUS ET SUPER HANC PETRAM AEDI-FICABO ECCLESIAM MEAM ET TIBI DABO CLAVES REGNI CAELORUM. YOU ARE PETER, AND UPON THIS ROCK I SHALL BUILD MY CHURCH AND I SHALL GIVE YOU THE KEYS OF THE KINGDOM OF HEAVEN."

Though far above him, the words called out to Pius XIII. "Wait for me while I pray. Do not sleep," he said to the guards, repeating the words Jesus said to Peter at Gethsemane. The guards looked at each other, uncertain, before bowing to the order of the Vicar of Christ.

Pius XIII began to climb what seemed to be an endless spiral staircase. After a lifetime compressed into a few minutes, Pius XIII stood on a marble balcony two hundred feet above the altar below, where the guards looked up at him, tiny as ants wiggling their antennae toward him in alarm. Feeling at the same time the heaviness of the world and lacy lightness of being, he experienced God taking control of every atom of his body.

Pius XIII kissed his dangling golden crucifix, then spread both arms like an angel. Supremely confident he would ascend to the right hand of God the Father, Pius XIII stepped into space.

GRAVES

Exuberant sailors streamed off the ships in Naples Bay to celebrate their victory with well-earned shore leave in the favorite port of America's Sixth Fleet. Famous for curvaceous women with long, shapely legs, Naples welcomed the young men and their money with open arms.

Confined to quarters while Admiral Littleton awaited orders, Ellison dozed in a bunk beside Miranda. Their disposition would be either to America or Rome for trial. Since all recent Popes had argued against the death penalty, he hoped it was unlikely that Pius XIII could force their execution under Italian law. But, helpless, he found himself tormented by all sorts of fears, especially for Miranda and the others who had followed him.

At the sound of a sharp rap on the door, Ellison flexed his aching muscles and stood, just before Admiral Littleton eased his huge frame through the door. Beecham marched one step behind.

"They want you in Vatican City," Littleton boomed.

"I'm sure Pius XIII does. So we're being turned over?"

"Hold on," Beecham cut in. "It's Cardinal Muldowney and Cardinal Lopez. They guarantee safe conduct for all of us in accordance with international law."

"What for? What about Pius XIII?"

"They wouldn't say, 'cept that it's mighty important. Right, Admiral?"

"Doctor, they're allowing some of our Marines to accompany you. I believe you will be safe."

"Once we are on Vatican soil, Pius XIII is king. He does not have to honor their guarantees."

"They said not to worry about Pius XIII. Disabled or something."

When the gray helicopters settled on Vatican gardens, Ellison's mouth went dry. He could see temporary scaffolding at the railroad tunnel, and dozens of heavily armed troops on guard.

Beecham chuckled at a private joke, "Europeans. It's like lockin' the barn when the bull's already out, my daddy used to say."

Cardinal Muldowney and Cardinal Lopez greeted Ellison as soon as he led the others down the ladder. In minutes they sat in a paneled salon of the Apostolic Palace, nervously looking at one other across a marble-topped table. Muldowney proceeded American style, getting to the point without preamble.

"Pius XIII died this morning."

Ellison and the others sucked in their breath. Miranda crossed herself and took Ellison's arm.

"Suicide," Muldowney continued, "Which, as you know, in our Church condemns him to eternal damnation."

"I mentioned your psychiatric observations to the College of Cardinals," Lopez added. "That is why we asked you here."

"At the request of the Congregation for the Doctrine of Faith, all of the cardinals remain in Rome for what we thought would be a reconsideration of Pius XIII's election. This painful and nearly unprecedented process was scheduled for day after tomorrow," Muldowney said. "Now we will have another funeral and conclave."

"Yes," Lopez agreed. "We must decide how to deal with his

death and what he may have done. Did he kill Hildebrandt III or not? That is what we need to know."

"If you want proof, exhume Hildebrandt III's body," Ellison suggested without hesitation. "Then we can test for poison."

"In secret, of course," Lopez responded, putting the tips of his fingers together.

Muldowney looked up from a book of Canon Law, "And the findings will go into the Secret Archives for at least seventy-five years before anyone can open them."

Hours later, with St. Peter's sealed off from visitors for the night, Ellison walked next to Dr. Morra in a solemn procession down the center aisle of St. Peter's. A dozen cardinals led by priests swinging incense led them in solemn order to the altar. After lengthy prayers, they processed to the crypt below.

Flickering candles cast ghost-like shadows that made the hair rise at the back of Ellison's neck. It was cool, and the faint odor of decaying flesh scented the air. Hildebrandt III's coffin rested behind a half-finished wall of brick and mortar. Young priests extracted his coffin, loosened the outer lids, and bowed out of the chamber, leaving Ellison and Morra alone with the entourage of cardinals.

"How much tissue do we need, doctor?" Morra asked.

"We have to assess the decay first, then decide."

Ellison and Morra donned thick rubber gloves from Morra's medical bag. With the help of three cardinals, they pried the lid of Hildebrandt III's lead coffin. When it slid ajar, a foul, rotten smell nearly knocked them backward. Stifling gags, they used a crowbar to force open the lid of the cypress coffin, exposing the Pontiff's remains to the flickering candlelight.

Three tiny insects crawled lazily over Hildebrandt III's upper lip and into his nose. His ermine blanket and hands resting on his chest, holding a jeweled crucifix, Hildebrandt III looked regal in his tiara. But the odor hurried everyone to complete the work.

"Bone marrow would be best," Ellison advised. "Or liver."

"We cannot disrobe him," Morra whispered, "but there is bone marrow in his thumb." Without another word, Morra took an autopsy scissors, heavy and strong, from his bag and, in an instant, amputated Hildebrandt III's left thumb.

An hour after dawn, one hundred forty-eight cardinals listened to Ellison with rapt attention while he concluded his presentation to the College of Cardinals.

"Who am I to say whether Pius XIII was an evil man? Some among you come from cultures that still believe all mental illness comes from demons. In your Rite of Exorcism you acknowledge the presence of Satan. Personally, I believe mania is a biochemical disorder, not evil. Sometimes it is controllable with lithium or other drugs, sometimes not. Under the influence of his disease, Pius XIII murdered a Pope, created immeasurable grief on earth, and took his own life. That is what happened."

"May God have mercy on his soul," Muldowney intoned, rising. "I wish we could have saved him. Thank you, doctor."

"What of him?" a cardinal cried out, his ringed finger pointing at Ellison.

"And what of our gold?" called another voice.

A general shuffling of bodies amidst a growing buzz made Ellison understand a large percentage of the College of Cardinals wanted his head on a golden platter. An august body of men, he knew, but one that had made a terrible mistake. Undaunted by them now, Ellison spread his feet and threw back his shoulders, willing to risk a direct challenge. "How dare you clamor for the gold! Most of it is Nazi war booty stolen from victims long dead. What claim do you have? The gold sat in your vault useless for more than sixty years. I know that someone, someday will find the gold, but believe me, it will not be soon."

He waited until the grumbling in the room attenuated. "I could lead you there today. But I will do this only if you agree to use the wealth to help the poor of the world, no matter what their religion. Nothing will change my mind."

The College of Cardinals remained in session after Ellison was escorted out between Swiss Guards and returned to his quarters with Miranda and the others on *Valkyrie One*. They were detainees of Italy but not arrested for diplomatic reasons.

Because all of the eligible cardinals were already in Rome, a unanimous vote suspended the rules and the conclave began immediately. Ellison did not expect any response to his demands until after the election of the new Pope. Along with much of the world, he waited as the College of Cardinals began the process he knew so well that he could imagine them inside chanting and praying. Shortly before he calculated the first vote would take place, he squeezed Miranda's hand as he led her into St. Peter's Square. Beecham and Eduardo wormed through the crowd behind them.

A cloudless sky shimmered gold and pink evening hues over the western walls. Standing shoulder to shoulder with hundreds of thousands of Romans and tourists milling in the huge square, Ellison was reminded of Francois' story of going to Mecca, of how in a great crowd a man senses his own insignificance. When Cardinal Strizzi, Vatican Secretary of State, had issued an order of the College that refused to press criminal charges against Ellison and the others, he had heaved a sigh of relief. Armed with the Vatican reaction, they had removed the remaining problems by evening, when Eduardo made restitution to the government of Italy. An unusually generous man, Eduardo had given a few million dollars for the railroad damages and large checks to anyone traumatized by the robbery. He also agreed to be chairman of an international foundation for the restoration of Italian buildings, pledging a fortune from his own funds.

For the first time since he had decided to fight Verdi, Ellison could relax. He knew from personal experience what was taking place inside the Sistine Chapel. He hoped the wait would be short. After the election, Eduardo planned to fly them from Rome to Bordeaux, to break the news to Francois' mother.

Miranda pointed to white smoke pouring from the chimney. "We have a new Pope!"

"And on the first ballot," Eduardo added. "So fast."

They watched the balcony of St. Peter's for the presentation of the new Pope. A flurry of activity signaled his arrival above them.

"Pope Leo XIII," *Camerlengo* Strizzi announced, before he pulled a curtain aside to allow entry of the white-clad Pontiff.

"Muldowney!" Ellison exulted.

"*Oremus.* Let us pray," Muldowney began. "We call for an end to the madness and strife. We pledge to use our wealth to help all mankind, as Christ asked us to do, not to convert them but to respect their ways. We pray as Pope John Paul II prayed at the beginning of our millennium. 'For the wrongs which the Church has done,' John Paul II said, 'be they out of intention or by mistake, we humbly beg God and man for forgiveness. Amen.'"

Two days later, a technician using the robot arm grasped Francois' coffin and clasped it to the submersible vessel for their dive into the deepest of the Mediterranean valleys. They were diving at the precise coordinates Ellison memorized when he sent *Aphrodite* and the Vatican Gold to the bottom of the sea.

"I remembered what Francois told me a few weeks ago," Ellison told Francois' mother, Sophie Francois, who despite her bent spine and aging hips had insisted on accompanying Ellison to her son's resting place. "What a memory your son had. He quoted Wittgenstein, 'I believe religion is the calm at the bottom of the sea at its deepest point.'"

"Yes, my son would have wanted it this way, somehow to be with his father."

"I knew," Ellison murmured. He wasn't sure how he would live with the knowledge that Francois had died for him, but he already knew something had changed inside him. For the past few days he'd been wondering about his own religion, particularly his belief in any divinity whatsoever. He had come to terms with not believing what had been inculcated in childhood Sunday School, specifically not believing that Jesus rose from the dead. As much as he wanted to believe Francois would have eternal life on another plane, Ellison was unable to find solace in the belief in an afterlife. The whole concept struck him as a *Deus Ex Machina*, as in a Greek or Roman drama, when a god lowered by stage machinery resolved a plot or extricated a protagonist from a difficult situation, something too convenient to be true. Yet he recognized the limits of his rational mind and acknowledged the existence of mysteries beyond human understanding. Troubled but unable to arrive at a sense of belief or the comfort of faith, in the end, he commended Francois' soul to the unknowable and hoped, with a sincerity so profound that perhaps it was a prayer, for the best for his friend, whatever it might be.

They descended rapidly into the eternal darkness of the Mediterranean depths with only a powerful searchlight to guide them. Even through their thick hull, they could hear the crushing sounds of Francois' metal coffin giving way, until finally it cracked and the cold sea water rushed in next to his body, equilibrating the pressure. He was glad Sophie Francois and Miranda did not realize what was happening to the corpse. Ellison could imagine Francois' body being squeezed to half its size, as all the gases and air in his chest and belly were compressed by four hundred atmospheres of pressure. The image brought tears to his eyes.

At a depth of thirteen thousand feet, side-scan sonar displays outlined the ocean bottom for them, a flat plain with few protuberances. Through the thick porthole, they could see an endless expanse of mud, its monotony broken by scattered clusters of tube worms and other strange organisms.

Ellison spotted their goal first. "Over there! A boxcar!"

They approached through the gloom until they were in the middle of boxcars planted ten feet deep in the mud, arranged in an eerie, chaotic Stonehenge. Hillocks of gold bullion that had ripped through the walls of the boxcars protruded like icebergs in polar seas, with nine-tenths of each pile buried in the silt. Nearby, a small rocky mound rose above the mud, with a shallow cave visible on one side.

"In there," Ellison gestured to the pilot.

"Yes," Miranda agreed softly, "Let Francois sleep there." She put her arms around Sophie Francois' shaking shoulders and dabbed away the old woman's tears.

With deft use of the jets, the pilot positioned the craft and slid Francois' coffin into the cave with a solid thunk. "Our Father, which art in heaven, hallowed be Thy name," Miranda began. Sophie Francois crossed herself, and they all joined in the Lord's Prayer while the pilot maneuvered to seal the opening with rocks.

Ellison thought it unlikely he would ever be back to visit this grave, and he was loath to leave. Somehow, burial was too final to accept, yet he'd been feeling that Francois' ghost could not rest until now. Just before the pilot shoved a large boulder across the crypt, Ellison stopped him. "Wait," Ellison said, recalling the single rose Francois had thrown into the sea at his father's funeral. "Put a single gold bar in with him, in case he needs it on his journey."

Miranda put an arm around his waist, while Eduardo embraced him from the other side. "Death gives rise to primitive superstitions, no matter how educated the man," she said. They stood silent as the pilot placed a golden bar on top of the coffin, nearest

Francois' plastic feet.

"Farewell, my friend," Ellison rasped when the watery crypt was sealed. He had a fleeting image that compressed a kaleidoscope of Francois' life into the blink of an eye. For an instant he felt Francois was there, whispering to him, "Love must contain the knowledge that everyone you know will die some day," but then he was gone.

Ellison shook his head after the ghostly visitation. He felt helpless facing Francois' mother, whose grief froze her face into a mask. "I guess there is nothing else for us to do," he said.

Francois' eternal wealth assured, they used the robot arm to load a steel basket with heavy bars of gold, the first delivery under the irrevocable salvage agreement signed by Pope Leo XIII, which according to Ellison's insistence guaranteed the wealth would be used for the good of all men. Those who were starving would be fed first with purchases from nations overstocked with grain rotting in storage elevators. Roads and bridges would be built so isolated villages could bring produce to the markets, the afflicted to hospitals, and industrial products to delivery points. Using wireless communications, electronic schools would be built worldwide, to give every human a chance to advance in the economic jungle of life. Properly managed, and coupled with judicious control of population growth, the Vatican Gold would reduce poverty on earth to almost acceptable levels, certainly creating the most halcyon age in mankind's checkered history. Such worldwide prosperity is what Ellison hoped would be the legacy of Francois, beginning with this first ton of bullion.

Treasure in their mechanical hand, from the eternal darkness they began their ascent, until, all around them, streamers of light from the sun above filled the sea with shimmering golden fans of the greatest beauty.

ABOUT THE AUTHOR

After growing up on the Great Plains of North Dakota and the haciendas of Central California, Tom Stern matured into a national record holder in swimming before graduating from Stanford University.

While a young man he picked fruit with migrant farm workers and rode the railroads of America as a brakeman, switchman, and freight train conductor to earn money for medical school.

Discoverer of gold on a remote island in the South China Sea, the author operated a gold mine there until a rash of killings forced closure. He also mounted five expeditions in search of the Yamashita Gold. These experiences inspired *Gold Fever*, his first novel.

Dr. Stern has traveled to Asia and Europe more than sixty times; and in addition to being a professor at a medical school and maintaining a busy medical practice, he has won a ***Humanitarian of the Year Award*** for volunteer work overseas. He has received ***The Great Seal of the Great State of California*** for exemplary work, as well as many other honors.

The author lives in California with his wife, Yolanda, and four children.